This book is a work of fiction. Names, characters, businesses, organizations, places, events and incidents are either a product of the author's imagination or are used fictitiously. Any resemblance to actual persons, living or dead, or locales is entirely coincidental.

Published by Griffyn Ink

www.griffynink.com

For ordering information or special discounts for bulk purchases, please contact Griffyn Ink at Mail@GriffynInk.com.

SAVANNAH KADE

WILDFIRE HEARTS #3

CHAPTER ONE

Leo Evans dangled over the side of a cliff. The wind kicked up and the light rain made the rock slippery, forcing him to grip tightly and pray.

He'd wedged his fingers into the small gap in the rock. It had to be enough, as his feet slid from their tenuous perch and he fell until his grip caught him and yanked at his arm. He took a deep breath and reminded himself not to look down.

He did, however, look up.

"You got me?" he asked the two firefighters hanging out over the cliff top peering at him.

"We've got you!" Sebastian Kane called out, but the new guy—new woman, actually—just stared down at him. She nodded once. She was the one Leo was most concerned about.

He told himself it was because he'd worked with Kane before, he trusted the man. He simply didn't know *her*. There might be more to it, but he wasn't willing to admit it to himself. *Not yet.*

The harness around him felt secure, thank goodness. The firefighters had tightened the line and he was able to breathe easier. Still, too much of his weight was hanging on it. Leo knew he should be supporting himself—the harness should only be a backup—but, with his feet dangling below him, the team above was doing most of the work.

Taking another deep breath, he opened his mouth to call up to them when the two people below him began yelling again. As the light patter of rain cranked up to a good cold smack, the man cried out, "Help us! I'm going to *fall*!"

It sounded more like a threat to Leo's ears, but he couldn't say so. The woman was pleading with them all to get the rescue going faster. Maybe to get away from him? He was nonstop making noise.

"Mark? Lindy? I need you both to be quiet so you can hear the instructions we are about to give you." He tipped his head back over his shoulder, hoping that using their names and speaking clearly would work.

It did—for about thirty seconds. And he wondered if the two below could see him heave a big sigh.

They were going to be the worst part of this rescue. Not the fact that he couldn't find a hold for his feet, not the way the webbing harness was cutting into his thighs, not even Jo Huston, standing above him holding on to his lines. Right now, the harness felt secure. He had to trust the people above him, or he wasn't going to be able to save the people below him.

"Help!" the man yelled up again, clearly not too happy with the speed at which the entire team had come to rescue him. Leo fought the uncharitable thought that he'd marched right by clearly marked signs that he wasn't supposed to be hiking in this area in the first place. He wanted to tell the man he could wait another ten minutes for Leo to get down there and that he should do so quietly. But none of that was allowed.

Looking over his shoulder, he called down, "I'm coming as quickly as I can, but I need to do it safely or no one gets rescued.

What I need you to do is to stay still and stay quiet, hold on to each other and hold on to that tree that's sticking out near you. It should be very well anchored."

With his foot out in front of him, now firmly braced against the rocks, he lifted a hand for a thumbs-up to Jo and Sebastian above him. Putting his hand back onto the rock, he felt the tension return to his limbs, the harness no longer holding him up. Now, he was supported by only his toeholds and his grip.

Leo lifted his right hand first, slowly moving it to a lower position, banking on the harness if it didn't work. Though he got his fingers wedged into the perfect spot, the toe of his left hiking shoe slipped out from under him again. The rock was slippery and wet.

"Fuck," he muttered under his breath as he slid several feet farther than he should have. A scream split the air and his heart stalled as he scrambled for a hold. The harness should have stopped him. His brain flashed images in slow motion and he was certain he was going to die.

As his hands fumbled for purchase in a mad effort to save himself, he reached for anything, but at last, the harness gave a good hard yank and he heard a grunt from above him as Kade and Huston finally managed to do their jobs.

Leo stopped moving for a moment, trying to catch his breath and close enough now to the fallen hikers to wonder if he'd accidentally kicked Lindy in the head. "You okay down there?"

"Yes," Lindy replied.

Leo was pretty certain that Mark's screams were still echoing off the cliff walls. They were certainly echoing in his skull. He stopped to regroup and found that one of his fingernails had been bent backwards. Now that he'd seen it, it hurt. Leo muttered another swear under his breath.

His breath soughed in and out of his lungs as he clung to the rock like a monkey. When at last he had himself together, he looked up to find Sebastian Kane looking down to check on him.

"Sorry man," the firefighter called to him. "That was me."

Leo narrowed his eyes. He'd never seen Kane make that kind of error before. Was the firefighter taking the blame for his new buddy? Didn't matter though. Leo had to get down the rock and he had to get the two people up.

It took another ten minutes until he had his foot firmly on the ledge where the hikers had managed to stop themselves. The two were clinging to each other, wet, cold, teeth chattering, and muscles shivering with wide contractions that he hadn't been able to see from above.

"I've got you." He reached into the pack at his waist and felt around for a moment until he found the small plastic bag. He ripped it open hastily using his teeth and watched as the plastic fluttered away.

Son of a bitch, he thought. But littering the pristine wilderness was the least of his concerns right now. The man reached out for the blanket that was unfurling beneath Leo's rig, but Leo quickly yanked it back and ground his teeth. "No, wait for instructions. I'm harnessed. You're not yet."

He snapped the blanket open, the sound of raindrops hitting the foil reminded him that they didn't have much time. "We're not out of the woods yet."

He was finally able to look them in the eye, sinking his weight a little too deeply into the harness. Rather than holding on for himself, he was once again trusting those above him. For a moment, Leo took another look down. Tall tree tops rose to extreme height but were still well below him, reminding him how far up they were; they would snap bones and die before they even hit bottom. He was reminded why the hikers were so petrified.

"I've got you," he told them. But even as he said it, he felt the line on his harness go slack.

He was no longer tethered, and his fingers dug into the edge of the rock trying to hold on.

CHAPTER TWO

Jo Huston watched as the heavy, static polycord began to pull out in front of her.

"Crap!"

She wasn't sure if she said it or if her new partner Sebastian Kane had muttered the word. He was reaching for the rope just as frantically as she and with his stronger upper body he had a better chance of stopping Leo Evans from plummeting to his death.

But Jo acted quickly. She might not have the arms for it, but she had the brains. Whirling around, she stomped on the line as it unraveled from the coil next to her.

Between them, they'd stopped the fall, but maybe only momentarily. She hadn't felt it give the hard tug she'd expected at the bottom, so maybe Leo hadn't plummeted. But this was not going well. She needed perfect execution, not slips and errors.

Foot still firmly in place, she grabbed the line as Sebastian pulled up the slack and she tugged it tight again. This rig was not exactly standard operating procedure. It was cornered around a tree trunk, at least giving her some leverage. It should be enough for her to hold Leo Evans alone, to keep him from falling and bashing into the rocks below.

She tried to listen above the sound of the rain and see if she could hear him. He was probably swearing up at her. He hadn't seemed too keen on having the new guy holding his rope, but Kane vouched for her. And now this ...

She was only three shifts into her new job in Redemption and she did not need to lose the local beloved Park Ranger. Gripping the rope tightly, she hollered behind her to Kane. "Don't reset the winch, we have to do this by hand."

She could see where Kane was now holding onto the rope rather than operating the machinery—the machinery that had just decided to quit doing its job. In her peripheral vision, she spotted a second pair of hands helping her partner as she anchored herself against the tree.

Kane leaned over the cliff and called down to Evans again. The ranger must have given some kind of word because Kane nodded and yelled back down, "We're hand lowering you. Something's up with the winch."

But it wasn't just 'something.' Jo knew. She'd commented when they set it up, wondering if it was adjusted correctly for this poly-braided rope. She didn't think it was the right kind for this machine.

So the settings weren't correct or the grips had been stripped, she didn't know—only that something was wrong. She'd not been able to articulate exactly what concerned her and, since no one else had agreed, they'd lowered Leo Evans over the side on a setup that was faulty.

She could only hope they remembered her early protests when the evaluations came in.

Jo sighed as the rope cut into her skin, despite the heavy gear she wore. It was going to continue to do so until they had everyone up. They were doing this hand-over-hand now. Technology and machinery often failed, the rescue couldn't.

It was another almost fifteen minutes before Leo called out for the second rope to be lowered. While she and Sebastian anchored him, Hernandez, Smith, and Kelly set up another handheld setup to bring the fallen hiker up.

Theirs was not a smooth job. Leo was a trained professional, mostly rock climbing himself down and using Jo and Sebastian as backup. He had slipped a few times, putting strain on the system ... though it should have held.

The hiker was another story and had to be hauled bodily up the face of the rock. If he was smart, he would use his hands and feet to not be dragged along it. Then again, if he was smart, he wouldn't be on a two-foot ledge off a cliff that he wasn't supposed to be anywhere near in the first place.

Jo questioned how smart the two of them were down there. She and the redemption Fire Department A-shift were out in the wind and the rain with a storm coming, saving these two. Still, she was glad for the gear and the work.

Luckily, once the first hiker was strapped in, getting him up was relatively quick work. The man cleared the top of the cliff less than five minutes later. Though they undid his harness and tried to rush him down the hill and toward the waiting ambulance at the base, he refused to go without his girlfriend.

Jo wasn't sure what she thought about that. He hadn't seemed all that concerned about her before he was safe again, and it was a waste of emergency forces not to do what they were telling him.

He stood at the edge, making her fear he would go right back over. Jo did not want to rescue this asshat twice. "Sir, I need you to move away from the ledge."

Though he nodded and quickly stepped back, he then slowly crept forward, wanting to see what was going on. Jo ground her teeth as they sent the harness back down and waited for Leo to strap the woman in.

When the signaling tug was followed by Leo's verbal command, the team of three firefighters pulled her up. She was probably the easier of the two jobs except when she cleared the cliff. She was yelling.

"I'm *never* going on another date with you again!" Her arm waved wildly, and she jabbed her finger at her date. "That's it. We're done!"

Jo almost snorted to herself as Lindy jabbed Luke by accident.

Her date should have gone down to the ambulance when he had the chance to go alone. This relationship was not going to work out well.

Others on the Search and Rescue team stepped forward, making sure the couple was snug in their foil blankets and staying away from each other. As they were ushered back down the mountainside, the only one remaining to be brought up was Leo Evans.

Though Jo wasn't looking forward to his expression as he cleared the top of the cliff, it still needed to be done. She couldn't watch, though she wanted to—Jo was still stuck at the tree, acting as the anchor. Using the trunk as a pulley system gave her extra leverage. When Kane gave her the signal, she began to pull.

Leo Evans cleared the top of the wall with his hands flat on the rock as he pushed himself up and over. He stood slowly, gathered himself before he accepted a fashionable foil blanket that Ronan Kelly held out for him.

At first, the ranger refused, and Jo wanted to shake her head. Rescue guys were the worst! They could talk anyone into taking the damn foil blanket and staving off hypothermia ... except each other.

Once he'd stepped out of the harness, and finally put the shiny, crinkly film around his shoulders, he looked up at them. "What the hell happened with the line?"

It was Sebastian Kane who answered, throwing Jo off her game. "Ask Huston, she knows."

CHAPTER THREE

"Today's training is on the ladder truck," Chief Taggert announced, and Jo offered a short nod in response.

She kept her hands behind her back, though she noticed the others were slightly more casual. She couldn't afford to be, not yet anyway.

Trying to stay toward the middle of the group wasn't an easy thing to do when there were just seven of them. New fire houses are always hard, new districts harder.

Chief Taggert stood at the front of the room as he gave them the instructions then asked, "Where are my volunteers?"

As he looked around, Jo made sure her hand went up—just not first. It was good to see that most of the guys also had their hands up. It probably indicated that whatever Taggert might do to her in training wasn't going to be too horrible. But of course, the chief looked right at her. "Huston, I want you on it. Both inside the rig and up the ladder today."

She nodded. It figured, every time she went somewhere new, they had to check out her competency.

Taggert wasn't done though, "But I want you going in second."

She felt an eyebrow lift in response, but still hadn't said a word.

"That way you can see what we do and, if anything's different, you can grab it before you go in."

That made sense, she thought. And she liked that he wasn't intending to throw her in the deep end and see if she swam. She could do it all, but different places had different protocols for different reasons … and they didn't always write them down for the new guy to study up.

The chief offered her a small nod with a smaller smile. But it was a smile. Jo felt her lips curve in response. It was good that the chief liked her, she needed to maintain that. Then again, her last chief had liked her, too. He hadn't been the issue. *Well, until he was …*

It was now her sixth shift and she wanted to be settling in, getting more comfortable. She wasn't there yet. Jobwise, yes, but she wasn't ready to relax around these guys. She was just grateful that no one seemed to have blamed her for the winch and the park ranger. In fact, they'd seem to appreciate that she'd had a sense that something was wrong before it happened.

Maybe they'd listen to her next time. Maybe they wouldn't.

She wouldn't know until there was a next time. And the nature of the business was that you never knew what would occur or when.

After Taggert made his announcement, she puttered around the station for about half of the morning. The calls were few and mostly medical related. Training would be at two or three in the afternoon. Or four, depending on when the runs came in and whether or not there was even time to have the training.

She polished one of the rigs entirely by herself, happy to be alone with a task. Then Jo hit the small weight room at the back. Only Ronan Kelly was in there when she entered, and he kept to himself then left about halfway through her workout. The trick with the workout was to stay in shape, but to never exhaust herself to the point that she couldn't do a run at full capacity.

By the time she headed back into the main room, she was ready to eat. She checked for food but resisted the urge to wipe down the counters. It was good policy not to clean the kitchen. For whatever reason, most stations assumed that because she had boobs, she should be the one to do it. She would do just about anything but wash the dishes and serve the food.

As she looked in the fridge a voice came behind her. "Hungry?"

Jo turned to see Kalan Smith standing squarely, almost as though he were inspecting her. "Getting there."

"Jose's got great subs. A handful of us are ordering. Want to join in?"

It could be a prank. She hated being so paranoid, but it wasn't an irrational fear—it was history. Even if these guys weren't after her specifically, pranking the rookie was a standard firehouse rite of passage. While she wasn't a rookie, she was definitely the new kid. Better to go along and get it over with.

Kalan was taking orders, writing them on a notepad like a server, and arguing with some of the people putting them in. "That mustard is too hot for you, bro."

"I can handle it, *bro,*" Patrick Kelly replied, stressing the last word.

Kalan turned to her with a sheepish look and shrugged. "I started saying it ironically. Now it comes out of my mouth."

Jo laughed at him. "You have recommendations, bro?"

At least he laughed. "Yes, I do. But I actually recommend you ride along with me on this one, so you can see what they have. Rather than just ordering off of this—" He waved a poorly printed menu at her.

It was either a good point, she thought, or just further embedding her into the prank. At least Kalan Smith didn't seem the trickster type. Once they arrived, she walked along the counter and ordered a Philly cheesesteak that made her mouth water.

She'd only barely been hungry before, but as she climbed back into the car surrounded by the smells of bread and meat and sauce, it was suddenly tempting to rip open the wax paper wrapper and bite into it right there. As they pulled back closer to the station, she spotted a car out front—an inauspicious but very high end model. She hadn't seen any of those in town and it bothered her now the way her stomach clenched as though her mother might actually be here.

Kalan pulled into the back lot and Jo popped out of the passenger side of the car, wishing that she'd worn her jacket. The cold air was biting against her exposed arms. Nebraska was colder this time of year than she'd given it credit for, though they kept telling her the summers were beautiful. She hadn't quite bought into that yet and she wondered if she'd be here long enough to see it.

They'd barely set the sandwiches on the table when Chief Taggert walked in. High Heels clicked the tile behind him. A long coat in the perfect shade of camel and edged with fur hung open, the cashmere ties dangling. The ice blonde hair was perfectly coiffed and Jo felt her heart drop.

Not again.

CHAPTER FOUR

There was no way this was going to go well.

Jo moved her head in the appropriate way, offering her mother a faux kiss on each cheek. She'd never live this down. Her mother and this moment would follow her the whole time she worked in Redemption. Jo had been through this before and she only wished her mother could have at least waited until she'd established herself before making sure all these poor guys knew she was a "Huston of the Boston Hustons."

She wouldn't live it down in her family either. For years, she would hear "Why weren't you excited to see me?" *Maybe because you dropped in unannounced at a place where I work, which I have specifically asked you not to do,* Jo argued back to a hypothetical mother in her head. At least in her head she won the argument.

"I wanted to see where you *work,*" her mother said, the smile on her lips belied the stress on the last word.

Jo hadn't even asked why her mother was here. Mother would tell her anything she thought was important and nothing that she didn't. But her mother would most likely remind her that she was horrified that Jo worked.

"Look at you, Joely, in that *uniform*." Again, just the slightest amount of stress, letting Jo now know that Marcia Huston did *not* approve.

She wondered if the guys heard the difference, but Jo was smart enough not to take her eyes off her mother. The best thing to do was go on the offense. Never mind that her sandwich was sitting on the table and getting cold. Or that she was now ravenous. "Would you like a tour?"

"Oh," her mother put her perfectly manicured nails to her chest as though getting a tour was a wonderful surprise after she barged in and already talked to Jo's chief.

Her mother's eyes flicked quietly to Jo's hands. *Yep, the nails.* Another point of failure for daughter Huston. She knew some firefighters who had perfectly manicured nails. She was not one of them.

"Why, that sounds lovely." Her mother held her hand out as though this were a ball or she were meeting the queen. Reaching out to take it, Jo pulled the woman out through the doors into the bay and away from the men. She considered hissing that she'd asked her mother not to show but she knew it did no good.

"You're a long way from Boston, Mother." It was the only thing she could think of to say that didn't involve swear words.

"I just flew in this morning. Rented the little Rolls out front."

Of course she had. The polite thing to do would be to ask where her mother was staying and offer her the spare room in her apartment. Jo was doing no such thing.

"I'm staying at the Magnolia in Omaha," her mother volunteered, making a point of letting Jo know that Joely Huston had not offered her mother proper accommodations. "It's a four-star. Best I could do."

"Oh, that's very nice." Jo kept her voice modulated and used her formal tone and hoped none of the guys were around to hear it. "That's more upscale than anything you'll find in Redemption, I'm sure."

She waved her hand around as if to indicate *everything* and continued with the tour. Finishing was likely the only way to get rid of her mother. "This is the bay. We have one water truck, one ladder, one ambulance—"

"I don't even know what those are," her mother interrupted as though she was superior for not knowing what a firetruck was.

Jo tried to continue. "The ladder is for tall buildings. We don't use it much. We'll probably get it out for training this afternoon, though. The chief jokes that he calls it *Christmas One,* since it's used more often for the parade than anything else."

"They're very shiny." Her mother doled the words out as though they were hundred dollar bills.

"Yes, they are mom." *Because I just cleaned them.* She wanted to say that the cleanliness of the equipment was directly related to their own safety. That the entire place was pin-neat and organized because everything they dealt with was messy chaos. But she didn't dare hand over anything she loved to her mother. It would be lobbed back as ammunition at some unexpected point in the future.

Jo felt the pinch in her chest and wondered just how quickly she could get rid of her mother. Marcia was staying in Omaha, which was a good distance away. *Little blessings,* she told herself.

She circled them around the outside and into the back hallway, opening the door to where the firefighters slept. Jo only did it because she knew no one was in there trying to actually sleep. The beds were laid out, neatly organized. She didn't pass through the doorway though, as it would be like walking into someone's bedroom.

"This is where we sleep."

"My!" her mother exclaimed, clearly distraught. "Joely! It's like an orphanage."

Yes, Jo thought. *If one had no idea what an orphanage looked like at all.* "Not quite."

As though sensing they were alone, her mother turned her head and narrowed her eyes. "What are you even doing here, Joely?"

"My job." It was an argument almost as old as she was.

She'd been a disappointment from the moment she'd climbed her first tree. She'd liked mud, cars with big tires, running track, and everything else a debutante wasn't supposed to.

There were no good answers here. But Jo opened her mouth to try to find the best of them. She had to stop her mother from saying, "It's time to stop playing. Come home. Marry Allan."

It was still a marvel that her mother still couldn't get it through her head that Jo was never going to marry that soggy piece of wet toast even if he was a doctor.

The bell rang, making Jo think *Thank you, baby Jesus,* even as her mother's head snapped up. Marcia Huston was clearly offended that the bell should dare to be so loud in her presence.

"Mother, I've got to go." She pushed past the woman because no matter what her mother might say or do or how awkward she might make Christmas, Jo was not going to hurt her chances at this job. Hell, her mother might have already harmed her just by showing up unannounced. Luckily, Taggert seemed to take kindly to walk-ins—everyone was allowed to have a tour and he loved when the little kids wanted to see the place. He was big on community service and getting to know the townspeople. Jo could only hope that her mother could be counted among her community outreach brownie points.

Heading into the bay, Jo let her mother find her own way out. *How much damage could the woman do if left behind?*

Dammit. It was a question Jo didn't want to have answered. But she suspected she would get the answer when they returned from whatever this call was.

The others were hopping into their gear and Jo quickly did the same. Kicking off her shoes in front of her locker, she stepped down into the waiting pants, boots, and suspenders. Then she was turning away, her mother forgotten as she climbed up into the rig.

She was assigned the back seat, right side, facing the rear. She stared at an empty seat and frowned until Ronan Kelly popped up in the still open door.

"I'm in, Smith!" he hollered as he reached out and hauled the door closed with a slam.

Kalan hit the gas, bouncing them out of the station and taking a right hand turn almost before the door had latched. Something about the bounce and roll put Jo at ease and quelled the similar churn in her gut. Her mother was left behind, her focus on the job.

She felt the growl in her unfed stomach and cursed her mother's timing.

"Here." Ronan held out a cut end of her sandwich. Not even half of the footlong she'd ordered, but it was something. "You were getting ready to eat when your mom showed up and now we're on a run. The rest of us managed to get our sandwiches down. So I thought you could use a little something."

Her heart twisted. As long as there wasn't wasabi hidden in it, this was maybe the sweetest gesture she'd seen when she was playing newbie.

"Thank you!" she meant every word and took a big bite. Wasabi or not, it was food. If it was a prank, she'd lean into it. She waited for the sting to hit her tongue, but it didn't.

Still, her gut clenched as she worried about a fire that would load every last one of them onto the trucks.

CHAPTER FIVE

Leo stood at the edge of the area marked for campsites, the front of him heated to the point of sweating, his back cold and clammy. He plucked at his shirt, letting air flow beneath it. No one designed a jacket for standing at the edge of a blaze.

He'd rushed out since getting the call from dispatch at midnight and he'd arrived still unsure what he was going to see. At that point, all the information they had was what had been relayed by the teenager who'd set the fire in the first place.

So Leo watched as A-shift aimed themselves toward the base of the blaze and tried to damp down the fingers of flames that now reached six, ten—and occasionally twelve—feet into the sky. The area had once been a family camp site but it was about to be ash and rubble.

Leo fought down the anger. It hadn't been a family camping, but kids. Had their parents simply not watched them? Had they not taught them proper fire safety before they were left with a campfire to tend? The night was cold and the kids had needed to make a fire. Maybe they were being kids and just dicking around. Still not okay. He stood and watched as the trees burned and threatened the entire area.

He wouldn't know the extent of the damage for a while. All he could do right now was pray that the fire department could get this under control and that this didn't become a hundred-thousand-acre blaze that required calling in the hotshots and making the national news. The park land out here was big enough—and there were enough new homes nearby—that it could happen.

With his jaw clenched, Leo turned and skirted the edge of the work, watching as the firefighters moved with brisk efficiency despite their bulky uniforms. He recognized some of them by height or shape. Many of them were simply identified by the names on the backs of their uniforms—Kane, Smith, Kelly, Huston.

He felt his jaw clench a little tighter on the last one. The guys swore she was not the reason that the rope had slipped. When he pressed, they swore they weren't covering for her. He told himself he could trust them. And he told himself he was being ridiculous not to trust her.

He and Taggert went way back. Well, the chief went back a lot further than Leo did, but they'd met when Leo was just a kid. Maybe that was why Taggert had earned his infinite trust. So he had to assume the Chief wouldn't have hired Huston if she wasn't as good as they said. It seemed she had a bit of a history, and Leo hadn't yet found out what it was.

It didn't matter now, though. He wasn't hanging from the side of a cliff and the team was here, moving as a yellow-suited unit. He completed the wide loop and sidled up next to Taggert where the man stood, slacks pressed and tucked into heavy boots, white shirt with the local firefighter logo and a heavy jacket. Quite the odd ensemble.

"What does it look like?" Leo pressed, though to him it didn't look good.

The chief didn't even turn his head, just held tight to his tablet—new gear the old man had fought, preferring paper for the longest time. His eyes kept scanning the scene. He ignored Leo and issued orders to his guys, discussing trenches and flanking before he finally answered. "Looks like a big pile of shit caught on fire is what it looks like."

If the truth of that statement hadn't been so dangerous Leo would have laughed, but he'd been through this enough times before. Campfires went awry and people weren't well enough trained to contain them before they got out of control. Sometimes tents had gone up when someone had thought they would bring a portable generator or a gas heater.

For all the times he stopped them before they actually caught anything major on fire, he'd ticketed them like the asshole that he was. But he still hadn't stopped them all. He sure hadn't caught this one.

"No one was supposed to be out tonight. It's closed here."

"You've got guys monitoring the entries to the park and the camp sites?" Taggert asked.

"Yeah. They were there." Leo had already questioned his rangers, but the fact remained that the national parks were big. People lived way out and there were lots of ways into the park that didn't involve passing one of the two rangers that had been on duty.

He told himself he should be grateful that the kid even called it in. Lots of times they didn't for fear of getting caught. Lots of times they left backpacks or gear at the scene—the good sturdy nylon that held up to very high temperatures. Sometimes it even had their name written in it with Sharpie. So, at least this kid wasn't as dumb as the others, he consoled himself.

He stood next to Taggert, his arms crossed over his chest much like the old man. Once again, his jacket protected his back from freezing but he left it open down the front, where he was still far too warm. "You seen the weather reports?"

"Storm coming in," Taggert uttered the words as if to say *yes, he'd seen them.*

The unit had been out here for several hours and though they'd managed to keep the fire from getting bigger, they hadn't knocked it back either. Leo didn't like the looks of it.

"The weather system shifted," he told the chief. Like the old man, he didn't look, but kept his eyes on the blaze watching as Huston and Kane ran a hose from the truck and Hernandez came up to report the water level.

Once again, Taggert barely turned his head. "Call the Beatrice department. Have them send a pumper."

Shit, Leo thought, they were in need of more water. Bringing in another department always seemed to Leo to signal that they were losing the battle.

Hernandez had already turned away, but Leo needed to finish what he was telling the chief. "The system shifted and the radar's looking worse."

The Chief offered a small shrug in response. "Rain would do us good."

"It's not rain," Leo told him. "It's snow and maybe ice, and lots of it. They're predicting high winds, too."

"Shit," was Taggert's only response. Leo wasn't even sure he heard it, but he didn't ask.

Only one of the kids had called in the fire. His two rangers were out searching for the other, though Leo didn't know the details, only that it had taken dispatch a while to get even that info out of the kid who'd called. He'd simply run when the campfire went up and tried to convince dispatch that he was alone.

When he'd finally confessed to the operator that his younger brother was out in the night by himself, Leo had sent the rangers out looking for the missing boy. He had three back at the station, trying to track down the cell phone that the 9-1-1 call had come from. He needed to know who exactly they were looking for and who they could question about where the 'brother' might have gone.

He fought the hard clench in his chest. Missing brothers always did that to him, even if he knew the circumstances weren't the same.

He wondered if his rangers were having any luck. He wondered if the storm was coming in as predicted and he looked up, as if the sky would tell him something. But it was too dark, the new moon giving no light to any approaching clouds. The wind kicked, cooling his front and forming ice crystals down his spine as his radio crackled.

Bethany's voice came across the line. "We located the boy who called. Sterling Winter. He's twelve."

Younger than Leo had expected. Quickly, he turned away, his face down to talk into his comm, grateful for the news.

"I talked to him a little." Bethany told him. She managed to have both that maternal ability to make kids feel safe and the schoolmaster tone that threatened them within an inch of their life. "It's bad news, boss."

Leo held his breath. "His little brother, the missing kid, is only five."

Dammit. He looked up at the sky again, the only heat he felt came from the blaze. The wind kicked up again, stealing his warmth as soon as he stepped away. A five-year-old wouldn't survive in this ...

CHAPTER SIX

Leo shoved the Ford Bronco into Park, once again wishing the money existed to upgrade to electric vehicles. It was the middle of the night, but the house was lit up and clearly active.

Though his adrenaline was pushing him to barge inside, he sat back and reminded himself that it wasn't the right thing to do. In fact, he should probably wait for Bethany, but she was still twenty minutes out. So he reminded himself that fires—though maybe not this one—were a natural part of the land's life cycle and were helpful.

He told himself everything he could to be calm and reassuring, including, *Think like* Bethany. He opened the car door and stepped down into the cold, brisk wind of the night. It had picked up while he was driving here, not a good sign for a lost kid.

For a moment, he frowned. It had taken him twenty-five minutes to get here from the fire site, though a good portion of that was because of family farms and open protected lands, which meant the roads didn't go straight through anywhere. This house was one of those places that you simply couldn't get there by any direct route. Even so, it was a long way from the campsite.

He'd have to ask how the boys had gotten miles away with no supervision.

Climbing the front steps, Leo knocked on the wide door and waited. At first it had looked like oak—a very expensive piece—but now he could see the wood grain was a print. The home was majestic, new with a variety of roof lines and edges. The white brick facade made it stand out from the open acreage around it. There were more and more of these houses coming up as the family farms got bought out in favor of neighborhoods.

He looked left and right, though. No houses in sight. This was an individual owner, someone who wanted to build in the middle of nowhere. They'd bought a huge entire property, if he was judging by where the trees had been cleared. Maybe close to fifty acres.

He shook his head. He didn't understand these people—all grass and no trees—but he didn't have time to think about it. The door opened and the mother practically threw herself at him before yanking him inside.

"We are so sorry! We didn't know!" she babbled on about the boys and how they'd lied to the parents, too.

How could you not know your children were missing from your home? He didn't have children and reminded himself he shouldn't judge. He'd seen it happen often enough that he couldn't fault the parents on this one, even if he didn't fully understand how it happened.

He held his hand out. "Leo Evans, National Park Ranger."

He didn't mention that he was head of the local unit, as he wasn't sure whether the honor was dubious or not. Though he was the supervisor for the entire area, that were only five rangers—including him. There weren't enough employees for him to have a full-time desk job. Brendan, the second cadet he had on the phones tonight, didn't even belong in his district.

But as he finished introducing himself, the mother smiled oddly then swiveled her head and yelled up the staircase. “Sterling, you get down here!”

She followed this with another yell. “Did you get warmed up?”

Leo simply stood there with his thumbs hooked into his beltloops and nodded along. There was nothing else to do but be grateful the child was warm again.

Betty Winter didn’t stop talking, though. “Paul, my husband, he's out in the truck right now. And he's picking up Bennett. Ben was with Sterling when they went out. You can ask him anything you want.”

Leo watched as Sterling stepped slowly down the staircase. His bare feet indicated he was a child who didn't notice the cold that crept at the floors of Nebraska homes this time of year.

“Hi.” Leo tried to make contact. Bethany had said the boy was twelve. He looked like he might be by his height, but his face certainly looked young and scared. Right now, he was missing any of the markers of manhood. “Will you talk to me, Sterling?”

Though Leo tried to ask as politely as he could, he immediately regretted it. *What if the kid said no?*

In fact, Sterling didn't answer at all. It was his mother who said “Yes, he most certainly will,” and motioned them both to the dining room table. Leo tried to sit down, unclench his fists, and not lean forward like a cop running an interrogation.

In under five minutes, Sterling had spilled a lot of the tale. He and Bennett had decided to go camping. The kid had paused oddly when mentioning his brother’s name and Leo thought he might be lying about something, but he didn’t interrupt. The Winters had a four-wheeler, and the boys knew where the campsite was.

Staying out overnight was a test. Sterling at least admitted that they'd failed to make it through their little personal challenge.

Leo looked up at Mrs. Winter, not sure how to ask his question. When he couldn't find the right words, he blurted out, "You didn't notice the boys were missing?"

She wiped her hands on a dish towel and glared at the child who looked away. "They said they were taking the four-wheeler to stay over with the Ryder boys. The boys are the same age. So when they packed everything up and climbed on the ATV, I waved goodbye like an idiot." Then she motioned to Sterling. "Tell them what you told me."

The kid mumbled the words with the too regular cadence of practiced guilt. "I told my mom I was going to Jason's house—"

The abrupt cut to the words bothered Leo but he didn't know what to do about it. His brain was racing too many directions to sort this out, too. How long had the boys been gone? Had the parents not called to be sure they arrived? How had they started the fire and when? When did they realize it was out of control? What had Bethany already asked?

So Leo only nodded. He'd told that lie as a kid, too. What he asked was, "And you decided to go camping?"

Sterling nodded, short and quick, as Leo heard a car pull up out front. *Was it* Bethany? He could only hope. She was so much better at this than him. Hell, she was better at this than anyone.

But as Mrs. Winter headed for the door and opened it, it wasn't Bethany that she let in, but a man and a small boy. They looked too much alike and too much like Sterling to be anyone other than the missing husband and spare child.

As Leo turned his head, only able to see a sliver of the front hallway from where he sat, he managed to make out the man assuring the small child was wrapped in a sturdy blanket.

Mrs. Winter was having none of that. "If he's warm, bring him in here!"

Leo wanted to get up and examine the child for himself, but

he fought the urge. Instead, he called out, "Hey, Bennett. I'm glad they found you. Are you feeling better?"

The child nodded and looked first at his older brother then at the floor.

Interesting.

"Your brother here tells me you guys were out camping tonight. Is that right?" Leo hadn't quite believed Sterling's story, but he didn't know where the problem was. He watched as Bennett nodded along.

The clench Leo felt in his gut was real and he wanted to curl his fingers into fists to match. He was mad—mad at these kids, mad that the land was going up in flames, mad that he hadn't heard from the chief that they'd put it out. He wasn't mad that he'd been called out in the middle of the night. That was par for the course. But the rest of it? He was fighting himself not to unload on these two kids who honestly hadn't done anything that other kids hadn't. They just simply managed to catch their world on fire.

"I'm glad you're both found, and you can get warm now," Leo told him, but at the last moment a spark caught in his brain and he tossed out a question. "It was just you and your brother out there, right?"

Next to him, Bennett uttered the one tight word, "Yes!"

But Leo knew better. Bennett and Sterling were lying and there was another kid still lost in the night with a fire raging nearby.

CHAPTER SEVEN

Jo was wrapping her hair in a towel when a knock at the door startled her.

Reaching out, and not liking that she wasn't dressed, she put her hand flat on the backside of the door. Holding it shut, she reminded herself that anyone with bad intentions wouldn't be knocking first. *Probably.*

"Yes?" she called out, almost relieved when she heard the Chief's voice.

"You good?"

Why wouldn't she be?

"Yes?" she called back wondering why he would even ask.

"Can you be ready in about five?"

Oh! she thought, *that was different.* Jo reassessed the situation. *Are you good?* didn't mean "the woman was taking too long in the bathroom." It meant "are you warm? Can you go back out?" That was an acceptable thing to ask her.

"Yes!" she said, this time with far more assurance. "What's up?"

"We've got a Search and Rescue," he told her, still calling through the heavy door. "Come out as soon as you can."

"Will do, Chief." She took her hand off the door, then turned around and toweled off as fast as she could. *Fuck,* she thought.

That meant going back out in this weather. It meant drying her hair completely. If she didn't, it would freeze and turn any mistake into a deadly one.

Jo wondered what the search and rescue was about. They'd heard the two little boys from the fire were found. The Beatrice department had come in and taken over and the blaze was mostly knocked back before A-shift had left. The fire had been declared "under control" and that the remaining firefighters could handle it. Her shift had been ready to be relieved.

Taggert guided them back to the station to warm up, eat, and rest. They would stay alert in case things changed—shift wasn't over—but no one expected anything other than the Beatrice crew to knock it all the way back and then go home themselves. If Taggert was still at the station in the middle of the night, that either meant he'd seen the fire get fully quenched or ... something worse had come along that required their attention.

Once she was dry enough—she dressed in just a few moments; she was a professional—Jo opened the door and turned to look down the hallway, catching Kalan Smith as he passed by. "Dude, can you tell the chief that I have to dry my hair and I'll be ready to go."

He offered her a small mock salute and the same response she'd given just moments before. "Will do."

She hated the drying her hair part. The guys had short hair. They dried it by running their hands over it and only used the hairdryers if they needed to head right back out and in bad conditions like today. She could have put her hair up wet if the temperature wasn't threatening to go sub-freezing.

Once again, she thought about chopping it all off. But, *one,* chopping it right now wasn't an option. And, *two,* she fucking wasn't going to cut her hair. The long hair was the only thing she held on to, everything else she'd given over to the job. She didn't make friends. She didn't have relationships with anyone at work other than getting the job done. She loved the work but didn't trust the workers.

She didn't rebel, did everything asked of her. The women on the other shifts here had long hair. Well, two of them did. She was just the first woman on A-shift, and that made her nervous. Why didn't A have women before? Was something wrong with it? She didn't need that.

But Jo didn't want to cut her hair. For some reason, that was the hill she would die on ... maybe with long wet hair. Shiny, long, wet hair that she treated with expensive hair masques. She had a damn trust fund and wore a poly-blend uniform that gave her mother heart palpitations. Jo wanted her hair!

She was who she was and she wasn't going to change that for the job.

So she pulled out her—also very expensive—hairdryer and turned it to the highest heat and the highest air. It wasn't good for her hair, but she could buy some expensive treatment to repair the damage later. She just had to get it dry enough now to head back out.

A short while later, she had it French braided flush against her head. She was in uniform once again, not having quite been sure what the situation would call for.

As she stepped into the chief's office, she noticed Sebastian Kane stood up from where he was eating a bowl of chili at the table and came into the office, too. Only after she sat down did she realize he'd carried a second bowl. He held it out for her, a square of cornbread sitting on top.

"Eat," he said, "I think we're going back out."

She took the bowl politely though she wasn't quite keen on the heavy handedness of his instruction. Jo held her tongue and reminded herself, it probably didn't mean anything. Most of it didn't.

When Taggert nodded at them, she dug in. And Sebastian spooned more chili from his already half empty bowl again.

"We're going out." Taggert told them, though it was clear he wasn't sending the whole shift. "You two and Kelly and Phillips."

Phillips, ugh. Jo thought. He was such an ass. She wondered if the expression had crossed her face, because Taggert immediately told them, "Huston, you're with Kelly. Kane, you're with Phillips."

Though he'd been mid-bite, Sebastian somehow managed to press his lips together. For a moment, Jo felt the satisfaction of knowing that she wasn't the only one who didn't like the asshole.

"We have two more kids out."

Holy crap, Jo thought but couldn't say as her mouth was full. The chili was damn good, and she wished she could slow down enough to enjoy it.

"The fire's been knocked down, basically out before I left. But Leo—," the chief paused, "—Leo Evans, the park ranger—" he made a motion with his finger as though that helped fill in what she needed to know, "—he interviewed the family of the first two missing boys."

"But they're safe?" Sebastian asked, his spoon making a noise as it hit the empty bottom of his bowl. Jo needed to catch up.

"Yes, but it turns out it wasn't just the one set of brothers. It was two sets." Taggert tipped his head as if to say, *what are you going to do?* "Each said that they were staying over at the other's house. The Winter boys were trying not to get their friends in trouble."

By leaving them out in the cold with a raging forest fire? Jo thought, but then again, she'd never quite understood how kids managed to reason their way through things.

"Leo's in charge. He's got a few of his own people. We're filling in. There will be a pair from the Beatrice department as well. I think only ten total, all trained."

That's why she was here. Why Kane was here. Why he wasn't out in the main room calling them all together. It was dark and cold and a storm front was coming in. Only the best were getting sent.

She hated that there were kids out there, but Jo relished the chance to prove that she was actually the best. Even if she wasn't the one to pull the kid out of a dangerous position, she could prove she was a worthy part of the team.

"So the four of you will head out. Hernandez will follow with the ambulance."

Jo didn't like the sound of that. They could have just as easily taken the truck. Hell, it would handle the roads up there better. If chief was sending the ambulance, then he was afraid they were going to need it.

CHAPTER EIGHT

Leo banged his fist on the steering wheel. It was the best he could do to let out the tension.

"You okay, boss?" Bethany asked from the seat next to him.

"Yeah." He let the word roll out on a sigh, though what he really should have said was *no*.

He wasn't okay. There were two kids still out there. The Ryder boys were thirteen and four. *Four!* he thought to himself. The littlest one wasn't even in school yet.

Leo was working hard to keep a lid on his rage. He was livid with the kids. What had they been thinking? Where were the parents? In his own mind, he sounded like his father. *They* weren't *thinking. That's what!*

Usually, he was more gracious. Kids did stupid things. Some kids had the misfortune of their stupidity turning into real trouble. Most kids just got out of it, no worse for the wear, and never realizing just how much danger they could have been in. But here he was, sitting in his truck, running the engine, with Bethany fidgeting next to him, not able to get going because he was stuck waiting on the rest of the search team.

Another car over, Doug and Bob also waited. And beyond

them, Bland and Stanford from the Beatrice FD. The others also ran their engines, as everyone was keeping as warm as possible before they headed out into the cold.

The minutes ticked by like eons. The storm was getting closer, and the kids were getting further away, or more injured, or making more stupid decisions. Probably, they were getting *colder*. And that was dangerous.

"We can check the provisions again," Bethany offered almost too cheerfully, as though she were trying to start a task to fill his time.

He chuckled. "I've checked them twice. There's nothing left to do but wait. I just suck at it."

She didn't protest his statement.

There were four firefighters coming from the Redemption FD. Depending on what the day brought, they could maybe get out a big community search team. But only if it cleared up. It wouldn't be the first time that Redemption and the surrounding areas needed to come together to look for a kid. He remembered everyone searching for his own brother when he got lost in the woods. That was the first time Leo had met Taggert.

Leo knew now that Taggert had been barely out of his rookie year but had been SAR before he was a firefighter. At the time, to nine-year-old Leo, the man had been a god. He'd saved Garrett and that had saved Leo's parents' marriage, too, though he'd only been viscerally aware of that at the time.

Even back then, a lot of the locals already knew about doing the searches. It was big country out here, and they understood the rules—hold hands, walk in a line, kick the plants, check up in the trees, that kind of thing.

But it was a different game in the pitch black, going on three am, near freezing temperatures and a storm rolling in. He glanced at the dash again. The temperature had dropped another four degrees, just since they'd been sitting here. He was going to grind his molars down to smooth, flat surfaces if it took any longer. So he was grateful when he saw the headlights coming up the road behind him.

Leo was out of the car before they were even close. That was dumb. It was cold and he should have conserved his body heat, but he couldn't sit still any longer.

He watched as the ambulance bounced its way up the long, rutted path, and he knew it had taken them longer to get here because they'd brought the cumbersome vehicle.

Slowly, it parked, the headlights cutting through the burned-out field in front of where they all sat now. He'd requested the ambulance, afraid of what they might find. But they were here now, and suddenly it was go time.

He watched as Kane, Phillips, Kelly, and Huston climbed out of the big truck that had followed. Kane and Kelly were solid. Huston was an unknown and Leo didn't know why his gut reaction was not to like her. Maybe it was because she was a little standoffish and he was used to the general warmth of the locals.

But Phillips? Conrad Phillips was a right asshole, and Leo wished he hadn't come. Unfortunately, the man had trained up for search and rescue. And he wasn't bad at it.

Well, Leo thought, grateful that he was in charge, *he won't be my partner*. In fact, the firefighters should probably stay together, so he wouldn't have to deal with Huston either. He and Bethany and Bob and Doug would be their own teams. Bland and Stanford could be theirs. Everyone would work with someone they already knew. His stomach settled a little with the decision made and he was getting ready to open his mouth, when Kane motioned with his thumb back toward the ambulance.

"We've got Hernandez in the back. The intent is to leave him there and keep him warm. So we can treat anybody that comes in."

Leo nodded. "Good thinking."

"Yeah," Phillips laughed. "Lucky bastard just gets to sit around and stay warm. He's probably got a book to read."

Yeah, and Luke could possibly watch his friends come in near death or hold a dying child in his arms. But Leo didn't say those things out loud. He quickly got down to business, anxious to be out and searching.

Dividing them into five teams of two, he pulled out a map and handed a paper copy to each of them. There was no telling what cell reception would be like in these areas and knowing that they were all well equipped to handle compasses and topographical maps made the paper a necessity.

He hoped Huston could handle it, then mentally berated himself. He didn't know her any more or less than he knew the guys from Beatrice. Was he being a sexist ass? Or was it just something about her? Was the problem that she was beautiful and seemed to have some kind of 'airs' about her, as his mother had always said? And was that sexist, too?

There wasn't time for self-reflection, but Leo figured he should examine that when he didn't have a four-year-old in need of rescue. Still, he pulled Kane aside, "Are you good with her?"

Sebastian frowned at him as if to ask why he was being an idiot, and Leo scrambled to explain. "She's new. We're searching the mountains—mountains she doesn't know."

Maybe that was why he was worried. That was legitimate.

But Kane tipped his head, considering it as though Leo had at least provided a reasonable answer for being a dick. "She was up here the other day when we got you—"

When she dropped me, he almost said, but again Leo held his tongue. The point was finding the boy. The point was releasing the deep clenching in his gut and holding the memories at bay just a little while longer, so he quit his line of questioning and got them all ready.

With instructions doled out, backpacks on, and high beam halogen lights in hand, the five groups stepped off into the dark, each aimed a slightly different direction.

Leo had gone maybe three feet before he felt the freezing rain hit his jacket.

This was going to get ugly. Fast.

CHAPTER NINE

"Check in." The voice came through calm and certain. It was a command not a question, Jo knew. She also realized the voice wasn't quite as clear as it had been the last time.

"Huston, Kane, all good," Jo replied back into her comm, then added, "Nothing yet."

They'd seen no signs of either boy. Though the parents had given a description of what they were wearing when they left the house, they now knew the Winter boys had brought extra clothing along with the camping gear they'd snuck out, knowing they'd be out overnight. The Ryder boys had done the same thing, and Sterling had been able to tell them what the other boys were now wearing. The good news was that Jason and Dalton Ryder were out in matching red snow jackets. Jo hoped it would be enough.

"Copy that," Leo's voice came back through the comm, the sound of it tugged at her , though she didn't know why. Then she heard another round of back-and-forth as he checked in with each of the other teams. Jo noticed for the first time that she didn't hear the pair from the Beatrice Fire Department reply.

She looked to Kane, who said, "We're all getting slightly further apart. We're probably just out of range with them … reception's not that good up here."

Jo nodded. There was a lot of land to cover and a lot of natural structure in the way. Not like in Boston or Dallas.

They'd been relatively quiet up to that point, sweeping their flashlights back and forth in careful motions as a pair. Together they checked a grid pattern, declared an area done, and then turned to check the next section. They were thwarted by trees, trails, underbrush, and more.

Though there weren't bears in this part of the state—at least none were expected—big cats were a worry as were a handful of very venomous snakes. Jo kept her eyes peeled—her biggest worry was getting surprised by dangerous wildlife in the dark, she wasn't ready for Sebastian to ask her a question.

"So, what's your story, Huston?" Apparently, out of the blue, Sebastian decided he was going to strike up a conversation.

She didn't answer, just looked at him.

But he pushed, just a little. "Seriously, did you go into firefighting just to piss your mom off?"

She almost retorted that she had a "Mother" not a "Mom," but she'd been too well trained to quip back without thinking. Or maybe not. "Well, aren't you a Chatty Cathy all of a sudden?"

Ugh, Jo thought, even as the words came out. The Chatty Cathy comment had been like hearing her own mother's voice come out of her mouth. It left a bad taste and gave her an epiphany right there in the National Forest in the middle of the night. Just because her mother thought it was horrifying to be a Chatty Cathy, it didn't necessarily mean that it was. "I'm sorry."

"I've been called worse." At least he seemed to shrug it off.

Jo followed her epiphany with a second thought. *Did it matter if she talked to Kane?* He seemed a decent guy. He was devoted to his girlfriend Maggie. Though Jo wanted to say that meant he certainly wasn't going to come on to her, it wasn't as if she hadn't seen it happen before. The job and the stress lent themselves to cheating and seemed to attract cheaters. Still, Kane didn't seem the type.

In fact, when she thought about it, A-shift seemed relatively solid, at least what she'd seen so far. She worried about her fellow female firefighters working with Conrad Phillips on C. But she hadn't gotten to know them well enough yet and she was too new to do anything about it. Certainly they could defend themselves.

Maybe the Redemption FD wasn't as bad as the guys back in Boston. Maybe Kane wasn't just another asshole. So for the first time, she decided to give it a try. But it took a minute to work up to it.

Jo swept her flashlight left to right, in careful lines, still keeping her eyes trained on the ground in front of her. She checked up each tree trunk and into the branches, in case a child had decided to climb, though she wasn't sure how a four-year-old might get up that high.

Then she took a breath. "I went into firefighting because it suited me. The fact that it pissed my mother off was just a bonus. However, by the time I figured it all out, I had also learned that, for me, simply breathing pissed my mother off."

"Ouch," Sebastian replied but it was more sympathetic than anything. "She didn't seem to appreciate much of anything about the firehouse."

Jo almost laughed. "Of course not. She didn't come to appreciate it. You didn't even hear the comments about how the sleeping quarters reminded her of an orphanage."

His light stopped moving as he blurted out "Are you serious?"

At least there was a laugh in his voice.

"Dead serious."

He thought for a moment. "She did fly all the way out from Boston to see where you work."

"Oh, no," Jo corrected him. "She flew all the way out from Boston to let me know I'm making a grave mistake. It was bad enough when I was a firefighter in Boston or even Dallas. But now I'm a firefighter who's moved to the boonies!"

She shone her light downward for just a moment, turning to make sure that Sebastian caught her expression. She whispered in harsh sarcasm, "Omaha doesn't even have any five-star hotels!"

Sebastian mock-gasped and put his hand to his heart, splayed open much the way her mother had when she first arrived, only Sebastian didn't have the perfect manicure to go with it and his shocked expression.

But quickly, his gloved hand fell away and as their flashlights began sweeping across the ground again, Jo felt she'd made the right decision answering his question. It was better to make a friend than hold everyone at bay. *Right?*

It was a few moments before he lobbed the next item her way. "If you grew up with debutante balls and finishing classes, then how did you even know about firefighting?"

This time, she almost grinned at the memory. "You know how you're not allowed to have hot plates or any cooking appliances in your dorm?"

He nodded. Probably, as a firefighter, he understood better than most anyone. Jo hadn't—at the time.

"It was my sophomore year and I had one of those lovely suite dorms with my own room and a main area kitchen that the four of us shared."

"Of course, you did. Any good debutante would."

Jo appreciated that he used the term mockingly but didn't seem to look down on her for it. She couldn't help that she'd been born into money any more than people could help that they hadn't. It had taken a long time before she looked any further than her own social sphere. In fact, it had been firefighting that had done that for her.

"Well, one of my suitemates decided to have a toaster in her room. I don't know what she did, but the toaster caused a spark or she put something stupid in it or that kind of thing. Anyway, the spark caught fire, the fire caught the curtains—"

"Were they a nice sparkly gossamer?" he asked.

And she knew why he knew that. "Oh yes! They went up in a lovely woosh! And, of course, we had fluffy area rugs."

"Ooof!"

He must be picturing the damage. They hadn't known it at the time, but the four girls had made a dorm perfect batch of kindling just waiting for a spark. And, honestly, looking back, Jo was more than surprised that her roommate who smoked hadn't been the cause of it. "Anyway, everything went up. I ushered everybody out, ran across the hall, banged on the door, directed them to run for the extinguisher. Then I made the guys give me a towel which I soaked in the shower and ran back into the apartment to get my roommate out. Honestly, she wasn't trapped. She just decided she was and that she would scream about it."

She remembered trying to coax TaraLyn out of the room. It was just smoke, but ... "As I was hauling her back out into the hallway, along with my purse, which I had decided to save, the guys showed up with the extinguisher from downstairs. They were yelling that they'd called 9-1-1. So as I pulled the pin and went back in, the firefighters showed up."

She didn't mention that she'd been in her shorty pjs. Or that she'd just been too pissed at Lara to even think about the danger she'd put herself in. Jo had been going along but then, maybe a little unnaturally, cut the story off.

Should she even tell him the last part? Even just telling the story had been a stretch, she was so used to work being just work. But she didn't have to tell it.

"Let me guess. They told you you did a good job and that you'd make a good firefighter."

That was close enough. Jo touched her finger to her nose. "You know it."

"And you were hooked."

"Hell, yeah," she replied with a phrase she'd only learned after leaving home and getting into the fire station. "All the adrenaline—turns out I'm a junkie."

This time he was the one who said, "You know it."

She was almost laughing. It sucked looking for a four-year-old. But they'd all learned to compartmentalize. If they let the worry take over, they would panic just like everyone else and the job wouldn't get done. So she enjoyed the moment, one she hadn't had at work since the first station when she'd been naive and thought the guys would be her friends.

Sebastian swept his light back and forth again. "So, you were in college, and you suddenly decided you want to be a firefighter, what did you do?"

She was opening her mouth again, to say she'd gotten her degree. That her mother wanted her to go to Wellesley. She'd wanted MIT. They'd compromised on Harvard. Jo almost told Sebastian that "Harvard doesn't offer Fire Science degrees," but it seemed so snobby that she held her tongue, even if it was just a statement of truth.

She opted for the truth, but simpler. "I changed my major to Chemistry—"

She was searching for something else to fill the space—not a lie, but not the snobby "I graduated Harvard cum laude" either —when the comm crackled to life.

"Searcher down. I repeat, searcher down!"

CHAPTER TEN

Leo wanted to scream into the sky. Had Bethany not been standing right next to him he might have done it.

The last thing they needed was a searcher down. Hell, they were on a skeleton crew as it was, and it was still three hours before dawn. That was *if* the sun came up. That the storm hadn't done more than spit the occasional icy rain at them yet was the only piece of luck they'd had.

The temperature was still dropping, and no one had seen any signs. The kids at least had red jackets. One had an orange hat and one dark blue—the dark blue would be harder to spot. But the good news was, the younger kid had the brighter hat. So at least there was something helping out the one who was more likely to hide from them or make other bad decisions.

He wished he even knew if the brothers had managed to stick together, but, from his own experience, he understood that it was far too easy to get separated when they were scared and the world was out of control.

Still, he and Bethany had been calling out the boys' names, as per protocol, every few minutes. But so far, they'd heard nothing in return. His hopes were not high and the frantic alert that he had a searcher down didn't help him.

Immediately, he grabbed his comm, squeezed the button, and asked, "What happened? What do you need?"

"It ... small ravine." He recognized Stanford's voice, but didn't like the way the line was cutting out. "We didn't see it ... too dark. Honestly ... pitch black on the ground over here. Bland went right into it."

"Sit rep?" Leo asked, now pacing as he tried to find a spot with better reception. It probably wouldn't happen, but he aimed for a slightly more open patch.

"Bland's pretty sure his ankle is broken. I think I can bring him up on my own. But I don't think it's wise to try that one my own."

"It's not," Leo responded. God forbid Stanford tried to haul Bland out and went down in with him. Then they would have two searchers down. "How much backup do you need?"

Ultimately, this decision wouldn't belong to them, it would belong to him. Still, he wanted to know what the on-the-scene assessment was.

"Can you send us two people?"

Good, Leo thought, that's what he would have offered. "I'll get them on their way. Once he's up, you assess the ankle and check in."

"Yes, sir. I'll hump him out of here," Stanford offered.

Interesting term, Leo thought, *military background*. Still, he imagined Stanford putting Bland up on piggyback and walking him out that way. The upside was that they could take the easiest, shortest path out, not the long meandering check they'd done on the way there. And Hernandez was waiting back at the ambulance.

But Leo still didn't like it. He was down four out of ten searchers until they got Bland up and on his way to the ER. And even if it all went well, he was still down two for the remainder of the night. *Son of a bitch.*

It had only taken a minute to get the situation and do his entire ugly rundown in his head. On the outside, he didn't miss a beat. He was on a first name basis with his own people, even though all ten were on the same comm channel. It was so they would all hear when someone found one of the boys, not so they would all hear when Bland had an accident. Then again, it was for that, too.

On the inside, he was mad at fate and losing hope.

"Bob, Doug ..."

"Gotcha, boss. Should we switch frequencies?"

He almost laughed. They really were on the same frequency. He liked his team. "No. Stay open, it keeps us all updated."

So they all listened in as Bob and Doug coordinated with the other two. So far, his cell still had service and the storm hadn't hit them, just the light, icy rain earlier. Even so, the night was becoming nothing but a clusterfuck.

"Broken ankles heal," Bethany said from right next to him, her flashlight still sweeping the ground and up into the trees.

Leo appreciated her optimism and that her concern was about a broken foot. But that was his problem: Broken ankles did heal, but lost children weren't automatically found.

His own brother had been gone for three days. He'd been in the hospital for a week after that, at only four years old. *Just like Dalton Ryder.* Leo tried to push the memories out of the way, but it didn't work.

Garrett was okay now. His parents were okay now. The one most traumatized by it had been Leo. And here he was searching for the next boy. Though Garrett had been out for three days in these same mountains, it had happened in the summer, not during a storm. The fears had been mountain lions and snakes—which were only concerning if you ran into them. There was no way to avoid freezing temperatures or icy rain.

The drops had stayed few and far between and Leo simply hoped that the weather report was wrong. It was the best that could happen, well, after simply stumbling across the kids in the next five minutes.

"Hey, Boss." Bethany reached out with her elbow, tapping his hard enough to be felt through the thick jackets they wore. She was only trying to get his attention, maybe get his head back in the game.

He nodded, but she'd turned away, already accomplishing her task. She headed down the path, easy to follow with "Search and Rescue" emblazoned on the back of the jacket in reflective tape. They all wore the jackets and bright red hats. He'd made the county spring for them, for exactly a night like this. *At least,* he thought, *Bland might be down in the ravine, but he'd be easy to spot.*

About ten minutes later, the comms crackled with Bob and Doug's arrival to where Stanford waited. Bethany commented, "Well, that's good. They've already arrived. I guess they weren't that far apart."

Leo nodded along, he'd been tracking them all via GPS tags—which was great, as long as he continued to get cell service. He swept his flashlight again. He wasn't just the team leader, he was also responsible for clearing his portion of the area.

Only now did he see that Bethany had stepped from the edge of their section of forest into an open field. As much as it might seem that a field would be easier to search, it was actually a bitch. The grass was tall and, while the rain had just passed them over, it left the grass wet. They would have to walk almost every inch of it, because they could get close to a small, hiding child and miss him otherwise. The grass hid everything. Including snakes and other things that bit.

"Jason! Dalton!" he called out. As he yelled, he put his hand out, effectively stopping Bethany. Together, they stood still and listened, but a crackle came over the comm. What he heard was details about getting the rope down to Bland.

All good news. But Leo had to call out the boys' names again.

Even so, even with the quiet the second time around, he heard nothing but the wind rustling the leaves of the trees. Another few hours of this and he would hate that sound. The comm continued to crackle with updates, ruining their chances of hearing any return cries.

Still, he yelled each boy's name, over and over, until Bethany made a motion to him and took over the job. Maybe they would answer a female voice. Maybe they would answer Bethany.

He yelled until he was almost hoarse, even though he knew better. While they did it, they continued their very methodical search of the tall grass. Sure enough, his pants legs were wet. But he'd dressed for the weather and, so far, he wasn't feeling it on his skin.

They weren't even halfway across the field when the comms crackled again with a shout of "He's up! We've got him!"

Leo took a moment to be relieved. Within a minute came another piece of info. "Yes, the ankle looks broken."

Gritting his teeth, Leo told himself that he was just as upset about Bland having a broken ankle as he was that he'd lost twenty percent of his already small team. He knew he should think more about them, but his brain was so focused on finding the boys.

The next announcement was that Stanford would, in fact, piggyback Bland out to the ambulance. Though Bob and Doug offered to go along, Leo let Stanford wave them off. It might be the wrong decision for the searchers. It was a good decision for the missing boys, and he hoped that Stanford had the stamina to get Bland to safety without hurting himself.

The comm crackled again, as Stanford chimed right into his thoughts.

"It's probably only two miles, Boss. I got this, but I'm sorry we're tapping out."

Leo didn't know what to say to that. He was sorry they were tapping out as well and he had no idea if the accident was a dumb mistake or an unavoidable mishap.

He said the only thing he could. "Thank you for your help and stay safe. Check in when you get there."

Bob and Doug headed back to their search area, not wanting to leave a grid section unfinished. But Leo would have to divide the most likely areas up again. He sighed just as Bethany once again turned to him.

"We'll find them, Boss."

He wished her optimism was more contagious. It wasn't. And even as he had that thought, he felt the icy rain start to fall, freezing on contact. They were standing in the open field as the clouds opened and the sky began to pour down on them.

Leo looked to Bethany, and saw her eyes widen.

"Run!"

CHAPTER ELEVEN

Jo and Sebastian were pulling out their rain gear and doing the awkward climb into it even as Leo's voice came over the comms.

"Rain gear on. Seek shelter."

It didn't bother Jo to be getting instructions that she should have clearly already known. It was simply par for the course. If they got wet, they could get hypothermia. From the tone of the transmission, it sounded like Leo Evans was already frustrated with the entire situation. Maybe because in addition to finding nothing, he'd already lost two of his searchers. She felt it, too.

Luckily, she and Sebastian had already been under the cover of trees. So they'd heard the icy rain hitting the leaves before they felt it. But it still took them a few minutes to get the gear out and pull it on.

It was another layer over already layered clothing. It was cumbersome, clear, and crinkly. Because it covered their heads more thoroughly, the gear made it harder to hear a child calling out. But not becoming another victim to be rescued was important.

So Jo wiggled into her gear, pulled her phone out, and checked her bars again as icy crystals hit and melted on her screen. "My signal's fading. But it was better just a few hundred feet that way."

She pointed back the direction they had just come from as Sebastian nodded. He didn't seem to fully catch on. It wasn't just about wanting to have a phone signal.

Jo had a point to make. "We're down two searchers. I'm going to make a call."

Sebastian followed along then leaned over her shoulder, opting to look at the screen of her phone rather than fumbling with his own through the heavy gloves at four thirty in the morning.

"Do you know Ivy Dean?" she asked him.

Sebastian laughed as she realized what a dumb question that was. Redemption was a small town, of course he knew the librarian. He replied, "I'm actually more surprised that *you* do." Then he tipped his head. "Though I guess you did come help when Seline was missing."

Jo nodded, wondering how Sebastian knew that ... *small town,* she reminded herself.

Jo had a few days between moving into her new apartment and starting her first shift. So she'd simply gone into the library to get a book. The librarian had been warm and charming and by the time Jo had several romance novels pulled from the shelves, she also had a new friend. Ivy had plucked it out of her that she was a new firefighter, that she was on A-shift, that she was search and rescue trained, originally from Boston, and had done a stint in Dallas before landing here.

Jo had learned that Ivy grew up in the Ozarks. That's she'd gone off to college after a few years working as a waitress and finding it wasn't enough for her. She had been on her own since she was sixteen. The thing Ivy hadn't told her, but Jo had quickly learned, was that the librarian was brilliant, resourceful, and stubborn.

"Ivy will know things we don't—at least things that *I* don't. And I doubt she'll mind if we wake her up in the middle of the night for a missing child," Jo told him as she searched for Ivy's home number.

"I think you're right."

Within moments they had a sleepy Ivy Dean on the line. But the voice quickly snapped to attention. "What can I help with?"

"We're down to eight searchers, and daylight is coming up soon," Jo told her. "We've been out all night searching grid patterns but we haven't found anything. No sign of the boys. And now, with the injury, a fifth of our territory isn't getting covered. I'm wondering if we can be a little more strategic."

Jo was almost yelling above the sound of the rain. The harsh pattering on the leaves above her and the crinkling of her rain gear around her made hearing difficult. Sebastian was leaned in close—too close really—but she had to press the phone to her head just so she could hear.

"That makes sense," Ivy said back, and Jo could picture her in prim, printed flannel pajamas, with a legal pad and pen at the ready for notes. "But how can I help?"

"Do you know the area? Where are the places to hide here? Where do kids go? Like where in the past have they gone?"

Sebastian was nodding along, and Jo was grateful that he wasn't trying to join the conversation. It was difficult enough as it was.

Unfortunately, Ivy replied, "I've only been in town another year and a half longer than you. So I don't know anything off the top of my head. I mean, I've hiked the trails a few times, but I don't go off trail."

Of course she didn't, Jo thought, but Ivy wasn't done.

"I'll tell you what, let me make a few calls. Because I don't know, but I'll bet I can find someone who does."

"That sounds good!" Jo wanted to gush, to thank Ivy, but it was too noisy for spare words, and she had to clear something up. She was nearly yelling her instructions now. "Call me back when you get the information?"

"Of course."

"But know that we're going in and out of cell signal range. So If you don't get me, text me a message and I'll see it as soon it pops up."

"Will do." Ivy told her almost yelling in response, even though she was almost definitely in her own warm bed.

Jo shrugged at Sebastian. "Ivy didn't know anything specific, she's almost as new as me. But she said she knew who to ask."

When he nodded, she pressed harder. "What about you? Do you know anywhere?"

He shook his head. "I grew up here, but my family wasn't the camping-hiking kind. I came out with the scouts but that was about it."

"You're too much of a rule-follower to go off trail, aren't you?"

"Even as a kid." He shrugged as if to say, *what were you going to do?*

"I know we've got our grids to do, but is it worth asking Leo to check out some specific places? Assuming Ivy finds us any."

"I'm guessing our assigned grid areas include the places he knows about. But he didn't mention anything specific." Sebastian shrugged again, the heavy gear and clear rain jacket only emphasizing his big shoulders.

Jo would wait and see. It was only a good idea if it worked. If it didn't, she'd woken Ivy for nothing, but it seemed worth the chance.

The two of them aimed their flashlights back toward the ground and started sweeping again. This time, she caught the silvery flashes of rain falling in the beam. The leaves moving as they were battered by the drops. They made it another ten minutes—searching and calling out to no avail—before the comms crackled to life again.

When Leo's voice came over the line, Jo and Sebastian looked to each other, and said in near perfect unison, "You have got to be kidding me."

CHAPTER TWELVE

It was an hour later that Leo watched as Bob and Doug carried Bethany the last hundred feet to the ambulance. She was strapped to the backboard, rain coming down on her and no way to avoid it.

Leo had carried her most of the way, apologizing for every bump and incline. She had to be in a lot of pain.

It was yet another mess in a night that had gone horribly awry. He would have scrubbed his hand over his face, but his gloves had water droplets beading on them. He couldn't push the clear hood back for air, and no matter what he did or how he positioned the visor on the rain gear, icy drops touched his face. He fought the urge to hiss out his reaction each time it happened.

What should have been dawn was no brighter than the night had been. In between the accidents and the errors, the search had been pointless. No one had heard a cry or seen a sign. There were no stray gloves—save one that had clearly been in the dirt too long to belong to this search. There were no marks on trees, scuffs on the ground, or fabric scraps caught on stray branches. Nothing.

These boys decided to go camping on their own. The youngest brothers were barely old enough to even agree to anything. It was about the dumbest thing Leo could think of. Then again, it hit just a little too close to home.

He'd been nine when he and Garrett had gotten lost. But he had left signs as soon as he realized he was in trouble. He'd grabbed a rock and scratched arrows onto the trail. He'd stolen his father's bright yellow field marking tape some time before, simply because it was cool. So he'd doled it out, leaving tiny scraps of it hanging from low branches as he went. The search team had found him quickly.

Now he was hoping that at least the older of the two boys, Jason, might have done something similar. But they'd found nothing and Leo was losing patience and hope.

His comm crackled to life, even as he watched the ambulance drive away and hoped to God no one else got hurt before Luke Hernandez turned it around and brought it back.

Bethany had slipped and fallen on a patch of ice they hadn't seen. Not even while they'd been running. Later, after they'd stopped. Of course, he now had everybody put on the traction cleats. His own gripped well enough that he didn't walk with his regular ease, but at least he wouldn't slip.

But for Bethany, it was too little too late. He didn't think she'd broken anything. But she'd be on muscle relaxers in bed, probably in screaming pain every time she tried to move her back for the next handful of days.

He felt like crap for not having them get the elastic and metal slip on covers on sooner. His only excuse was that it was a pain to stop and affix them properly. They liked to tangle … and in rain gear and thick gloves, it hadn't been easy. But his excuse was shit in the face of Bethany's pain.

Bethany, of course was her sunny self, apologizing even as she grimaced with the pain. "Don't worry, Boss. This was on me. It wasn't the first time I slipped, and I should have been smart enough to put on my own cleats."

He still felt like it was his fault though. At least the ambulance was warm. Bob and Doug were standing at the edge of a makeshift parking lot. Just a patch of grass where Leo had made everyone meet up.

Being the closest, they'd come immediately when Bethany had her accident. They'd help stabilize her, but then there'd been nothing to do but sit in the rain and wait until Luke arrived with the backboard. The four of them had rotated shifts carrying her out. Though Bethany herself wasn't heavy, the board was awkward and the ground uneven and now icy.

He looked at Bob and Doug now. They looked barely the worse for wear, but they were his old guard. Both were pushing sixty and, though they were in excellent physical health, if anything did happen to them, Leo was afraid the recovery would take twice as long.

He couldn't afford to lose them in their regular capacities. Not for a search that was dangerous and yielding nothing. He was considering sending them home.

No, he admitted to himself, he wasn't considering it, *he was doing it*. The decision was made.

So he was down to fifty percent of his original search force.

He was opening his mouth to tell them his decision when his comm crackled.

"Where can a guy get some hot coffee around here?" Phillips asked.

This time Leo did scrub his face with his wet glove before he thought better of it.

Jesus, Conrad, he thought, *you don't get coffee on these searches unless you bring it with you.*

Maybe the guy thought he was being funny. Leo had coffee, but it was for when everyone came back. It was for the victory of finding the boys. The better part of valor right now was silence.

He started to push the button on his own comm, trying to think of a neutral reply, but Phillips voice came over the air again, sharp and this time serious.

"What's the word? Are we calling this off?"

The angry sigh escaped him, and he was glad no one was close enough to hear or see it. This was the third time Phillips had asked. Leo was tempted to tell him to just turn around and haul his own ass home. There was every possibility his attitude was hurting the search more than it was helping.

But they were all on the same channel and everyone would hear. Doing that would leave Kalan Smith without a partner … though, the more Leo thought about it, it made sense. Get rid of Conrad, and have Kalan replace Bethany. He was down a search partner himself.

But he didn't get a chance to reply. Jo Huston's whiskey-colored voice came over the line before he could say anything.

"Kane and Huston here. We're still in."

It was followed pretty quickly by Smith's deep voice, even though he was probably standing right next to Phillips as he said it. "Smith. Still in."

Leo couldn't help but smile. There were others. It wasn't just him. They could find the boys. But poor Kalan had been out all night with Conrad Phillips by his side. It was time to regroup and get a new strategy.

Even as he had the thought, lightning cracked overhead.

His head whipped up, the indigo sky cut with white fingers arcing through the air.

At the same time, he heard multiple voices over his comm. Sebastian had hit the button in time to catch both him and Huston yelling, "Oh shit!"

CHAPTER THIRTEEN

An hour later, Leo was down to the final three of his original SAR team.

The *Oh shit* he had heard from Huston was them reacting to a tree getting hit by lightning nearby.

Very nearby, it turned out. Leo hadn't heard the actual crisis, but they'd called in their report immediately afterwards. Both of them had managed to get out of the way, but one of the branches had been close, and it ripped open Sebastian Kane's rain gear. They hadn't said it, but the guy was probably going to have a rough bruise and some bad scratches if it had torn through the thick plastic.

The problem was the tear ruined the quality of his gear. By the time they'd regrouped, one entire side of him was wet. Though Kane had protested, Leo still had sent him home. The last thing he needed was to actually lose someone.

He made Conrad Phillips head back to town with his fellow firefighter. Unfortunately, Kane—wet as he was—had to be the driver. Phillips had managed to pick the wrong foot gear. His ice cleats didn't fit and though Leo hadn't caught the error at the beginning of the night, it was clear now that his boots were soaked through.

The last thing anyone needed was the next three weeks of complaining—or maybe a lifetime of it—if Phillips lost any toes to this incident. There wasn't even a found child to counter the trouble they'd gone to tonight. Leo was losing hope. It was down to him, Kalan Smith, and Jo Huston. They stood together at the edge of the makeshift parking lot.

Everyone had lost their partner now, Leo thought as he watched the taillights head down the driveway. Conrad Phillips' truck bounced away, Kane at the wheel taking them to warmer places. Leo could admit he was jealous of that.

"It's almost seven am," he told the others, because apparently he was still in charge of the clusterfuck. "I was expecting some light by now."

Hell, he was expecting anything better than this, he thought. He had hoped the storm would pass through early. Instead, it had rolled slowly in, almost too slowly, and now it seemed to be lingering.

With the weather the way it was, there was no Command Central. No volunteers putting up the red-topped tent and handing out granola bars or hot soup. The locals came out in force when they could, but this was by necessity a bare bones operation.

He hated it. But he made the call. "Everybody in my truck."

Everybody was just the three of them. Though Smith and Huston looked at each other clearly wondering if they were getting called off, too, they didn't disobey the order. He noticed Huston aimed for the back door, setting herself separate from the two guys.

But he pulled open the other back door, reaching for the things he'd packed. He'd known there wouldn't be volunteers to help them, so he now handed out peanut butter and jelly sandwiches, energy drinks, and apples. For a moment they all ate in relative silence as the storm raged outside the truck. He turned on the engine and waited for the heat to kick in. Even he hadn't realized how cold he'd gotten until he closed the door and shut out the wind and rain.

Leo calculated that at least, if they had to stop searching for a while, he'd made it coincide with the ambulance being gone. They shouldn't get hurt sitting in the truck and eating, but they wouldn't find the kids from here either.

Exhausted and disheartened, no one spoke. The only sounds were the three of them chewing and popping the lids on the drinks. He wasn't even sure how much time had passed before Huston handed up the reusable sandwich wrapper.

"I'm guessing you want to keep this?" Then she passed the empty sports drink bottle over the back of the seat to him. She'd eaten everything, no delicate flower pretending she hadn't burned calories out there tonight. He was grateful, but didn't get a word in before she added, "And I'm sure you have recycling for the bottle?"

Kalan had laughed. "Leo's the sustainability guy."

Was that a dig? Leo wondered. "I'm a park ranger. It's what I do."

But no comment about it came from the back, only Huston's voice asking, "So is there any chance you have anything hot?"

"Coffee."

"What? You have coffee, and you're holding out!"

"It's in the bag next to you," he commented then talked her through getting into all the different compartments. He'd paid a pretty penny for the thermal bag that could store cold or hot in any pocket. "It's the silver thermos."

"What's in the red?"

"Chicken noodle soup."

"Damn, Evans. You are prepared."

He shrugged. "It's my job." It was. If he didn't feed them, who would? If they weren't fed, they'd go home. There had to be some perks to this miserable night. "There are cups in the front pocket. Pour some for everyone."

It took her a few more minutes to get everything found and then balanced. But she graciously handed him the first cup instead of keeping it for herself. Something about the way she offered it spoke of high tea, but Leo took the cup and sipped at it, grateful it was still almost too hot.

She offered another up to Kalan, but he didn't take it. Somehow the two of them managed to look at the same time and see that Kalan Smith was out cold. Leo almost laughed if not for the fear that he would wake the big guy up.

"You firefighters really can sleep anywhere."

"He worked a double before this," Huston told him, and Leo felt his head automatically tip back hitting against the seat.

Jesus, just what he needed. He should have asked before they started. "I need to send him home, don't I?"

Once again, he hated the way this night had gone. But Huston didn't answer, she just shrugged at him. So Leo asked his go-to question. "What would you do if you were in charge?"

"I would send him home." She answered this time with confidence. And Leo nodded.

Her phone pinged several times in a row just then. Even that jarringly odd sound didn't wake Kalan up, confirming Jo's diagnosis of having been awake too long. She was rapidly sending text messages, raising Leo's irritation again.

"Are you missing a hot date?" he quipped.

For a moment, she didn't reply, and he felt his irritation grow.

Sure enough, when she did speak, her ire at his stupid and maybe sexist assumption came through her tone. "Because I'm new and I don't know the area, I asked the town librarian—"

He interrupted, though he shouldn't have. "You know Ivy?"

"She's a friend." He could hear the grind of Jo's teeth and wondered how she was too new to know the area but had been here long enough to befriend the librarian.

Leo tried a different tack to cover for his error. "I'm sorry, I shouldn't have said it that way. Ivy is amazing."

"Yes." But the grind stayed in Jo's words, maybe coming back harder. This time it was accompanied by a sarcastic or bitter undertone. "She's beautiful. She's smart, and she's sweet. I'm sure you're just as in love with her as *everyone else*."

But the emphasis on the last words made him realize that, in trying to correct his first error, he only screwed up again. He thought about protesting that he wasn't in love with Ivy, but clearly now was not the time.

Jo was telling him with clipped words how far off base he'd been. "Ivy spoke with a handful of locals. And she's come up with three locations for us to check out—one of which is apparently a set of caves about eight miles northeast of here. I was double checking for exact directions."

He'd fucked up. Jo Huston was his only surviving searcher and he couldn't go out alone. He'd insulted her, and it hadn't been a mistake. He was mad that he'd been dropped when he was on the ropes and she'd been at the top. But so had Sebastian. Leo guessed that—because he knew Kane—he'd just assumed the new girl was the point of failure. But nothing about Jo Huston had indicated anything other than competence, and he needed to start treating her like it ... if only for his own well-being.

But ... "We don't have caves in that direction."

"Well, according to Mr. Gentson, and this article that Ivy found on an old case, you do. Mr. Gentson said he and his brother used to hide there when they were kids."

Holy shit, Leo thought. Joely Huston, new person and possible pain in his ass, may have just provided him the best lead.

"Are you willing to go back out?" He asked because he

couldn't go alone. She was the last man standing and he needed a partner.

But before she answered, lightning cracked the sky, cutting it in half again.

CHAPTER FOURTEEN

"So where are you from?" Leo asked into the silence of the car.

What was it with these men and their questions? Jo wondered.

They had decided to sit and wait for Luke Hernandez to return with the ambulance, as well as for the bulk of the storm to pass. They were trained for rain, but the lightning and the heavy, icy downpour meant they wouldn't be able to see past the end of their own arms. Basically, they were stuck now waiting for the chance to go out again.

"I'm from Boston," Jo told him, not elaborating.

"I don't hear it in your voice." Leo had broken out the chicken noodle soup after they'd agreed to send Kalan home with the last of the coffee.

Her fellow firefighter still hadn't texted that he'd made it safely, and Jo was running on faith that he hadn't fallen asleep at the wheel. She'd become a firm believer in his ethics, though. Smith would simply pull over and sleep on the side of the road before driving if he was really too tired to do so.

But she was stuck here now, in the front seat, alone with Leo

Evans. And no way to avoid his personal questions. "Of course, you don't hear the Boston in my voice."

For a moment, she wondered how he'd missed her mother's visit, but he wasn't at the fire station. Leo didn't know that not only had her mother shown up unannounced, she'd come back at eight am the next day, demanding that Jo change clothes and come for a nice breakfast ... in Lincoln. Maybe her mother didn't know how far that really was. Or maybe she didn't care that her daughter had just come off a twenty-four-hour shift.

Jo had gone along, knowing it was easier to placate the woman than argue with her. Certainly not when the rest of her very life was an argument with her mother. "My mother made sure that I had classes in etiquette and deportment. It more than made certain that there was no trace of Boston left in my voice."

He frowned at that for a moment, as if to ask *why would anyone even do this?*

Jo decided to throw it all out in the open. Why not? She might not last that long in Redemption anyway. She trusted Sebastian Kane, but Leo Evans, not so much. Trying a different tactic from playing her life close to her vest, she dumped it all in his lap ... well, not *all* of it.

"I'm a trust fund baby. I grew up in a mansion outside of Boston ... in Brookline. I went to Harvard. I drive a BMW. And this is my fourth fire station. Are we good?" She shouldn't have added the last part, but she didn't want to sit here for half an hour, reliving everything she'd tried so hard to leave behind.

There was a long moment of silence before he asked. "Do you want to know about me? I mean, since we'll be out there in horrible weather as the only ones who have each other's backs."

Jo didn't usually ask questions about people's pasts. Lots of people didn't want to volunteer it. So she didn't press, but what should she do now? Just sit in silence and stare out the window? And something about Leo Evans made her want to know. So she said, "Yes."

"I grew up the oldest of two boys. In Pleasant Hill."

"Where is Pleasant Hill?"

"About two hours north, in the middle of nothing."

"I haven't heard of it." She thought she'd heard of a lot of the local places by now.

"Of course you wouldn't. It doesn't even have a good state road that runs to it, and it makes Redemption look like Lincoln, and Lincoln look like Los Angeles."

Ouch, she thought. But then again, a lot of people liked that kind of life.

Leo kept going. "The nearest kids were five miles away and the bus ride to school in the morning took fifty-five minutes."

Jo had no idea what that meant. She'd never ridden a school bus. So she simply nodded as though she understood.

"And my brother and I got lost in these mountains when we were kids."

Holy shit. Growing up in Pleasant Hill with no one nearby was probably not that big a deal. But this was likely why he'd become a park ranger. "How long were you lost for?"

Jo tried to nonchalantly drink her chicken noodle soup with any semblance of lady-like decorum. It was next to impossible, but maybe it covered up the fact that he'd piqued her interest.

"I was out for eighteen hours, petrified and alone. Part of me was having a grand adventure—that part was the part that had taken my brother and run into the park in the first place. The petrified part was that I had lost my little brother and I thought they were going to kill me when they found me."

That made sense. SAR training dealt with finding kids—kids hid from searchers, and didn't respond when they were afraid they'd been bad. This story was ringing a little too true to the current situation.

"My brother was lost for three days."

"Holy shit!" This time she said it out loud. Then she asked the part she might not want the answer to. "They found him?"

"Oh yeah, and he was none the worse for wear. I mean, it was summer, so he wasn't that cold. He said he'd made friends with the birds and squirrels, and he'd eaten berries, which petrified my mother and the hospital staff."

As it should! Jo thought but managed not to say. Had his brother poisoned himself?

"But Garrett has the luck of the gods. Apparently whatever berries he ate are not only non-poisonous, but perfectly tasty. And he said he stumbled across a stream, so he had plenty to drink. He even managed to not get wet, though I promise you he was constantly falling into the creek at home."

"It wasn't like this," Jo said, waving her hand toward the storm raging beyond the windshield and she wondered if the rain had actually let up at all. Would they make it back out or was this just a small truck party with her and Leo Evans? Hell, rumors from that would be the last thing she needed.

Leo had pulled out his phone again, the charger linking him to the central console where he'd lined them both up. He'd made sure they had everything needed going forward. They had fresh batteries for the flashlights and, this time, they would take extra food. Leo, of course had a second cooler in the back. He was prepared for four people for three days.

"Looks like the storm's passing over," he commented with his head still down over the screen.

"There might even be light in the distance." Jo pointed off to their right where it looked like a small dawn might finally be happening. "So let's pull up these articles from Ivy and see where we need to go."

Ivy had sent screenshots of old print newspaper. The article was close to one hundred years old. But Mr. Gentson said it was the same cave that he and his brother had played in. Together, Jo and Leo tried to find a direction to aim.

Fifteen minutes later, Luke had arrived with the ambulance

again, and they had their bearing though it was still raining. Leo declared it time to go. And though Jo could see more light edging in from the distance, there was a sour pit forming in her stomach.

CHAPTER FIFTEEN

Five hours later, Leo was as frustrated as he'd ever been. Though the trees basically kept the light rain off of them, the air itself was wet and cold. And a hike through the woods on a path that was getting mushier and muddier by the minute wasn't helping anyone.

Jo, though she was hiding her disappointment better than he was, seemed to have the same issue. "There are no signs. The boys left nothing, no trail to follow."

"Are you a certified tracker?" He bit the words out, realizing too late how blunt they'd come out. They rang with the accusation that if she wasn't certified, her words didn't mean anything.

He was opening his mouth to correct his mistake. When she said, "No. But I've worked with a few and I've tried to pick up everything I can. And whatever is here, it's above my pay grade."

He was opening his mouth again to say he was sorry he was being a bear, when she waved her open hand in a gesture to indicate everything. "The rain has taken out anything we might have found. So if there was a sign it's not here now."

Unfortunately, Leo agreed with her. He meant to say so, but he wasn't quite sure how to get words to work properly. All his frustrations about the search and the way the boys had gone missing in the first place were overshadowing the fact that he'd found Jo to be more than competent, and even decent company while he was becoming less so.

He was carrying this stupid, heavy satellite phone, too. And he was getting tempted to use it, because he should have heard something from someone by now. That the boys had wandered home, or someone had seen something. But he was guessing everyone was socked in by the weather.

"Do we need to go back?" Jo asked.

"No!" He snapped the word far too harshly only a mere five seconds after making a vow to be less irritable. "We're not tapping out on this!"

Or at least he wasn't. But he wasn't allowed to search by himself. That would be stupid, and he prided himself on not being stupid.

Jo lifted her hands as if to surrender and backed off. Her flashlight still in one gloved hand even though the daylight had filtered in a little. It was two pm., this was probably the best they would get all day. But Jo wasn't backing down. "I wasn't suggesting that we quit. I was suggesting that there might be enough good weather coming in that you could set up a Command Central and operate a full-scale search. Someone else might know where these caves are."

Leo took a deep breath. Ivy might have found someone who knew better than old man Gentson where the caves were. But the sat phone hadn't beeped at him, nor had his cell. If anyone had found anything that would help, they weren't using the proper channels to get that information to him and Jo.

Maybe it was time to stop. His irritation wasn't serving anyone. And most importantly, not Jason and Dalton Ryder.

Leaning over for a moment, Leo braced his hands on his knees and sucked a few deep breaths into his lungs. The cold seared his tissues from the inside out and it was probably what he deserved.

When he stood up straight, he looked to Jo calmly. "I'm sorry. I'm being an ass. As I've already mentioned, this one hits a little too close to home."

Though she nodded, she showed no real emotional response and he wondered what it would take to see a true spark in a woman so controlled.

"There's more bad weather coming in." He added that to see how she would take it.

When she simply nodded again, it was at least with the added understanding. It wasn't just that the boys were missing, it wasn't just that there was no trail and no sign, and it wasn't just that this whole shitshow reminded him of losing his younger brother—it was that the situation was about to get worse.

There was nothing he could do to bring in the larger search group, like they both wanted. It was just a nasty trick of fate. The weather prevented the searchers and at the same time it made the boys' chances of survival much lower. A double whammy that was likely to leave him with no wins in this case.

But he was finding that something in him believed Jo Huston when she told him she wasn't giving up—cushy Boston upbringing or not. She'd not complained once. She had all her gear with her and on properly. She was still here when eight of the others had been sent back. And she'd been smart enough to contact Ivy and get the information she hadn't known for herself.

"Let's keep going." He turned away and pushed along the trail.

They weren't doing grid searches anymore. Since they'd left the comfort of the truck and the stilted conversation, they were moving from one point to another ... checking all the places they hoped the boys might hide.

Leo first had them check a spot that had originally been in Bland and Stanford's section, but they'd lost Bland before they checked it. Neither boy had been there. They'd next hiked to a cliff that Leo prayed the boys hadn't gone to, but there were no signs there either—thank God. And there was no indication of either child along the way.

The caves were the last specific spot that Leo even had a clue to check. If they were empty, he was shit out of luck until he got a big team. They were now aimed in as straight a line as one could get out here to the location of the promised caves. Having not been to this spot before, he didn't even know if it was a wild goose chase.

Wrong decisions meant dead children.

But there were no right decisions and he wasn't psychic at all.

He was going to be incredibly disappointed if they actually found the caves and there were no kids in them. But there was no reason to believe that these boys had found these caves other than the fact that they would be looking for shelter.

Leo took point, even though he didn't know this particular trail. The parks were far too big for him to know all of it. He only knew the general area better than she did. He pushed on, setting a brutal pace for the conditions, but Jo didn't protest. She just followed behind, following proper protocol for being in the rear.

According to the simple map they had drawn up, they had maybe another four or five miles to go before they hit the area where the caves were. Even the article was unclear about the location—the paper certainly hadn't provided GPS coordinates or geocaching clues a hundred years ago.

He found himself wondering if two young kids could have covered this kind of distance. But again, it was the only real lead they had, and time and the weather were crushing down on them with no trail to follow.

Leo only made it another ten feet before Jo's hand came down on his shoulder—a soft, silent signal to stop.

Leaning forward, she whispered in his ear, "I think I heard something."

CHAPTER SIXTEEN

Jo shoved her hand out to her side, holding Leo back.

She'd practically slapped him, and she heard and felt the crinkly fabric of his raincoat. The last thing she needed was extra noise ... or to be touching him. She lifted her gloved finger to her lips.

Just then, thunder rolled above them, ruining her request for silence and indicating the storm was getting worse and not better.

Though Leo looked at her for a moment, his expression indicated that he hadn't heard anything.

She didn't hear anything now either. *Son of a bitch.*

She could have sworn she'd heard something human. Hopefully it was one of the boys. But if it wasn't, then it was somebody else who was in need of rescue. Though they stayed still and tried to listen through all the noises of the storm and the woods, eventually Jo gave up and shook her head.

She hadn't heard it again. With the alarm declared false, they continued on their way. Five minutes later, her arm shot out again of its own accord. She'd heard it again. And it did sound human.

This time when Leo looked at her, he raised his hands, shrugged his shoulders and shook his head, all of it asking, *what are you hearing?*

Clearly, he didn't hear it, and she couldn't answer. She needed everything quiet to hear the soft cry again. Unfortunately, the rain was bouncing down through the leaves like thousands of tiny pinballs. The wind was blowing, rustling every leaf and branch.

For a moment, she left her hand on his arm, closed her eyes and tried to shut away everything that didn't matter. The cold was seeping in at her toes, the boots having held up well, but not quite well enough. Near her ears, tiny patters made a constant static as raindrops hit the plastic of her own raingear. Jo shallowed out her breathing. The sound of it was trapped by the hood she wore, but she couldn't pull it back.

If she did, her head would get wet. If her head got wet, she could freeze. So instead, she tried to listen beyond the sound of her own breath passing through her lungs and what must be her own blood rushing through her veins each time her heart beat. There was no way to shut everything out.

In her own mind, she counted down. At some point she had to give up and walk away. Five ...

Four ...

Three ...

There it was again!

She tapped at Leo, suddenly excited. "I heard it! I think it sounds like *help*."

She could totally be making that up though. It was so easy to hear what you wanted to. It might have come from a bird or an animal. But Leo seemed to believe her and there was something about him trusting her that felt a little too good.

"Which direction?" he asked, clearly not having heard anything.

Pointing toward the right of the path they'd been on, she

watched as Leo called out again, throwing his voice the best he could. "Hello? Jason? Dalton?"

Together they waited through a roll of thunder and then he called again. Jo was afraid the kid might have called back but the booming sky ate the sound. Just in case this day couldn't be awful enough.

But when they heard no reply, they realized it was time to move on again. Again, it felt good when Leo turned and stepped off path heading in the direction she pointed. The walk, however, was going to suck.

The paths were bad enough, but breaking covered ground was going to be worse. Jo kept moving, happily letting Leo take point. Though she'd heard the sound, he knew the woods far better than she, and it was no hardship to have someone else push through the dense underbrush and figure out where she should be stepping.

Despite the long day, Jo had energy to burn. Her mother had often referred to her as a shark—in an unkind way—that she'd always needed to keep moving forward in order to stay alive. It had been hell at her private boarding school, where girls were expected to wear skirts and sit quietly with their knees and hands tucked together. At least now her physical energy was useful.

Unfortunately, Leo had to crash through the underbrush, which covered any sounds they might have picked up. But they stayed aimed in the right direction.

About fifty yards later, he stopped and motioned for the two of them to stand still and listen together. When they didn't hear anything, he quietly told her what to call out, and they yelled together for the Ryder boys with their voices in unison.

She hated to admit it, but they worked together pretty well, despite the fact that Leo didn't completely trust her.

When no reply came, she began to lose hope. They were closer to where she'd heard the sound, it should have been here.

Anyone who could have called back should have. Jo wondered if she'd lead them off trail on a wild goose chase, or maybe even a wild *mongoose* chase. She sighed and told herself she hadn't been in town long enough to learn if there were mongoose. But she should have learned more about the local wildlife and now she didn't know what they might encounter.

They headed onward, but Leo stopped more frequently now. This time when they called out for the kids together, she didn't hear anything, but Leo did. Maybe his head was just aimed the right way, or his hood had funneled the sound to his ears. He looked at her excitedly and this time he yelled louder, stronger, enunciating every sound. *"Jason? Dalton?"*

And they waited.

CHAPTER SEVENTEEN

"I'm going down," Jo told him, though Leo shook his head. They'd spent almost ten minutes walking back and forth, finally deciding the descent should happen at this point. It was a shitty section of mud that would likely slide out from under whoever went down, and it was sadly the best option they had.

Jo sounded like she wouldn't take an argument from him, but he was in charge. And descending was the more dangerous position. They also didn't know what they might find when they hit the bottom—other than Jason Ryder.

At least they'd gotten close enough that the kid had begun talking back. He'd told them how he was stuck on a rock in the middle of rushing water at the bottom of a ravine. It appeared there was a full creek running at the bottom, not just a trickle of runoff. With the rain coming down all day, the boy was plausibly in the middle of a strong current that would only rise, which meant they had to get him out as soon as possible.

"I should go down. It might be dangerous." Leo told her.

"It's going to be dangerous no matter what." Her reply was quick and harsh. "Are you suggesting it's too dangerous for me, but not for you?"

"For anyone." He was quick, too, but it was the same reply that he'd always given. He didn't expect people to take the kinds of risks he did, but Jo was having none of it.

"Why you, then? Why not me? Why do you think you're better than me?"

An odd phrasing, he thought, and he tilted his head at her. "I don't think I'm better than you. It's just that this is a serious risk—"

"And you have more medical training than I do," she countered.

He hated that she was making sense and that she was still going.

"I'm lighter. Therefore, *you* should anchor *me* and I should go down and rescue the kid. And when I bring him up, you'll be fresh to treat him."

Leo was opening his mouth to say ... something, but it didn't matter. She beat him to the punch again. "And you don't trust me to belay your line."

"That's not true!" But even as he said it, he felt the lie. The last time he had slipped, it had been at her hands. When he was being honest, he also admitted it was at Sebastian Kane's hands. And when he was being even more honest, he admitted that though he'd worked with Kane on rescues before, Kane had never held his belay line. Sebastian Kane was also zero for one.

But he didn't mistrust Kane. Maybe it was because Sebastian Kane's confidence was quiet and reassuring. Jo Huston's was almost demanding. She didn't wait to show you she was competent. Sometimes she just told you. There was something about her that rubbed him the wrong way.

It bothered him that she rubbed him at all. She was beautiful. If he'd met her in a bar, he would have been elbowing everyone else out of the way just for the opportunity to have her brush him off.

Maybe it was because she shut down sometimes when he asked her questions—which made him think she was hiding something. But her argument about the rescue was solid. She was smart and—in this case—correct. What he said to her was, "You're right, you're lighter, and I have more medical training."

It didn't make sense for the lighter person to hold the rope for the heavier one. So he called down to Jason with instructions to stay put while Jo carefully put her harness on and double checked everything. The harness over their regular gear was cumbersome on any day. There was a reason climbers wore thin, tight clothing. None of that was going to fly now. Not only did Jo need gear against the cold, but also against the rain. And she had to carry a pack of medical supplies down with her to help Jason when she arrived at the bottom.

Leo didn't like that—while they could call to the boy—he was stuck where they couldn't see him. Jo was going in blind, or at least with only the information a pre-teen boy was feeding them.

According to Jason, he thought his arm was broken and his ankle twisted. But Jason was thirteen and Leo wasn't about to make any decisions based on that diagnosis.

When they stood at the top of the point they had chosen, Leo took another look and decided he liked it even less each time he checked the course. As Jo had pointed out, it was the best of a variety of bad options. The creek had cut its own path through the land, and was settled deep, maybe twenty feet below where they stood. Unlike a cliff, there was no rock and no clean edge to send Jo over or brace her line against. There was only mud, and the rain had ensured it was all slick. There was no safe place to walk out and peer over, so Leo had to stay far back.

As the newly appointed anchor, the worst thing he could do was lose his footing and slide down after her, leaving all three of them at the bottom of the ravine. Though he had anchored her rope on a tree, in hopes that if both of them went over, at least one of them might be able to find it and haul themselves back up, it was a last resort, not a plan.

He couldn't see Jason or the water below—though he could hear it—and Leo hated it. He held tight to the line, slowly letting out slack as Jo faced him and began tracing her way backward away from him. Being smart, she planted her feet flat, and at perpendicular angles to each other.

She knew all the techniques, he thought, and was being as safe as she could be. He watched and let a little more of her line out as she reached toward a small but sturdy tree and braced herself.

Then, as she walked farther backward, the ground started sloping out from under her. He could tell by her movements that her footing wasn't solid. He watched as her gloved hands clenched tighter on trees and then rocks as she slowly descended.

She was a professional. Why was he so worried about her?

He was slowly lowering her down, watching as she began to bend at the waist and moved to crawling backward down the slope. She made comments telling him that her feet were sinking into the mud and that the sides of the ravine were getting slick.

It was slow going. The need to pull Jason Ryder quickly out of whatever predicament he was in at the bottom of the ravine was crucial. However, making Jo go faster and giving them two victims to rescue would be a huge mistake. So Leo held his breath and slowly let her go.

The slope was not harsh, and it took forever for her to get a distance away from him to where he could only see the top half of her. He called out, "You good?"

She looked up at him, having to move her whole head to

move the visor on her rain gear out of the way. When he could finally see her eyes, she didn't smile. Jo Huston wasn't much for sunny dispositions and overt optimism, he'd found. But she held one thumb up and gave a nod.

But just as she did it, she screamed and disappeared.

CHAPTER EIGHTEEN

Jo felt her feet slipping away from where she'd had them braced against the mud. She did the only thing she could do: pushed with her feet that had no purchase and tried to twist as she swung out and back toward the side.

She braced for the inevitable full body smack against the dirt.

The ground didn't slope enough to save her.

"Are you okay?" Leo's voice filtered down to her and she almost laughed.

Leo Evans sounded very worried about her.

"I'm fine," she called up knowing that the tone of her voice conveyed her irritation. Hopefully, the fact that she was irritated would convey that she was okay. "Just muddy and wet!"

All of her weight hung on the harness now, and not where it was supposed to be—on her own feet and hands. Carefully, she tried again to brace herself, only this time she knew the mud wouldn't hold her as she began the awkward journey of climbing down.

"Are you okay, sir?" the little boy called up.

Sweet kid, she thought. "I'm fine. My name is Jo."

But it was Leo above her who simultaneously corrected. "She's okay and Jo is a ma'am."

Well, damn. She didn't care if a thirteen-year-old thought she was a man from the backside of a harness coming over a mud slope. That was probably not the best time for anyone to be worried about being misgendered. But now she was laughing so hard, that it made it more difficult to get down the slope.

Reminding herself she was a professional, Jo forced her attention back to her position, slowly making her way downward. When she finally reached the bottom, she turned and for the first time got a good look at Jason Ryder.

He was huddled on a rock. His butt was sitting on what had to be very cold, wet moss. His knees were pulled up under his chin and his teeth were chattering. His brown eyes were wide in dark skin, but he'd kept his hat and gloves on.

The rock he perched on—that she thought he might just slide right off of if he moved!—was about a third of the way out into the creek. She really wanted to ask how he got in there, but this wasn't the time. Jo reminded herself that she didn't always like the answers people gave her while they were in trouble, so she pushed that aside.

Jason had his arms wrapped tightly around his legs, and he had on a good coat and the hat his parents had told them about. He was doing as well as he could at conserving his body heat.

Smart move, she thought and wondered about his twisted ankle and broken arm. Maybe it wasn't as bad as he thought. However, she had to get across the rushing water to get to him. Maybe she did need to know ... "How did you get out there?"

First, he shrugged, but then quickly added, "I fell in the water. And when I climbed out, I was up here. I don't know how to get back to the side."

The kid was already wet, and she didn't want to be wet, too. If she got wet, it meant she went home. It meant Leo Evans was the only one left to search for Dalton Ryder.

Jo didn't like those numbers. It was against protocol to search alone, and she didn't like the idea that Leo might go out by himself. He knew better, but she also didn't quite trust him not to do it.

So she talked as she rigged a line between Jason and herself. "Don't reach out. Don't slide off the rock. I'll just keep tossing it until I put the end in your lap."

She talked him through, taking another throw before hauling the rope back—wet—for another attempt. She kept him engaged while she did it, asking about his ankle and his arm.

"My ankle feels better now," he said. "I can move it okay."

"What about your arm?" Jo walked him through a quick field test of getting him to squeeze the arm as she watched to see if he flinched. When he didn't, she hoped again that he'd completely over-diagnosed himself the first time.

Fifteen minutes later, she'd managed to climb into the thin waders she'd brought down with her. They didn't really fit her —more of a one size fits no one thing. They would protect her legs just enough to make it through the water ... if they didn't tear and if the water wasn't even an inch higher than it looked from here.

Jo narrated all her actions loudly for Leo above and then added extra instructions for Jason after telling the boy that she was narrating to her team member. She explained that Leo was out of sight at the top so that he didn't slide over the edge.

When at last she had Jason in her arms, the extra weight of the boy made her walk back through the rushing water ever harder. When thunder and lightning split the sky directly above them. Jason squealed and grabbed on to her tighter, disrupting her balance.

Jo barely managed to hang on, keep them both upright, and not let his actions topple them both into the roiling creek. But in a split second, as she did all of that, she turned her head at the heavy pounding rushing noise that followed the end of the thunder.

For a moment she'd thought the sky was just rumbling extra, but it wasn't the sky making the noise. She stood in two feet of water with her lower body encased in the waders she'd brought down for just this purpose, but it wasn't going to be enough.

She watched as—upstream from her—the rush of oncoming water caved the muddy walls of the ravine in as it passed. Everything churned from clear to brown as the rush came at them like a tidal wave.

For a moment, Jo froze. But she quickly broke the mental lock and yelled up to Leo.

"Mudslide!"

CHAPTER NINETEEN

The muddy water rumbled and rolled its way down toward her, almost like a cross between a crashing wave and a roll of mud and debris that moved like lava.

It wasn't quite as quick as the creek water had been, but it was tumbling toward her more than fast enough to be petrifying. Jo knew exactly what it was: the mix of branches and rocks that rolled with it would pummel her if she was pulled under. The thicker quality would act like quicksand, only much faster. And Jason? If the child, already weak and cold, was caught up in it? He simply wouldn't survive.

The rock Jason had sat on was a little downstream of her entry point. So Jo had to aim *toward* the mudslide; it was her only means of escape.

"Leo?" she yelled up again. But even as she said it, she realized he'd heard and understood her the first time she'd called.

Her line had gone tight. There were too many things that needed to be done simultaneously, but she couldn't do all of it. Her heart pounded, but she refused to let the fear take over.

Jo opted to keep moving, despite the fact that she was

holding the boy cradled in her arms. Jason Ryder was small for his age, and she'd intended to carry him this way for balance until she could get to the edge of the creek. She'd planned to set him down, take off her waders so that she could have the traction of her boots, then harness the boy in a second rig and send him up first.

There was no time for any of that plan now. Jo aimed directly toward the oncoming mud and water in order to reach the point where Leo could haul them up. She splashed her way through with high steps, praying she made it in time. Just walking through water was difficult, walking through oncoming water was worse. But there wasn't time to be petrified or truly stop and think or even to let the exhaustion that was taking her have its way.

Jo had angled directly toward the extraction point. When the water and mud appeared to be coming too fast, she thought, *screw it,* and changed her aim. She had to go to the side of the ravine. It didn't matter where, she just had to be "up" so they didn't get caught. She could figure out how to get to the extraction point after she got them out of the mud.

They couldn't afford to be in the water any longer. If she could get above it, and they could wait it out while it went below them, then that's just what they would have to do.

Jo managed to get her foot onto the bank just moments before the mud barreled down behind them. She felt as it hit her heel and grabbed and sucked at her, as though it were actively trying to pull her under.

The feel of it as she fought to reclaim her own foot was terrifying, and her arms clenched tighter around the boy.

"I know you're cold. I know this is scary," she told him. "But I need you right now to climb around onto my back. I'm going to piggyback you up."

It was the only option. There simply wasn't time to send a second harness down. The mud was rising behind them and Jo tried to climb another foot higher even as he moved slowly trying to get into a safer position.

Her harness line was in front of her and it had already been effort to avoid getting Jason tangled in it. Now she leaned forward, giving him a platform, she wished the kid would climb faster.

"Up!" she yelled to Leo. And even as she felt the kicks and inadvertent elbow strikes of the boy trying to get into place, she felt the tension on her harness.

Thank God.

Jo reached for the nearest sturdy thing she could grab. There wasn't much down here by the rushing water. One hand landed on a rock, and she decided that would be the best she was going to get. The other hand anchored on a small tree that she was afraid would come out by the roots if she put any weight on it. But she tested it, and she'd have to trust it.

With Jason firmly clinging to her back, she took a step.

The mud was rising behind them. Each time she got a little higher, thinking she was out of it, the water and mud lifted as far as she did, encompassing her feet and tugging at her.

The single use waders slipped. They were lightweight and not holding against the mud. It wasn't the job they were made for, but there wasn't much she could do about it. She didn't have time to pull out her ice cleats. She wasn't even sure they would work, but where would she even find a spot to stop and put them on? She couldn't.

Jo would have to get the two of them out of here with only what she had. She climbed another few feet higher, disappointed as once again the mud caught up as soon as she gained any ground. Her harness held tight, and thank God.

Leo must have the rope wound hand over hand holding her up. And—as scary as it was down here—she was grateful she wasn't the one hauling him.

"Slow and steady," she whispered to herself, keeping her

thoughts on one thing, though she quickly realized that Jason nodded along.

They'd crossed upward at a little bit of an angle at first. This worked since she'd entered the climb not directly below the harness. She worried that Leo still couldn't see them. There was no safe way for him to peer over the edge and check on them. So he called down periodically and she called back up.

"Jason's good!"

But she still couldn't see him behind her. The boy shifted a little bit, his face buried into the back of her neck. She could feel his terror in the clench of his arms around her neck. So far, he'd managed to not choke her out, but she didn't put much stock in that remaining the case.

For every step she managed to make, one foot would slip out from under her. Each time her heart clenched, she would flash to a sudden fear that this would be the time they would slide down.

What if she fell and hit the mud hard, and it jolted Jason loose? There was nothing holding the boy onto her, except his own strength and terror. Reaching up with one hand for one moment—she couldn't spare it any longer than that—she patted his arm around her neck and said, "Good work. Let's keep going."

It took an eternity to reach the top even though there was no real top. She just kept climbing. By the time she was far enough up to see Leo, she was on her hands and knees, digging the toe of each boot into the mud for whatever purchase she could find. Jason's extra weight now pressed her downward into the mud, rather than trying to pull them both off the steep upward side of the ravine.

"Jo?"

Her head snapped up to look at the same time Jason's did.

"Thank God!" Leo seemed relieved but it didn't change his stance. He was braced against a sturdy large trunk, one booted foot against the base. His hands slowly pulled in the rope and anchored it every time she gained another foot toward the end.

Despite his obvious relief at seeing them, the tension on her rope didn't change. *Thank God.*

When she finally got close enough that he let some slack into the line, her breath cut and her heart stuttered as she realized she was okay. She wasn't sliding backward. Leo had made the right decision.

He moved with speed and precision, his hands quickly lifting the boy off of her back. Only then did she realize how heavy the burden she'd been carrying was—not only the physical weight of the child, but the concern that she could lose him at any moment.

She heard Leo's voice talking calmly and rationally to the boy. She watched as the steady ranger set Jason onto his own feet and moved him carefully away from the sloped edge and the danger.

Breathing a sigh of relief, Jo moved one foot forward in an attempt to stand upright. But as she did, the mud gave way from underneath her, and she slipped and fell backwards into the ravine.

CHAPTER TWENTY

Something moved at the corner of his vision.

Leo had his hands on Jason Ryder's shoulders, steadying the boy while making sure he was upright and assessing him.

The kid needed a foil blanket and heat. He needed food.

And Leo needed Jo.

His head whipped around and he saw her arms fly up as she slid backward and down the ravine out of sight.

He'd not anchored the last several feet! And she was falling.

Leo's first instinct was to run toward her, but he fought the urge despite the clench in his heart and the need to rescue her. If he went over the edge, he'd either wind up going into the ravine and needing a rescue himself, or if he was lucky, and he caught her as he went by, he'd add to the weight load on her harness system. Neither was good.

He'd screwed up. The rope was dragging along the ground, her weight uncoiling it as she slid backwards into the ravine. It dug into the dirt, making it nearly impossible for him to grab.

"Go!" He pointed and yelled to the kid even as he ran toward the rope and the edge. The earth slipped away under his feet with each step.

He knew to keep one eye on his rescue ward, and he watched as Jason Ryder slowly moved backwards—too slowly for Leo's tastes, but there was nothing he could do right now. Jason Ryder was old enough to take care of himself for these few moments.

Leo needed to get Jo.

Every movement felt like running in a nightmare. Each time he stepped, he slid backwards. Still, he fought to get closer to the tree, to where the rope was anchored. When he finally got his hands around it, it was taut and his feeble yanks felt like they accomplished nothing.

It was absolutely wrong form ... everything he was doing and, for the briefest of moments, his brain flashed back to when he'd been on the harness. There had been a light rain when he'd been saving the two hikers on the ledge, and he'd slipped. In that moment, he forgave Jo for every bit of blame he'd carried.

"Jo!" he yelled out, his voice carrying through the woods.

They shouldn't have come out here, just the two of them. But they had found Jason Ryder! It wouldn't matter if he lost Jo, though.

So he grabbed the rope, wrapped it around his arms, and felt the bite even through all of the gear. He pulled with everything he was worth.

It took forever. He rested only on the faith that something was on the end of the rope. He felt the weight as he pulled upward and he reminded himself that something could only be Jo.

She hadn't had time to get out of the harness and that had been the saving grace. Slowly, her head appeared once again over the sloped edge of the ravine. For a moment, he stopped pulling and just held steady. His breath soughed and his mind didn't question the relief that flooded his heart.

"I've got you!" he said and pulled again. Beside him, small hands latched on to the rope ready to help. But Jason Ryder's hands were now bare, his dark skin concerningly ashy.

"Thank you, but let go. If it slips, you'll burn your hands," he told the boy and watched as the small fingers reluctantly let go from 'helping.' "I've got gloves, you don't."

Leo managed to turn his head far enough to see the boy's expression as it fell. "Just step back, I'll have her up in a moment."

It took well more than a moment to get Jo Huston once again to the top. She emerged on her hands and knees as she came up and over the rounded edge. Though this time she came farther in, still crawling until she was almost at his feet.

Leo reached out, putting his gloved hand in hers, their joining squishing mud as they held tight. But he didn't care.

He just breathed out a heavy sigh of relief as her grip entwined with his, firm and steady.

"Can I get you to your feet?"

He hauled upward, helping, as she said, "Please."

The word rang in his ear with a weary heaviness. For whatever reason, at that moment, his brain twisted it into something far sweeter.

Even as he pulled her to her feet, he thought he could not develop feelings now for Jo Huston. But when she stood—her big blue eyes framed with wet dark lashes, her full lips slowly widening into a smile of relief—he felt his heart kick.

The moment drew out, soft and warm. Connection in the middle of the hellscape of the wet wilderness.

Shit. He couldn't fall for Jo Huston. *He couldn't.*

But the reason he couldn't do it now was because *he already had.*

"Jo!" the young boy yelled before hurling himself at her and hugging her despite the mud she had all down her front from her fall.

Jo's arms went around Jason and she shrugged as if there was no point in not hugging him back. Both of them were already filthy, Jason's gloves had been discarded onto the soaked ground. And the moment was gone.

Had it ever even happened?

Leo turned his thoughts toward figuring out how to get them cleaned up here in the middle of nowhere. He had to get Jason warm. And their next task was to get the hell out of dodge.

He put his own hand out, touching Jo's shoulder. He enjoyed it too much, the feel of it as she leaned into him with one arm still around the boy. She was opening her mouth to say something when a lightning strike cracked the sky and a nearby tree suddenly lit up white.

CHAPTER TWENTY-ONE

They'd run as fast as they could from the tree as it cracked and burned and threatened to fall.

Jason was the weakest link, holding them back. Jo had grabbed one of his hands, angry that her own hands were still so muddy and it was difficult to get a grip on him. Leo had him on the other side, and they pulled the boy along. His shorter legs having difficulty keeping up. The two of them were also trained for endurance and distance, while Jason was weak. He'd been out—lost—for almost a whole day, with no food, or at least none that she knew of.

When Jo felt Jason pitch forward, she glanced down and saw his feet stumble and twist. Once again, the only thing that kept him upright was Jo and Leo on either side.

She turned to Leo and made a motion. "We have to stop."

"Are we far enough away?"

The tree had lit up like a blaze. The noise had cracked the air like a gunshot as the trunk had come apart. Luckily it hadn't exploded embers on them. Maybe it had vaporized in an instant from the direct hit. She didn't know. And she hadn't hung around to find out.

That was the second time a strike had been too close. But at least this was a little farther away than the last time. She'd not had any damage from this aside for a racing heart rate.

She was breathing heavily, waving her one hand that wasn't anchoring Jason, who was now trying to lean over and put his hands on his knees. At least the exertion would warm him, she thought. It made sure his blood was pumping.

"It's the only upside of all this rain!" she yelled to Leo over the crackling almost thunder-like noise of the rain once again coming down in torrents. "The fire shouldn't last long, and it surely won't gain a foothold on anything nearby. Everything else is too wet to burn without a direct hit."

He nodded and said only, "Thank God for small favors."

They needed shelter and heat and she had no idea where they were. Given that they'd run away from the ravine and the mudslide, she hoped that if they kept going they would aim the right direction. But she couldn't say she was certain.

She did know they could no longer search for Dalton Ryder. They had to get Jason home. They couldn't sacrifice the child they'd found for the one they hadn't.

"Are we headed back toward the car?" She asked Leo when she caught her breath.

He nodded and she watched as he scanned the area. She should be scanning, too, but the threat of animal attack was minimal with the rain coming down the way it was. And she wasn't certain she had the energy to be on the lookout for anything.

She didn't want Leo to see that she was exhausted from going down and then up the ravine side several times in the thick mud. She didn't want to sound like she was tapping out, or holding him back, so she held her tongue.

But the fact of the matter was, she was nearly done for.

Jo watched as the park ranger pulled a compass out of yet another pocket and opened it up. The rain beaded on the curved glass and ran off, but it didn't seem to interfere with his ability to use it. Leo pointed. "We should head back this way. But we need to take a moment and get the mud off of you. And get Jason covered."

Jason was soaked. They had three spare raincoats, and she watched as Leo reached into his pack and pulled one out. It was a small size as they'd known they were looking for children.

The mud normally would have dried and flaked off. But in this weather it had only somewhat washed away; it wasn't going to dry. She was looking at her own mess as Leo pulled the clear garment around the little boy and gave him instructions.

"Keep your hands inside." He said as the boy began to poke them through the ends of the sleeves. "We need to keep you warm."

He helped close the front of the raincoat when the boy's fingers didn't seem to want to work, then grabbed chemical hand warmers from his bag and activated them, pushing them through the elasticized ends of the sleeves into the little boy's hands.

She watched as Jason's face relaxed, finally getting some heat.

"When's the last time you ate?"

The kid shrugged. "I had three granola bars with me and I ate them all."

"Did you drink anything?" Jo chimed in. She wasn't going to get clean, so the least she could do was help.

"We had water at our campsite." His eyes darted down and to the right, clearly ashamed now of the fact that they'd run off to go camping. They hadn't even begun to discuss the fire the boys had set. But Jo reached in her pack for water.

Leo's hand reached out and stilled her. "Let me take care of him. You take care of you."

For a moment she frowned before she realized that she was more of a mess than she'd thought. She didn't just have mud on her hands and feet, she had it all down the front of her. It was slowly beginning to wash away with the rain, and there wasn't much she could do to make it faster, nor could she just take off the gear.

But her gloves ... *shit*. They were caked and that was no use. She didn't have an extra pair of the outer gloves. But it was time to let these go. Taking them off meant her hands were going to get wet and cold, which would be a huge problem. But as messy as the heavy gloves were, leaving them on would be worse.

At least the temperature had gotten above freezing. That would be a small consolation though, as the rain was still cold and stole body heat from all three of them. Still, she peeled the gloves, held them up into the rain to rinse them and then tried to figure out where to put them.

They were far too expensive to just throw them on the forest floor and walk away. But they were wet and muddy and ... *screw it*. She shoved them down into a pocket as Leo handed an open water bottle over to Jason Ryder, who clutched it between his two covered hands still clenching the heating packets. The kid drank greedily, and Leo was trying to get him to slow down.

"If you drink too much too fast, you'll barf it back up."

Jo almost laughed. She wouldn't have expected Leo Evans to say the word 'barf' to anyone.

Then he looked up at her, those hazel eyes catching in a way she'd not expected.

"Do you want the good news?" he asked with a small smile.

Well, hell, she thought, *if there was good news ...*

"Luke and the ambulance are close. As soon as we get there, we can get Jason into it and get him warm."

That *was* good news, she thought.

"And you," Leo added even though she was shaking her head. She didn't need an ambulance, just a warm bath and a few hours of sleep.

She thought how heavenly that would be even as she

accepted the water bottle he was now holding out to her, already half empty. She realized they'd reached the point where they were sharing. Whether it was some level of intimacy, or necessity—maybe they'd already gone through their stash?—she didn't know. Jo didn't question it.

The water was slightly warmer than the air having been kept close to Leo's body heat the whole time. It shouldn't feel intimate out here in this mess. Nothing should. But it did.

"We have to get going again," Leo said before she was ready.

She'd managed to eat half of a granola bar. And she shoved the other half into the pocket without the dirty gloves.

The ground was still wet and slick. The mud making the going slow. Leo kept them aimed, and she trusted him. He knew these woods and he wouldn't let anything happen to her or the child.

They kept Jason in between them for his own safety, though Jo wondered if maybe she wasn't using the kid as a buffer against softer feelings that seemed to have sprung up.

She would have liked to have carried the poor kid, but he had to make his own tracks. One—because there might come a point when they needed to carry him, and they would need their energy saved for it. They were both tapped already. And two, because when he walked, he kept his blood circulating. It was the thing keeping the little boy warm.

But as they went further and further, she noticed the shivers racking his entire body. Jo became very concerned that they'd managed to save the boy, only to have him die out here on the trail.

She tried to be inconspicuous, but she called forward, "Leo. Leo!" in a soft voice.

It took several tries to get his attention, but at last, he heard over the sound of the rain and the wind that periodically kicked up the leaves, making rustling noises all around them in a sinister way. It sounded as though the forest were closing in, and it did seem to be claiming Jason.

Jo pointed to the back of the little boy's head as they all kept moving forward, hoping the kid wouldn't notice. But the sudden alarm on Leo's face, as he took in the boy's condition, made her heart kick.

CHAPTER TWENTY-TWO

Leo checked the dash on the car. Though he was confident he could feel the heat on his feet, the engine temperature gauge showed him the car was still quite cold. He looked over to the passenger seat to find Jo leaning her head back against the headrest.

She shouldn't go to sleep. Neither of them were warm enough to sleep.

"You okay?" he asked.

"I'm fine." She probably knew that single word really meant that she wasn't fine.

Leo only nodded as he stared ahead. The red taillights of the ambulance blurred and bounced in front of him as he followed it down the trail road. "You can't go to sleep."

"I'm not sleeping," she protested. At least the strength of her words was convincing.

Still ... "You have to keep your eyes open. I can't drive and monitor you."

She opened them wide and turned to smile at him, but it wasn't sweet or friendly. Leo laughed at her, then they both jolted as he managed to hit a rut and the moment was lost.

His brain was going five different directions. They'd handed Jason Ryder off to Luke Hernandez in the ambulance. Ronan Kelly had arrived and was checking the boy over, and Leo had checked in with the office. Bland had taken over Bethany's spot at the call center. He'd contacted the boy's family and Leo was grateful that he didn't have to do it himself.

Ronan was driving the ambulance in front of them, and Leo knew that Luke was in the back, helping warm Jason and keep him lucid. They were lucky that he'd been alive in these temperatures. One day, Leo might get to tell him he did a good job staying alive.

But for now, it was still a little touchy. They had instantly put the boy under a warming blanket. And even Leo could see that Jason had perked right up. Unfortunately, he was also asking about his little brother.

Leo had been in contact with everyone via his sat phone, and there was no news about Dalton miraculously showing up on his own. There had been no other searchers to join them in the nasty weather, not that Leo had expected it. And now, there was no one out looking for Dalton Ryder.

The only way to console that horrifying thought was to take care of everyone around him. Leo had a complex and he knew it, but he tried to get Jo to go in the ambulance with them.

She'd staunchly refused. He'd tried to enlist Hernandez' help. But Hernandez had only said, "Absolutely. Huston you can climb in, head to the hospital with us, and get checked out. But if she goes, you do too, Leo."

Well, he'd felt that like a personal attack. "No, I'm fine."

Damn, if Jo hadn't echoed those same words to him just now.

"What?" Luke had looked innocent enough. "If she's in bad enough shape to go in, then so are you. You were both out in the same conditions. So you either monitor each other and get each other home, or you both hop in the back."

While Jo had stood there with her arms crossed, one hip

cocked out, and a sly grin on her face, Leo had been forced to concede. It was either that or climb into the back of the ambulance.

He was confident he didn't need any more medical care than he could provide himself. Then again, he was driving down the trail road when he probably shouldn't be driving. Maybe he wasn't making the best decisions. He sighed.

He looked again and saw that the engine still hadn't heated enough to crank the air up. He turned to Jo. "You feel any better yet?"

She sighed, a soft simple sound that struck him straight in the heart. "I do. It's good to be inside. It's good to have the heat on."

"Yeah, about that ..." he said, and pointed to the dash. He hadn't meant to make her lean over almost in his lap to look, but she did exactly that.

"Well, shit. I guess the heat isn't on."

They both felt heat where there wasn't any. Not a good sign. "Who can I take you to who can monitor you?"

"I've got it." She tipped her head at him and raised one eyebrow. He knew it meant she was new in town. And he realized a moment too late that she was going to use Luke Hernandez' trick against him.

"Who can I take you to? You got a nana in town who can help?" She smiled.

Well, at least her brain was still functioning. Maybe his wasn't.

"My Nana is less help and more work these days." Though he almost laughed at the fact that she nailed his name for his grandmother on the first try.

Neither of them wanted to deal with the subject and it seemed she handled it the same way he did, by dropping it.

They followed the ambulance until the trail road met the main highway, and the engine temperature gauge finally began to move. Leo reached out and turned it up, blasting heat onto their feet.

The sound of the air hissing through the car was unmistakable and he watched as Jo leaned forward, putting her hands down toward the footwell, warming them up, too. She hadn't yet taken off her gloves. Neither had he.

They were in trouble. He knew the signs. They were both far too cold to be left alone. He hadn't noticed it when they were out, but didn't he always tell the searchers *that's why there are protocols?*

And here he'd gone and run an off-book search. They'd both known it wasn't protocol but both of them were cocky enough to count their training to make it okay.

Well, they were okay, at least so far. And they had found Jason. Both points in the favor of their dumb decision. But they weren't done yet.

Leo wasn't one to back down for much of anything. And he got the feeling that Jo Huston wasn't either.

"Listen," he told her having no idea what she would decide in the end, but he wanted to give her all the options. Tell her what he was thinking. Despite the first incident with the harness, she was a good rescue worker with great technique and wonderful instincts. "I want to go back out and find Dalton."

"You and me both." Her reply was quick, but she still held her hands down in the footwell and the heat was barely on.

"Others will come out soon if the weather changes. And you and I are in no shape to go back out right now."

She nodded along. At least she wasn't pushing him to turn around.

"Do you think they can find him?" she asked. She didn't tack on the dreaded word *alive.*

Leo nodded. "I've seen rescues in worse cases."

She nodded. She probably had too, that was probably part of why she hadn't given up.

"If we're going to go out and search again—" He didn't add together or in separate teams, "—then we've got to take care of ourselves right now."

She nodded again. "We need a warm shower and about four hours of sleep."

Not quite. "We need a hot bath—immersion is better. And *six* hours of sleep," he said, neither of which was still as much as protocol would indicate.

She merely shrugged at him, as if to say he wasn't the boss of her. Though Leo wanted to add that he, in fact, *was* the boss of her, he couldn't make her sleep and he couldn't force her into that warm bath either. "We both need someone to watch us. We need to be monitored for the next several hours or until our body temperatures are up to normal."

"Are you suggesting we follow the ambulance to the hospital?" Jo pointed ahead to the empty road where the ambulance had long since dusted them.

"No," he sighed. This wasn't good, but he hadn't yet thought of an alternative. Any of the people he would trust to monitor him had other things to do. They'd be going out and doing the search if the radar held true and the weather turned better in the next hour.

So he took the plunge. "I know you've got your go bag in the back seat. I live right on the outskirts of Redemption. It'll save me half an hour of driving." He didn't have to say it, she would understand that meant an extra thirty minutes of sleep. "There's a hot tub at my place ... and a guest room."

He tacked the last part on at the last moment.

"Neither of us is ready for a hot tub." She held her gloved hands up, and finally peeled the polypropylene layers to show him her fingers. Probably not surprising to either of them, her nail beds were a pale, ashy blue.

"Agreed. Neither of us can hop right in. I do have one of those deep, old Victorian bathtubs," he said. "Do you?"

"My apartment has a nice steamy shower."

"That's not immersion," he countered. He sounded like he was trying to convince her to spend the night. And he was, but not like that. He wanted to get back out as soon as possible. Unless he got word that Dalton was found while he slept, he'd be gearing back up at first light. That was only nine hours away now. The night was full dark around them. It had taken too long to walk back, and without the tension of the search, they'd probably lost what little adrenaline was keeping them warm.

It was just enough time to get his body temp up and sleep. He didn't want to waste half an hour driving her home. And he really didn't want to hear that she was sick—or worse—because he'd dropped off the new firefighter alone at her apartment and she'd fallen asleep before she was healthy enough.

So Leo asked again and waited for her answer.

CHAPTER TWENTY-THREE

"I'm not getting naked," Jo protested, feeling the fight in her voice, even though it shouldn't be there.

Leo shook his head as though she was being ridiculous. She was.

"I didn't ask you to. Get in with your clothes on for all I care. I have to scrub the tub later anyway."

She stood at the side of the huge old tub thinking what she wouldn't give to close the door and fill it with bubbles and fall asleep. It was, however, not her tub, and locking him out of his own bathroom was incredibly poor form. Especially when his body temperature had registered just as low as hers.

He was not going to try anything. He wasn't in any shape to.

That's what she told herself.

They'd taken off their raincoats and left their muddy shoes near the back door. She would have liked to have admired the house, but it was dark and she didn't have the energy to spare. The night had fallen around them as they walked Jason back to where the ambulance waited. In the end, they'd taken turns carrying the child.

But Jo pushed that out of her thoughts and admired what

she could see. The place was gorgeous. An old Victorian on the outside, it seemed modern on the inside with a few touches of country, including the huge clawfoot bath in front of her.

She wanted to tell Leo *Thank you.* Her apartment was high end with a wonderful standing shower with multiple streams and a sauna feature. But it wasn't a tub, and the thought of *standing* right now was clearly beyond both of them. Hence why the two of them were now staring at the water level as it rose in front of them.

The house, for all that had been remodeled, was small and had only the one bathroom.

Beside her, Leo must have declared the water high enough because he began peeling his shirt. The long sleeve, sports fabric pulled away and revealed what Jo had known she would see and wished she hadn't. It didn't help that Leo Evans was damn fine.

She stood still while he undid the buckle on his pants. And he must have seen her tense up. She'd signed up to monitor him and him her. They'd already checked their temperatures and both of them were woefully low. The tub was necessary. So was the water that was barely ninety degrees. It was going to feel like it was burning them both.

Leo stood on one foot, though whether he was wobbly because he was impaired or because he was normally bad at that, she didn't know. Now he stood there in a pair of unexpectedly bright green boxer briefs with smiley faces.

"You have smilies on your ass," she told him.

Leo shook his head at her, his hands planted on his hips. "You don't get to make fun of my underwear unless you're showing your own."

But that was all he did before turning away and slowly stepping one bare foot into the water as he cringed at the feeling.

Jo knew. She peeled her own shirt and stepped out of her pants, grateful that he wasn't watching her. She joined him on the side of the tub, but she plunged both of her own feet in and clenched her jaw against the growl that wanted to emerge.

It felt like sticking her feet into fire. But she sat forcefully still and waited for the burn to pass. She'd been here before—you knew you were cold when the cold water felt like it was burning. It was just going to hurt, so she leaned over and plunged her hands in as well. Though it felt bad, it shouldn't cause any actual damage. The water wasn't warm enough to do that.

Leo, it seemed, was more of a slow goer. After a moment of watching her grit her teeth, he put his other foot in, his hands still gripping the edge of the lovely porcelain lip.

Jo was in no position to look around, hunched over like she was, but she tried to do it. The bathroom was cream with stark white features. The pedestal sink seemed a bit impractical for being the only one in the house. But the tub was boxed in with a closet that seemed to have been added later. Though the molding around the door and the door itself matched the rest of the house, many of the features were far too modern to be original.

"It's a lovely place," she said, trying to make casual conversation. She sat in her underwear next to a man in his own underwear. He'd not commented on her matching neon pink bra and undie set. They were hardly lacey seduction material, more of a sport set designed for the comfort one might need if, say, searching for a missing child in the Nebraska wilderness during a storm.

She did however, regret that she'd not gone full sports bra. There was a deep V in the front of this one. Nothing she could do about it now, she needed to get warm. Slowly, she slipped down the side, letting her whole body slide under the water. She was grateful the water felt cooler to her torso, almost too cool. That let her know just how cold her hands and feet had been.

"Leo, you need to get in," she told him.

He only tipped his head one way then the other before conceding and slowly sliding down next to her. The tub was huge, but two adults just barely fit.

Lord. She'd not expected to be taking a bath with Leo Evans, of all people.

"Did you decorate the place yourself?" She was still trying to keep things casual even as she was aware that her now wet underwear was anything but casual. There was no way to do this gracefully.

But he seemed the perfect gentleman, kept his eyes up and shook his head and laughed at her question. "Somebody flipped it. I bought it this way. I am *not* handy."

That caught her by surprise. "How can a park ranger not be handy?"

"I am excellent—I'll have you know—with a wounded bobcat. I can repair a trail trap with the best of them. And I can create a shelter out of anything. But home repairs are out of my league."

She laughed, threw her head back and felt the smile form on her face. The casual conversation she was pushing was ridiculous self defense. This wasn't Dallas. It wouldn't ever be Dallas again, at least that's what she told herself.

But laughing like that just drained her of all her energy.

Leo, too, she thought as she watched him lean his head back against the wall the tub was up against.

She was just getting ready to say they couldn't go to sleep, but he popped up and pulled the chain to the plug, letting some of the water drain out as he claimed, "Time to add warmer water!"

Even as he turned the faucet on, he explained, "It'll take a minute to get warm. It was a good remodel, but they didn't go for the instant hot water."

"Not handy enough to add it yourself?" she teased, but he took it in stride and shook his head again.

Neither was she, Jo thought. She liked to believe she might have been better at repairing things had she been raised in any environment where people fixed any of their own appliances. She was certainly mechanical enough. But when the trucks or the jaws of life or the chainsaws needed repair, she was the assistant at best.

She leaned back against the sloped edge of the tub, created for exactly that purpose and she watched from under her increasingly heavy eyelids as Leo added hot water. She felt the tub and her own body temperature rise.

Her eyes slipped shut and his hand touched her arm, soft and warm as he tapped on her wet skin. "You can't go to sleep. You know better."

So she sighed and sat up. He was close, too close. Leaning in. Worried maybe she'd actually fallen asleep for a moment though she would have sworn she'd just blinked.

She couldn't sit up like she needed to without getting even closer. And she couldn't help the way her heart kicked at the intense gaze that she saw in his face. Or the fact that she knew it was all wrong.

But she leaned in.

CHAPTER TWENTY-FOUR

"Hey, stay awake," Leo told her again, reaching out and tapping her smooth, wet skin. It was hard enough to keep himself awake, let alone someone else.

It was equally difficult to ignore the feel of her under his fingers, but he tried.

If they stayed in the tub too long, the water would cool. Without their own bodies working to keep their temperature up, that could be dangerous. So they needed to keep increasing the temperature, slowly bringing themselves back to normal. He watched as Jo didn't really respond, and he said, "We need to add more hot water."

She merely waved her hand in a small circle. "Go ahead, I'm awake."

But she didn't look awake. Her head was tilted back against the curved edge of the tub and her eyes had drifted closed, long, dark lashes resting against her cheek.

He was in trouble.

Had she rubbed him the wrong way the first time he'd met her because he was attracted to her and he hadn't wanted to be? Or was he finally just seeing that the irritation and concern he'd had about her was his own and not anything that she'd said or done?

It didn't help that they all knew that she'd come from Dallas, and from Boston before that in relatively rapid succession. Jo Huston had arrived at the Redemption Fire Department with a black mark trailing her around.

"We have to talk," he blurted out. At least that made her open her eyes.

"I'm sorry," she said as she stared at him coolly, almost regally. "Are you breaking up with me?"

He laughed then, a loud amused sound that bounced off the walls of the old house. He tried to ignore the issue that they were sitting in a tub full of clear water, both in their underwear, no secrets left for either of them. "No. We have to talk so we stay awake ... Tell me about your childhood."

"Oh, dear Lord," she replied. "I guess you weren't there when my mother just showed up at the station last week?"

"I heard about it," he said.

"What? You did? Are the park rangers and the firefighters this really tight knit group?"

Leo thought about it for a moment. A lot of the guys on the shift were his friends. He didn't work the same "24- on-48-off" that they did, so he had friends from all three shifts.

When he didn't answer immediately, she sat up straighter, causing little ripples through the water. "Oh, my God. It is. It's a boys club!"

"Not really," he countered. "It's not a *boys* thing." Though even as he said it, he realized the majority were "the guys" and it could easily look that way.

He had not yet seen Jo at any of the outings. "Have they really not invited you?"

She didn't really answer yes or no. "I've been here for—what?—four weeks. And yeah, I guess they did invite me a few times. The timing was just bad."

"You should go next time," he told her. "You should make an effort."

Something about the way she nodded told him that not only would she maybe not make the effort but that there was something about "making the effort" itself that concerned her.

"Why Redemption?" he asked next. He'd grown up around here. A lot of them had. The imports tended to have a variety of reasons for moving to a place so small. He wondered what hers was.

But once again, Jo shrugged it off.

Curious, he thought, and he told himself questioning her was just an excuse to stay awake. He phrased it another way. "Then why did you leave Dallas?"

"Didn't fit," she said too casually.

That's what he'd heard, too. Now, it seemed strange that he'd heard it. But he knew chief Taggert from back in his own lost-kid days and even though he was a full generation younger than the man, he was a family friend, a national park ranger, and not specifically on Taggert's crew. Leo realized he'd been privy to interesting information over the years. One piece of which was Jo Huston's past.

Taggert had liked her but been leery of hiring her.

"What?" Jo asked, leaning forward now, looking him in the eyes as though she'd read on his face every thought that crossed his mind. It was unsettling how she seemed to be looking into him rather than at him.

So he told her, "Taggert and I are friends."

"Okay ..."

"Your rec letters said she's a good worker, very intelligent, always working to train herself better. Yet, for whatever reason, she just didn't fit with their crew. And that the chief hoped you'd find a good position elsewhere."

He watched as whatever spark that lit her up faded suddenly and Jo disappeared behind shuttered eyelids. Her mouth pressed tight, clearly angry and clearly not going to let him in on any of it.

Leo shifted the topic back, not quite sure where it had gone so wrong. "So, after Boston and Dallas, Redemption's a big change. Why Redemption?"

"They had an opening," she said, her thoughts still shuttered to him, the words making it sound as though it were just that easy.

He waited her out, until eventually she gave in and said more.

"The women on the crew have been here for years."

Leo frowned. "Lots of fire stations have women. In fact, lots of fire stations have a lot of women who've been there a long time."

She nodded. "You're absolutely right. And a lot of fire stations *don't*."

Something about the stress on the last word piqued his interest, and also warned him it was a topic that was none of his business. He tried again to steer onto friendlier ground. "So tell me about your childhood."

"Oh, please," she countered, the tone alone friendly, but her expression still closed to him. He hated it. But she asked. "It's your turn now. Why are you a park ranger?"

He told her about Garrett. About his getting the two of them lost, and he watched as she slowly sat further and further forward. Her top half emerged from the water and he tried hard not to notice.

"This search that we were on …" She made a little circling motion with her finger over the bath water, her tone icy. "This was personal for you."

"I try not to let it be." He felt attacked, but she was right. "But they're all personal, aren't they?"

Jo ignored the part where he'd tried to get out of it. "It would have been nice to know that before I was left alone in the freezing rain with you."

That hit him like an open hand to his rib cage—not enough to hurt but enough to let him know he'd done wrong. "You're right. I'm sorry."

He watched the tiny flare in her eyes that she tried to conceal, surprised at his sudden apology, and he added more. "I should have told you."

She nodded slowly. "I don't begrudge you doing it. I really don't. We all have personal things we go after." She motioned to herself, her hand moving up and down as if to say "Case in point." "But I would have liked to have been let in on *why* you were making the decisions you were making."

"That's fair," he said. "Although, honestly, I'm not always sure why I'm making the decisions I'm making. I tell myself it's because there's a lost kid and I have to find them. But you're right, I can't dismiss the similarities and that my past is probably influencing me. What about you? Why did you stay out and search, even when we knew we were going off book? We both know the protocol is not to step foot in the wilderness in those conditions. I think it's easier to see why I stayed. Why did you?"

CHAPTER TWENTY-FIVE

Jo's initial response was just to shrug in answer to his question. But that was always her initial response wasn't it? *Give nothing away.*

She didn't know why she was starting to trust Leo Evans, but she told him, "I always start from a deficit. And, as you can tell, I'm pretty driven. So I feel like I have to go and do everything."

She paused, but he didn't say anything and she filled the silence, the warm bath maybe soothing her into saying more than she would have otherwise. "And there's also the fact that I picked a job where I really like going and doing everything."

Leo was nodding along. "But you don't have to do everything ... Why do you think you start from a deficit?"

That was rich. He figured it was her own personal flaw to think that way. She heard her own laugh and the brittle undertones. "Are you serious? I'm a woman in a firefighting rig."

He shrugged again, almost as if she was being silly. "But you aren't the only woman. Redemption has women on the other shifts, you're just the first on A."

She tipped her head at him and motioned for him to refill

more warm water. "It'll be time to check our temperature again."

She said it because she was thinking it was past time to get out of this tub and out of this conversation. But Leo seemed to truly not understand.

She gave in and explained. "It doesn't matter how many women are on the team, we all start from a deficit. We're all expected to not be as good or to not be able to lift as heavy of things, to not run as fast, to not perform as well. That's an inherent expectation each time we walk in."

She watched as his eyes darted to the side. "What?" she asked, and then—when he didn't answer—she pressed. "What?"

"Maybe you're right." He paused a moment before adding, "You and Sebastian were working that rescue when my harness slipped. And I assumed the problem was you."

He clearly hated acknowledging that, but Jo nodded. "That's exactly it! Granted, you know Kane better than you knew me at the time. But that's another deficit I have: constantly being the new kid. No one has any background to judge me by."

She hated this conversation. She'd lived it and that was enough. But Leo seemed to genuinely want to hear about it. Frustrated, she slapped at the water, just a little, as if that would make a difference and relieve some of her anger. "Apparently everyone here already knows that I'm coming in with black marks against me from my old units—whether or not they're actually true."

The words seemed to absorb slowly into him as though he were a sponge. His expressions changed and softened, as if considering for the first time that maybe everything he'd heard about her wasn't flat out right.

In the end, all he said was, "That sucks."

It disturbed her how good that made her feel, just to have him acknowledge that without trying to fix it. "It does. And I know if I want to get promotions, if I want to be the same as everyone else, then I have to fit in and have to work a little bit harder to be thought of as good. It's just the way it is."

"Well …" He seemed to think it through. "The women on the other shifts seem to like it there. And Taggert and the crews think very highly of them."

Jo nodded. It was part of what had brought her here, made her apply and made Redemption her top choice. That was what had thrilled her when Taggert had called and asked her if she wanted the position.

Applying for firefighting positions was a complex web of figuring out where you were willing to move, exactly what skills you had, and whether that fit the missing puzzle pieces of a particular station. So Jo told him, "I'm bringing yet another deficit, beyond just being a woman."

"What's that?"

"I'm a Huston."

"Is that supposed to mean something to me?"

"Well, thank God that it doesn't!" She smiled. It sure had in Boston. So she sighed. "You know the houses on the hill just outside of Boston?"

"I guess I've seen pictures … Oh my God, is one of those yours?"

"Yes."

"Ooh." He raised one eyebrow at her, a charming expression that she couldn't afford to fall for. "That might actually change how I feel about you."

"I know. Right?" She leaned forward, because at least this time he was smiling, rather than seeming to either be shocked or dealing with the fact that he was telling her he knew all about her past. Even though he didn't quite know …

"No one appreciates a trust fund baby." Jo tried to look sad and watched to see Leo laugh again.

"So you don't even need the job."

"See, that's what everyone thinks." She talked now over the

sound of warm water rushing into the tub once again. She couldn't help the sigh that came out. "Oh, that feels good."

He shifted with an agreeing sigh of his own and her eyes darted to the bright green underwear with the smiley faces soaked through, grinning up at her, and she tried to quickly avert her eyes. Looking was inappropriate.

"Hopefully this is the last round," she said when he turned the water off. They would be warm enough and they could get out ... she hoped.

Leo looked at her solemnly, too solemnly for her almost religious enjoyment of the now actually hot water. He looked at her and said, "Okay. You want to know the real reason I became a park ranger?"

"Do tell." She could see the red starting to creep up from his chin at even just the thought of what he was about to say. Now she was horrifyingly curious.

"So I stole my parents tractor when I was sixteen."

Didn't everyone out here do that? She motioned for him to keep going. No way was that bad enough.

"I drove it on the freeway ..."

How many times had she been caught behind someone on a tractor, taking up the road? She had to be frowning at him. This needed to get bad, fast.

"I drove it to my girlfriend's house." The red creeped a little higher and it was damn cute, but she didn't say so. "And then I stole her father's car."

"What?" Jo leaned forward. "You *what?*"

He nodded in admission. "She convinced me it was okay. Said that she had the keys and she was allowed to drive it, but she wanted *me* to drive. It was one of those things where you know it's wrong. But none of it was wrong enough to make you stop doing the thing you *really* wanted to do."

Jo knew.

"So I'm driving her father's car. I thought I kind of had permission, but I got pulled over for having stolen the car."

"You little thief." Jo grinned at him.

"Oh, wait, it gets better."

Now she was laughing openly. She was definitely awake and he'd won that round. Though she was still exhausted and in dire need of a bed, she wanted the rest of the story. "So what's worse than that?"

"The cop who pulled me over pretty quickly identified that I had forged my own license."

Her mouth fell open. He'd stolen a car and forged a license? Not the Leo Evans she was expecting. It made her slamming a coworker into a wall a little less scary to talk about. But his transgression was at sixteen. Hers was less than sixteen weeks ago …

Jo paid attention to the story.

"See, the thing was, I wasn't sixteen. I was fourteen. I was tall and I thought because I was tall for my age that I could pass as being older. If you ever get a chance to see a picture of me at fourteen, you'll understand just how mistaken I was."

She tried to fight the silly grin at the thought of a gangly teenaged Leo.

"I don't think the cop pulled me over for a stolen car. I think now that he did it because he saw a *kid* who was clearly far too young to be driving."

"Did you tell your girlfriend you were sixteen?" she asked.

"Oh yeah. And she bought it … or she seemed to. It turned out I really had stolen the car, because she'd lied to me, too. She was only fifteen, and not allowed to drive."

"That's why she talked you into it."

"Uh-huh. So I was underage, in a stolen car—"

"With an underage girl."

"D—all of the above." *He looked so chagrinned!*

"So why did this make you want to be a park ranger?"

"Because a park ranger who knew my dad—"

"Oh," she interrupted. "So fourteen-year-old you had connections?"

"I guess I did. I didn't see it then, but I do see it more now for what it is. But I was sweating bullets and the ranger talked the officer into letting me off. It was the ranger who drove me back to my tractor. And I had to drive the damn tractor home at fifteen miles an hour in complete and utter embarrassment. It was pretty bad."

For a fourteen-year-old, she thought.

"Did you ever have a fake ID?" Leo asked her.

She shook her head. "Nobody carded me."

He motioned up and down her warming skin as if to say, *Well, why would they?*

But she hadn't always been an adult. She'd simply always been a Huston, but instead what she told him was, "I'll go one better ... I've practically been handcuffed on the side of the road for impersonating myself."

"How?" He was grinning at her, nearly laughing, and it pulled her in. She would have said *yes* if this man had picked her up at a bar. She was going to have to work hard to stay neutral and this stupid bath wasn't helping, but dying of hypothermia in her own apartment or even just getting pneumonia would be stupid. The entire FD would make fun of her and she would have deserved it. So she told Leo her embarrassing story.

"I had my driver's license done as my mother always told me to. I got dressed up for my picture. Hair, all the makeup."

She wondered what Leo might think if he saw her like that. She'd been raised in charity event ball gowns and she could do it. Leo shrugged as if to say, didn't all women do that?

"I think a lot of people make sure they look nice, but when you get pulled over in your firefighting gear, no one believes that's actually you."

"Oh!" he finally caught on.

"So I went into the DMV in Lincoln two weeks ago with no makeup and my hair in braids hoping that at least the officers would recognize it was me when they pull me over."

"That's pretty funny."

"It's actually pretty sad that I can put on enough makeup and change my hair enough to be completely unrecognizable."

He opened his mouth, but then closed it and whatever he'd been ready to say disappeared. Instead he said, "We should take our temperature again."

He handed her the thermometer and at the beep, Jo smiled and handed it back. "Oh my god, I am high enough. Your turn!"

She watched him with the plastic digital home thermometer, thinking that it shouldn't be sexy to place it under his tongue. The man was sitting there buck naked except for smiley face underwear and sucking on a dumb thermometer and she was getting turned on.

Fighting her urges, she stood up and announced, "I am ready for bed."

A quick, wild expression crossed his face.

It mirrored the feeling she'd been pushing down for a while. And Jo knew she'd opened a whole can of worms with those five words.

CHAPTER TWENTY-SIX

"Your guest bed is a futon, Leo." Jo leaned in the doorway of the spare bedroom, her arms crossed.

"It's a good futon. It's fine."

"If it's so fine, why didn't you offer it to me?"

He'd offered her his bed—a queen, covered in fluffy comforters stacked with pillows. He'd offered to change the sheets and sleep in the guest room himself, playing the perfect gentlemen.

It almost bothered her just how much that attracted her. Had the men she'd been around just been so shitty that a guy being decent was too much for her to resist?

She rarely dated. There hadn't really been anyone she'd wanted to. And she'd had her mother shoving her at society milquetoast men her whole life. She kept telling herself that later she could find the right person, maybe get married, settle down, once she got her career taken care of. Her career had not taken care of itself. It had kind of done the opposite of that.

So she stood quietly now, while Leo peeled the blanket off of the futon, revealing that this bed wasn't made at all. It was more work when they were both already exhausted. She was going to sleep like the dead.

For a moment, she considered just walking the few feet over to him, taking his hand, and pulling him from the room. The hallway was short and narrow. It would take ten seconds to drag him back to his own bed. He could peel the yoga pants she'd slipped into, and the too large t-shirt.

That and her clean underwear had been rolled up and stuffed in the corner of her go bag for situations just like this. He could have her out of everything in three seconds. In her imagination, Leo agreed to all of it. She wondered what it would be like to come apart in his arms, then roll over and go to sleep curled into a warm man ... into Leo Evans.

It sounded wonderful. They didn't have to be anything to each other or mean anything to each other; she could just have a warm, wonderful, wild night. But it had been a long time since she'd been with anyone and even longer since she'd been with anyone that she truly had feelings for. Jo was getting the idea that she could fall hard for Leo Evans.

But before she could even reach out her hand and set the whole wonderful plan in motion, she imagined all the fallout. It would be enough that people would know she'd stayed here tonight. If she slept with the park ranger, she'd have to see him again. For some deep reason that she didn't want to examine too closely, it mattered to Jo what Leo Evans thought about her.

It shouldn't. But it did.

She added in the issue that she'd been his anchor the last time he'd been dangling over the side of the mountain from a harness. It wasn't that long ago. What if the situations were reversed and he didn't think very highly of her? What if she was the one in the harness and all the people who would be her anchors were people who thought she was sleeping her way through the ranks? Would it make a difference? It shouldn't! But it wasn't just their respect of her, but her life on the line, if it did.

What if she slept with Leo and he talked? She already knew he talked to the other firefighters on her shift.

"What? What's wrong?" His voice startled her but still moved through her system smooth as butter.

"I should go home," she said.

"You should go to sleep," he countered. "You're falling asleep upright in my doorway."

"You're right. But do you mind if I borrow your car for the night? I'll bring it back in the morning." It was the only thing she could think of that didn't make him more responsible for her.

"It's a nice bed." He pointed across the hallway. "It's comfy, and I'm more than happy to change the sheets, if that's the issue."

"It's not that." She closed her eyes for a moment, then jerked them open. Had it been a moment too long? Was she falling asleep on her feet?

"It's just the fact that I'm here."

"That you're not at home in your own bed?"

"No, it's that I'm in some man's bed." She couldn't help the slightly bitter tinge that colored her words.

Leo nodded as though that all made sense. "You're not the first firefighter to stay here. And you're not the first person who's been in that tub after a cold day of searching. This is not unusual for me."

That didn't make her feel better. "But am I the first woman?"

"No."

"Did you sleep with the other one?"

There was a pause before he said, "No."

"So you did sleep with at least one of them."

"She was my girlfriend."

That sparked something inside Jo, a worry lightning bolt that made this even worse. "Do you have a girlfriend now? Am I not only going to get accused of sleeping my way around, but also of breaking up a relationship?"

"I don't and you're not going to get accused of anything," Leo assured casually as his hands worked quickly to put fresh sheets on the futon. "Is it really that problematic?"

"Yes!" She answered it emphatically. "You don't know because nobody ever accuses you of sleeping around. Not that you're trying to further your career by fucking someone."

"You're right. I don't. But I will tell you this: I know the guys at the station. I'm in charge of the Rangers. I don't think anyone would even dream of saying anything. But if they do, I will shut down any talk."

Her smile was slow and sad. "Do you really think that works?"

He looked at her as if to say *why wouldn't it?*

"Did you vehemently defend everyone else who came through?" She waved her hand down the hallway as if to mention anyone in the past that he'd helped. But their existence didn't matter to her situation. It didn't make things any better that at least one of them had been somebody he was sleeping with. "Because if you act differently toward me, it will just be evidence that something happened."

"But it didn't," he said it as though the night had already passed.

"You can tell people not to say things, but you can't change what they think." And she hated to admit that it mattered what people thought of her. Not in the general world it didn't. But at her job, it was everything. It was promotions, it was getting sent in first, it was being trusted to fit into the pipe and save the kid. It was the guys who held her lines when she was dangling over the side of a cliff . . .

"Worst case, they'll think I'm sleeping my way around. Best case, they'll think I didn't, but that you want me."

He turned away, suddenly furiously tucking the sheet under

the edges of the futon and snapping out the comforter he had set aside with a little too much anger.

Was he angry on her behalf? On behalf of women everywhere, who'd been accused of screwing their way to the top.

He didn't turn around as he said, "Well, I can't help that part."

Her heart kicked and stuttered at the admission.

Leo Evans wanted her.

Heat flooded her.

Did it matter what she did?

Maybe it didn't matter when everyone was going to say she did it anyway. Jo took a step into the room …

CHAPTER TWENTY-SEVEN

Leo woke to a slightly sore back and a lonely futon. Though he was more rested than he'd been when he laid down, he was also more stirred up.

He'd dreamed of Jo Huston. Of having her long naked legs wrapped around him. He dreamed of her making noises—breathy sighs and orgasmic gasps—in response to him touching her.

He'd woken up rock hard and unsatisfied.

For a moment last night, after he admitted that he wanted her, she'd stepped into the room. His brain had flashed to a fantasy of her peeling off that gray Redemption Fire Department t-shirt that looked better on her than it had on anybody ever before. He imagined his arms around her and him kissing her until she begged for more. He'd held his breath, not even realizing he was doing it.

But whatever had seized her to make the first step had stopped her there.

The heat that had flared momentarily in her eyes and shot through every cell of his body had once again shut down. It was like the door had closed. She wasn't cold, just neutral, and maybe that was worse.

Jo had offered a calm and simple good night, before she turned and walked across the hallway, and closed his own door behind her.

Leo now swung his legs over the side of the bed and pushed those thoughts away to check his cell phone. He first saw that the weather had, in fact, turned. More search teams had gone out last night and it seemed they were still out.

Unfortunately, there was no news other than that they were looking. That meant no one had yet found Dalton Ryder. But the weather turning better meant that not only could more people search, but that Dalton would have a better time on his own. It meant he was far more likely to survive.

Leo thought about climbing back under the covers and sleeping longer. If he and Jo weren't needed, they could certainly use the extra rest. But he was already awake and, with his thoughts churning about everything Jo had said last night, he wasn't going back to sleep.

He also had the feeling that she would get mad if he simply made the decision for her that they were sleeping in.

He stood up, stretching, and feeling every muscle ache this morning even though the sun hadn't quite come up yet. He took a moment longer than he should have, needing the time to adjust to both letting his muscles wake up and figuring out how he would face Jo, after what he'd admitted last night.

Should he just let it pass? Act as though he hadn't said anything? Should he dive in and address it? Maybe he should just say something along the lines of, *I know what I said but it won't interfere with our work.*

Would she even work with him any more after that? It would be a shame if she didn't feel comfortable around him anymore.

It hit him then. And he hated himself for it. He had done exactly what she complained about.

It wasn't anything he'd asked of any fellow worker ever before. He didn't date within his work groups. And the girlfriend who'd come over that he'd slept with after a search? She'd already been his girlfriend before that.

It hadn't been difficult before to not be attracted to any of his coworkers. In fact, it only just now occurred to him that Bethany, one of his favorite employees, was actually a female.

Shit. He was the problem.

Stepping slowly and softly across the hallway, he knocked lightly and turned the knob.

He didn't step in the room. Just looked in and saw that she'd kicked the covers off and slept in the shirt and underwear. *Aaaannnnnd he shouldn't have seen that.*

What was he doing? He liked this woman. A lot. And he was making really shitty decisions because of it.

Even as he realized he should pull the door shut, because he was acting like he was in his own home with a family member and not a coworker, her alarm went off.

Jo rolled over groggily and he appreciated the sight he was suddenly privy to, that he shouldn't have been. But it seemed dishonest to back out now and act like he hadn't been there. He wished this was all occurring under circumstances where she wanted to be there for him.

He was going to have to clamp this down hard and be a damned professional.

She sat up, relatively bright and cheerful for such a quick transition. But then again, he thought, she was a firefighter to her core. She didn't move the comforter to cover her legs or act as if he was doing anything wrong. She just sat up and put one hand up to her head, her long, lean fingers shuffling through her hair.

Leo decided now was as good a time as any. "I'm sorry about

what I said last night. I shouldn't have put you in that position. And you can rest assured—" he kept talking even though she opened her mouth, "—I won't let it affect how I work. And I hope I didn't make you uncomfortable."

There, it was all out.

He waited.

She shrugged.

"We can't help what we feel." It was almost too casual of a dismissal. Was it worse that he hadn't made her uncomfortable or that she didn't even care?

He offered a nod and hoped his tight expression didn't convey all of the feelings crashing through him like waves on opposing courses.

"It's going to be worse," she offered up, grabbing and holding his attention yet again. "All the talk will be worse because I can't hide how I feel. I've always been very bad at it."

Maybe that was why she was so standoffish. She'd come across as cold. It wasn't just him who'd thought that; the others had commented on it. But maybe she went for *cold* because she was afraid of coming across as *hot*.

Leo nodded again, his hand tightening on the doorknob, once again ready to pull it closed and end this third circle of hell torture.

But Jo spoke one more time. "Because once everybody sees that it's mutual. All they're going to do is talk."

CHAPTER TWENTY-EIGHT

Jo sat at his breakfast bar facing him as he made breakfast for them. Her elbows were casually on the counter, a coffee mug cradled in her hands. Her hair was a little wild from having woken up, but to Leo it seemed more than a little intimate that he got to see that. Every time he'd seen her before, her hair had been military neat, appropriate for the job.

"Peppers?" he asked, holding up the small bowl that he had diced earlier. He had red peppers and yellow peppers and he felt a little fancy for it.

"Anything hot?"

"I'm sorry. No."

Jo held the mug in one hand and held the other up to stop him. "I don't do spicy."

He wouldn't have guessed that, and he tucked the small bit of personal knowledge away for later.

She nodded at him once they'd established nothing would burn her mouth and he added them into the eggs he was scrambling. He would have liked to have showed off with an omelet, but it wasn't a skill he had.

Leo worked diligently staying somewhat silent. He

simultaneously tried to appear perfectly normal and also to impress her. He was probably doing a shitty job at both.

"Cheese?" he asked. *Ah yes, the ultimate seduction effort. Offering cheese.*

This time she didn't answer, just took a sip of the coffee as she motioned for him to put all of it in. It made him grin.

"Are we going back out?" she asked.

"I don't know." He'd been thinking about that since he woke up and he hadn't come to a decision yet. So he figured he'd run it by her. He scrambled more things into the eggs, proud that he had steamed broccoli from the other night that he could throw in. It was enough to make it look like he knew enough to actually cook up a proper breakfast. The toaster dinged behind him and he turned.

"I've got it," she told him, and he talked while she buttered toast and he checked the eggs to see when they were fully cooked.

"We don't even have a full night's sleep," he started in. A good reason not to go.

"True, but you know the woods better than anyone."

"And you're one of our better trained search people," he smiled at her. Good reasons for them to go out.

"But we're only two people." She was arguing both sides, just like him. "What does the team that's out now look like?"

The day was gray, but warmer. Leo had checked the weather report, looked out his own window, and stepped onto the back patio earlier to make sure everything was accurate. "Most of the original team is back out. Stanford's down, but Bland is back. Bethany is down. Lincoln sent us a guy to work my desk. I think his name is Joel."

Leo didn't like it. He didn't like having someone work his desk that he'd never met before. Then again, Joel from Lincoln was probably able to handle the phones and having his own people out in the woods that they knew, directing the searchers, was probably more important. His people had set this up while he slept, and he couldn't fault their decisions.

Jo set the plate of toast beside her, sat back down, and picked up her mug. She'd cut the pieces into triangles and took a bite from one. She chewed thoughtfully while he plated the eggs and asked, "Are you going to feel bad if somebody else finds Dalton? Or if they find him and you aren't even out there at the time?"

Interesting question, he thought she must have that same drive he did, but he answered immediately. "No. I won't feel bad."

He slid a plate across the bar to her then walked around to take a seat next to her. He could feel her body heat, they were so close, but he missed seeing her wonderful expressions. She was right, she couldn't hide them.

He should have suggested they eat at the table. But it'd be a little hard to suggest that now. So he just answered her question. "I won't be upset if somebody else finds him. I need him found and I'll feel better once he's safe. Will I be jealous? A little. We had a rough shift out there last night."

"Not finding Dalton—for all that work and all that risk—it hurts," she added. She did understand. Even though they'd found Jason—which was *good*—it wasn't a full *win* until both boys were home—alive and safe.

"How is Jason doing?" she asked, seeming to know that he had the intel and that he'd managed to get all the details before she'd even woken up.

"Still in the hospital. He's stable and they expect a full recovery."

"Thank God, he isn't going to lose any toes or fingers."

Leo agreed. It would be a hard thing for a kid. Hell, it would be a hard thing for anyone, he thought. Leo hadn't had to go through that, but what he and his brother endured had been traumatic enough. He hoped the family was getting Dalton counseling, but it was his job to find the kids not fix them afterwards.

"What about you?" he turned the question back onto her. "Do you have a need to go out and find him?"

Jo shrugged. "I'm the same as you. I always want to be the one who finds the lost hiker, but I do know it's far more important that he's found than that I get the glory. I'd like to be there. If nothing, I want to cheer when they bring him in. But if other people are out searching ... I don't know that we are more help than hurt. We're the people who already put in a full shift, risking hypothermia and barely slept. I want to go, but I'm smart enough to admit if it was someone else, I would emphatically tell them not to go ..."

She let the thought trail off and they finished eating in silence. When she pushed her plate away, it was as clean as his. Leo gathered up their dishes and walked around to the other side of the breakfast bar and began to load the dishwasher. Only when he stood up, he bumped into her.

Jo was hand washing her mug before she set it in the dish drainer at the side of the sink. If they weren't going back out, then they weren't going to be search buddies. If they weren't coworkers ...

He let the thought trail away.

She'd said it was mutual.

She stood at the counter, facing him, an odd look on her face as though she didn't know what should happen next. Her wide eyes stared at him, her wild hair framed her face, her full lips parted slightly.

Here she was, having breakfast in his kitchen, and he hadn't even kissed her.

But he could remedy that, Leo thought. Slowly, he moved forward, making his intention clear. A small smile forming on his lips as she leaned in, too.

CHAPTER TWENTY-NINE

Heat shot through her as Leo's lips touched hers.

He tasted her softly, as though she was something precious, rather than the hardened warrior she'd worked to become. Every cell caught on fire. And though she'd seen him coming from a mile away—and had thought she could keep this casual—one touch and she'd been done for.

She wrapped her arms around his neck and leaned in further, pressing herself against him. She was relatively tall, but still she pushed up on her tiptoes, aligning them and enjoying the slide of her own body against his.

When was the last time a kiss had lit her up like this?

High school? College? Honestly, she didn't remember.

His fingers laced through her hair, and her head tipped back, cradled and secure. When his tongue swept in, her back arched, and she realized she could easily fall into bed with this man.

Maybe she should have last night. Maybe she could now.

It seemed nearly impossible to get close enough. But she was trying. Leo Evans was a man she could get lost in.

Jo felt the counter press into her back and she felt Leo at her front, all hard muscle and warm flesh. She considered reaching behind her and popping herself up onto the counter, as though that might be a nicer place to be. But like a deer in headlights, she tried not to move too much, afraid that any wrong gesture would end this. But so far, none of the gestures she'd made felt wrong.

Leo's hand slid from her shoulder and trailed down her side, tracing the edge of her breast, but going no further. His touch slipped lightly along her ribs and dipped in at her waist before following down to her hip. He elicited a sigh from her as his fingers clenched and tried to pull her even closer. Her leg slid up the outside of his, rubbing against the jeans he'd thrown on earlier. He was wearing far too much clothing for her taste.

Given his own bold touches, she let her hand slide under the hem of his t-shirt and trace the skin at the waistband. It was smooth, warm, enticing, and Jo leaned even closer into him.

She ignored every warning, every possible consequence, and every bit of fallout that she knew would happen.

It was done. She'd kissed him, and she couldn't un-kiss him. If she was going to suffer the consequences, she might as well enjoy the crime. Because being talked about, or shunned, or even fired for something that she hadn't done—or hadn't done the way it was insinuated—was bad enough. At least, if this came back and bit her in the end, she would have had this.

Her hips moved. She could feel the length of him behind the denim, growing hard at her touch. But as she moved proactively against him again, his cell phone rang. The harsh digital sound cut the air between them and pushed them apart.

As Leo stepped back, he looked at her through glazed, now-green eyes, heavy lidded, like her own, his mouth open, breath coming harsh.

It wasn't just her. Thank God.

His hand reached out for the phone and she wondered if there was news about Dalton. She too, turned everything off and focused. It was a wonderful skill even if, right now, she wished she could have lingered in the moment longer.

"Hello?" The excited tone in the word let her know that he, too, was hoping maybe there was word about the Ryder boy. "Yes … Yes?"

The second *yes* seemed a little more concerned. Leo's eyes darted back and forth across the room. "I can. Okay … hold on."

He held up one finger to her and walked out of the room, leaving her wondering if that kiss would fade into the ether. Then she wondered who the hell he was talking to that she couldn't even hear the half of it.

CHAPTER THIRTY

"She assaulted someone?" Leo couldn't believe what he was hearing.

"I don't know the details," Ronan Kelly told him from the other end of the line. "I just wanted to warn you because I got the feeling you liked her."

Leo didn't answer that. He could only appreciate that what he'd been feeling had likely shown and if Ronan had picked it up, had been there before *he'd* even realized it.

He scrubbed his hand over his apparently far too expressive face. "Are you sure? How can you be sure?"

"Well, I have the paperwork the Dallas station filed in my hands. Otherwise, I wouldn't have called you. I don't like to spread rumors, but this isn't rumors." Leo could hear the reluctance in Ronan's voice.

He still couldn't wrap his head around the idea that Jo had assaulted someone. She was bold and forward, but she wasn't mean, and she certainly wasn't stupid. He was trying to talk his way out of it. Though he recognized what he was doing, Leo still did it. "Taggert knew, and he still hired her!"

"Apparently, Taggert didn't know."

Leo was so confused. Jo had been at the Redemption Fire Department for well over a month. "How far back was this?"

"Not far, which is maybe why Taggert didn't know. Maybe she shifted jobs before all the paperwork went through."

"So it filed now and they sent it to him?" None of this was making sense.

"No, not even that." Ronan Kelly sighed—apparently neither of them liked this call. "Conrad Phillips looked it up. He got it in his head that he didn't like her and didn't want her on shift, and apparently he's been investigating her."

"Are you serious?" Leo asked. Phillips was a misogynistic piece of shit. He managed to barely keep himself together enough for the two women who worked on his shift. But Leo had no idea if Conrad had simply decided that they were the exception, and he was okay with it. Or if he just bit his tongue the whole time. Or if they'd gotten him by the balls and put him in his place. None of them would mind seeing the man go. But, apparently, he was out digging up paperwork.

"We can all call up the line," Ronan pointed out. "Make an official inquiry. That will at least get the truth out. Conrad said he contacted his rep."

"How is he considering filing a complaint against someone not even on his shift? He doesn't even work with her."

"I think he used the search this weekend as an excuse." Kelly had apparently become privy to all the dirt. At least he wasn't picking and choosing which parts he dished but …

That little bastard has been busy, Leo thought. What he said was, "That's pretty shady."

"It's super shady," Ronan replied. "But the problem is he did turn something up in the official paperwork. Within twenty-four hours before Jo Huston left the Dallas Fire Department, she assaulted one of her fellow firefighters on her own shift."

CHAPTER THIRTY-ONE

Jo puttered around in Leo's kitchen, finding it odd that he had disappeared to take his call. His voice carried a bit from the other room. But that was no surprise, the house was fairly small.

She couldn't make out the words, only the tone, and he sounded concerned. Jo became worried about Dalton. She could have sworn she heard Leo say goodbye and hang up. At least, that's what the tone and cadence sounded like.

But, though she turned and waited, he didn't come out of the room. Giving up after a minute, Jo checked out the decor and looked at the pictures on the walls.

The place had clearly been built with one idea in mind—very modern farmhouse. Though it was Victorian on the outside, the interior walls, paint, molding and fixtures all had white and gray tones, even the plank wood flooring.

Leo's furniture, however, was slightly different, more eclectic. Jo let her eyes sweep the place.

She didn't judge. She didn't have a talent for decor; she had a talent for tying knots and climbing cliffs. Her apartment was two bedrooms and very spacious for the money. Not surprising, given the land values here.

And she'd let Ivy Dean steer her to Marjorie Kane, a local decorator, who looked old enough to want to put up cabbage rose wallpaper and quaint farm signs. She would not have used the woman if she'd known at the time she was the mother of a fellow firefighter, but Marjorie had quite an eye and Jo now lived in a warm-toned, comfy apartment that managed to mix neutrals and colors with ease.

None of it she'd chosen herself.

So she didn't fault Leo the puffy green couch. And the brown leather side chairs flanked by black painted end tables. The built-in, white bookshelves held three or four rows of books, but the one at eye level was entirely populated with photographs.

Jo couldn't help herself, she moved in for a closer look.

The other man who looked a lot like him must have been his younger brother. The older couple were clearly their parents. But the pictures were so different from her own family photos.

The Hustons had portraits done almost annually at the photographer's studio or on location in some field blooming with wildflowers. The casual photos she had weren't casual at all. They were shots from galas, charity events, and ribbon cuttings.

The other photos she liked enough to display were from search and rescue missions. Those were the groups where she had had friends. There were none from the firehouses she'd worked at and, for a moment, she began to wonder if maybe she was in the wrong profession.

She loved the work. The hoses kicked and bucked when the water came through. She loved the challenge of knowing what would burn faster or slower. What materials would cause a flashover. What you needed to vent and what you absolutely should not. Where to stand and where to aim the water. It was all an art and a science.

She loved every minute of it. But she'd never been welcomed.

Though she'd done her part, she'd not been part of the team. Maybe that was because in Boston, she'd walked in as a Huston. They'd all thought they knew her before they'd ever known her. She'd been in the local papers with three inches of makeup and five inches of hair and a gown that cost more than their annual salaries.

After two Boston fire houses, she'd gone to Dallas. Had Dallas gone wrong because she already had a black mark on her name?

She'd never really know. But if that was the case, then she'd come to Redemption with two black marks.

Jo had considered taking her case to court, getting the history removed or at least straightened out. But in both cases, she'd been so happy to leave everything behind that it hadn't seemed worth the effort. Her transfers had come with rec letters—probably the kind that said, "We don't want this person but you should take her!"—and those were contingent on her walking away.

Besides, taking the cases to court might get the marks removed, but it could also get her known as litigious. Another black mark she didn't want.

Leo came out from the room then, leaving the door open behind him, where she could see the futon he'd slept on and the corner of the desk where he apparently had his office.

His expression told her that her reading of the call had been correct and the news had not been good. "What is it?"

"The weather's turning." He was looking out the window, not at her.

"I thought it was going to hold for a while."

"We all did. But they've already begun calling back the less experienced searchers. If it goes the way they think, everyone will be in shortly."

Silence hung in the air between them, and Jo waited for what she knew was coming.

"I'm going to try to go back out."

"You need a partner," she stated the obvious while wondering about the distance that seemed to have sprung up between them.

That call had come in the middle of a hot and heavy kiss. Yet now he stood on the other side of the room. Though invisible, the barrier between them was suddenly obvious. Was it just that the job had interfered? Or was it something else?

She hadn't said the words, but her offer to be that partner hung silently in the air between them. It took him far too long to respond and Jo felt that old, familiar sinking sensation. That moment she'd known when the fire was going to take the house. The moment right before she found the child, and knew he was no longer alive. The moment right before the job went to shit.

"I will." He let those two words hang in the air for far too long. Before he asked, "Do you want to go back out?"

But he still hadn't said they should be partners.

CHAPTER THIRTY-TWO

"I need three more minutes!" Jo called out from Leo's bathroom.

She couldn't help but glance at the tub. It hadn't been that long ago that she'd been in there with him. Now, she was defiantly braiding her hair, pulling the strands close to her head. The style was easy to take care of, but it took too much time. Leo had simply sprayed something on his fingers and run it through his own hair.

She thought again about cutting it all off. And again, she got mad. She wasn't going to do it. She shouldn't have to change who she was to be thought good at her job. Her fingers worked quickly, tying the braid up. She'd learned how to do the whole thing firmly anchored with just two ponytail holders.

Her arms flexed with the movement, heating her up at just the action of braiding her hair. She was back in her searching gear. She and Leo had tossed it into the washing machine before climbing into the tub, and then into the dryer before climbing into bed. They'd known this could happen—she'd expected it.

Now, she tucked the end of the braid under and secured it down before opening the door. She was almost too warm. And she would definitely be overheating in a few more minutes. But out in the weather, she would be more than grateful for all the layers.

Leo stood at the end of the hallway, all business now. His gear didn't mold to him, but it gave her the same thoughts it'd given her the first time she'd seen him in it. She'd suspected then that he was built like a Greek god. Only this time, she knew it for a fact.

She'd been held up close against those muscles, touched and tasted until she melted. But now the heat had been replaced with ice and she worried about the search.

Turning her brain to her professional side, she pushed all the emotion away. No one had found Dalton Ryder. And, so far, they'd only found evidence in the form of one of his gloves. His parents had identified it, confirming that the little boy had made it at least that far.

Jo and Leo had work to do. They checked and rechecked their gear, this time packing better. He'd pulled out two backpacks. Unlike the small ones they'd carried last time, these had frames and were ready to go. All she had to do was add her own water, food, and any of her own supplies, like her ropes and rappelling gear. It wouldn't be easy, but they'd be in better shape to handle the weather.

"You have everything for when we find him?" she asked.

Leo nodded, not commenting on the fact that she stated it as though it was a done deal. "Let's get going."

He turned and headed out toward the car without so much as a comment, or even a glance that referenced their earlier interlude. She told herself that he was simply in "search mode," and the Leo she'd seen last night and this morning would come back when the search was over.

But if they didn't find Dalton, would he come back at all?

And what would he tell the others about her?

It didn't matter, she thought. She'd done the deed. She might not have slept with him, but she'd spent the night at his house. And, because she'd kissed him, neither would be able to say it was simply about work. The fallout would be what it was.

Leo drove them down the freeway in silence, his SUV deftly avoiding any potholes. The shocks took most of the work to cushion the bumpy ride once they turned off the main road. They passed other cars and trucks coming the other way as more searchers tapped out, trying to get ahead of the incoming weather. Knowing it was dangerous to be out in this.

More than one stopped and asked them what they were doing. Each time, Leo made it clear they were going in when everyone else was coming out. When people questioned the wisdom of their move, he merely pulled rank. Jo stayed silent.

The thing was, she thought, everyone was right. They *shouldn't* be out here. They were violating protocol. If something happened to them, someone would come looking for *them*. They were gambling not only their own lives, but the lives of anyone who would come after them. And they were gambling it to find Dalton. She could only hope that—if they became more problem than solution—that anyone who came after them would do a better job of following protocol than they were doing.

Before she knew it, they were parked and Leo was getting out. Her boots hit the ground, and the weather pushed in around her. The cold bit at the exposed skin it found as the temperature plummeted. She pulled on gloves as the wind tried to un-braid her hair for her. Any nice weather that had come by the area, they'd slept through.

With the packs pulled out of the car and the straps slung over their shoulders, they aimed in the direction of where the searchers reported finding the small glove.

Leo had pulled out a map and handed it over to her, showing her the mark of the exact location. He no longer stood shoulder to shoulder to point things out. Something was definitely different.

But like any good rescue worker, Jo couldn't let her personal life or her emotions interfere with doing the job. Well, if Leo could leave everything from this morning behind, then so could she.

"The good news," she told him as she handed the map back. "—is that glove is directly on the path from the initial fire to the caves that Ivy suggested we check out."

They'd not made it all the way out the last time, having gotten sidetracked by hearing Jason. They'd found one boy. But the younger one was still out there.

Leo nodded. "You're right. That's where we need to be headed."

Central command, where they now were, had been set up at a different location than where they'd started before. So they were aiming a new way, one that left Jo just as unfamiliar with the landscape as she'd been the day before.

With no more than that one comment, Leo turned and headed out leaving Jo to simply follow along. As she did, she looked around, checking out the trees and watching the ground where she was stepping. More than that, she literally watched Leo's back. He moved with an easy grace, carrying the pack with comfort.

But it was the pack itself that was beginning to concern her. Leo had prepped them for far more than a simple search.

CHAPTER THIRTY-THREE

"Can I ask you something?" Leo almost had to holler the words above the rustle of the leaves, but he'd led them too far out to go back now. Whatever he learned about Jo, he was already stuck with her.

The temperature had plummeted again in the two hours they'd been out, and rain was a constant threat. Leo worried about Dalton more and more. They'd periodically stopped and called out for the little boy. The two of them might be breaking certain protocols not to search in dangerous weather, but they hadn't broken all the rules. Leo figured if Dalton had drawn a straight line—or even a relatively straight line—from the fire to where the glove had been found, he'd probably kept going after that.

They weren't even close to finding him yet.

Leo was grateful that Jo had all of the gear necessary to be out searching in freezing and sub-freezing temperatures. It was certainly something she'd eaten the cost for, something they couldn't request of most of the rescue team.

But so far, the hike had been awkward. What Ronan Kelly

had told him was disturbing, maybe more so because it simply didn't fit what Leo believed—or wanted to believe—about Jo.

This was a horrifying and blunt way for him to ask, but he figured they'd both appreciate just getting it out of the way. The walk had been silent until now, both of them angry and confused.

Jo proved his suspicion right when she called back, "Go ahead. Ask."

The tone in her voice indicated that she knew things had changed between them and that she was mad that he hadn't told her what. Well, he would tell her now.

"Did you really assault someone at your last job?" He paused. "Right before you left?"

The last part had tumbled out of his mouth. Leo realized after he said it, that he was clarifying as if she might have assaulted a handful of people and he was making sure she knew that he was talking about this one particular incident.

Jesus. What an idiot he was. For all the time that he waited, hiking in jaw-clenched silence, he still hadn't planned this very well.

The noise behind him changed. *Shit.*

He turned around to find that Jo had stopped several feet back on the trail.

She stared at him harshly. Even though she was almost entirely covered in several layers of polymer fibers keeping her warm and a head covering topped with a knit hat that left only her eyes exposed, he could see that she was pissed. Leo could even tell her mouth was hanging open and she was glaring at him slack jawed.

Even though all the clothing and the packs had been designed to be as comfortable as possible, maneuvering still wasn't easy. He took a few halting steps back towards her. Closing the distance, hoping to make the conversation easier, or at least make the hearing of it easier. The conversation was clearly going to be difficult as hell.

Sure enough, as soon as he stepped close enough, she said, "Obviously, you already know that I did."

That was it, it seemed. She'd said her piece, but her anger was the more important part. Jo's expression was clear that she was done with him.

But just when Leo waited until he felt compelled to fill the silence, she ground out, "That's what that phone call was, wasn't it?"

"Yes."

"Great. Who called you?"

"Ronan Kelly." He hated this. She had every right to be mad.

"So it's all over the fire department?"

He didn't know. "Were you hoping to bury it?"

"Since that was literally the agreement I struck when I left, yes."

Everything he felt must have showed on his face.

Jesus, she'd not only assaulted someone, she'd tried to cover it up. Why had she been foisted off on an unsuspecting department? Why hadn't she been fired? Who the hell would write her a recommendation letter after she'd assaulted a fellow firefighter?

And that was the mystery of it, because she'd gotten the rec letter. Taggert had hired her. He'd said he liked her in the interview. Leo was confused, scared his mentor and friend had been scammed, and worried that he'd had his own tongue down her throat just hours before.

Jo stood and glared at him and Leo stared back, trying desperately to understand.

Had she simply snapped? Would she assault him? Did he need to be worried about her walking behind him?

He'd not thought so. Left to his own devices, none of that

would have occurred to him. Was he really that bad of a judge of character?

"What did you do?" he asked.

He could almost see her, making decisions licking her lips, sorting her options.

But then her expression changed, she looked sad, scared, almost on the verge of tears. That couldn't be right, could it? Jo glanced quickly down and to the side, then looked up. Something about her changed in that moment.

Steel replaced the bone in her spine and ice replaced the heat in her eyes. "I slammed his head into a wall."

"Holy shit!"

Jo shrugged as if to say, *Well, what else could I do?*

She simply glared at him as if waiting for something. But Leo didn't know what else to say or do. This wasn't a provoked punch or a shove. That was a *real assault* by her own admission. What if she was watering the story down? People often did.

She stared at him, this time with no moving, no fidgeting, no glancing to the side. "Well, Leo. What are you going to do? Do you want to send me back? Do you want me to walk in front so you can keep an eye on me?"

These were all the things he'd been thinking. She'd nailed all the questions he hadn't yet answered. And Jo was demanding answers.

She stared hard for a moment, waiting for his decisions, but Leo didn't know what to say. He didn't say anything.

"Well," she replied calmly. "I'm sure that you're such a great searcher that you'll be just fine out here on your own. Certainly, I can find my own way back. If I find Dalton, I'll bring him in safely. And as soon as I find someone with a satellite phone, I'll have them contact you."

Jo Huston turned and marched away.

CHAPTER THIRTY-FOUR

Wait.

Jo thought she heard Leo's voice, but with everything covering her head, she couldn't be sure. So she kept moving as she fought the tears that formed, pressure pushing them to the edge of her eyes. She couldn't afford to cry. Her tears would freeze. She couldn't afford it emotionally either.

How many angry tears had she shed when she had left Dallas? Tears she would have liked everyone to believe she didn't even have.

Wait.

The sound was a little stronger this time, but she still didn't quite believe she'd heard it.

She kept marching forward, her feet stomping flat on the ground. It was safer than shuffling, but still dangerous if she hit something that rolled her ankle. Right now, she didn't care, and that was dangerous.

When she left Dallas, she'd been mad. But now, she was just hurt—hurt at having to deal with it all again, hurt that it was coming back to bite her, and hurt that it was stealing a fire department she was growing to like. Stealing a job where she was just beginning to feel appreciated. More than that, it had destroyed anything between her and the first man she actually liked in quite some time before it even started.

That was the first kiss she'd had in forever that had melted her bones and turned her to the kind of mush she'd sworn she'd never be.

This was exactly why she'd sworn she'd never do that.

She'd made it far too easy for him to stab her through the heart.

"Wait, Jo. Wait!"

That was him. He was calling her, nearly yelling now. So Jo slowly came to a stop and turned around. He'd been running to catch up with her, and it was everything he could do with the added momentum of the pack to stop before he slammed into her.

Leo looked her in the face as if he were searching for answers in her eyes.

She blinked anything away before he could find it and wondered if he could still see the remnants of the tears that sheened in her eyes.

"Jo, I don't want you to go back."

She just stared at him. That was not an admission of undying love—not that they had even gotten close to that—but it also wasn't an admission of trust.

"What happened?" he asked.

Really? She thought, *that's what it always came down to.*

She wasn't going to fillet herself open and hand him all the tools to hurt her more just because he'd asked. Because he'd already hurt her once.

"Fuck off," she told him. "You either trust me, or you don't."

Her hands splayed out to her side, as if she were giving up. It was on him now.

Leo nodded as if seeming to understand. Whether he actually understood or not was a dilemma. She simply wasn't going to tell him. Maybe, just maybe, he'd figured out it wasn't his to know. He nodded again. "Okay. I'm going to trust you."

Jo waved her hand forward, indicating he should turn around and get back on the trail. They did, after all, have a child to find.

Though it was morning, the day was dark before they'd come out. Just once she'd like to search in sunshine. But even the day before, the daylight hadn't lasted long for them. Now they'd come back out here during the worst conditions, worse than it had even gotten last time, though it hadn't started raining again.

Kind of like her and Leo, their little 'daylight' sure hadn't lasted long.

Leo reluctantly turned back around as if not quite certain about having her behind him. But they were both burdened with layers of clothing and the heavy pack. There honestly wasn't much she could do to him even if she wanted to. If she somehow went psychotic and tried to attack him, she'd be too slow and he was protected by so many layers.

So they moved forward in lockstep, back to their usual system with Leo leading the way. Occasionally, he would point out an obstacle she should be wary of—a root that stuck up higher than it looked like or a rock that appeared flat but would roll if she stepped on it.

They stopped periodically and called out for Dalton, listening for any return cries from a four-year-old. Honestly, Jo suspected that if the boy was still alive, he was already hypothermic. *If* he even heard them, he probably didn't have the mental power, or even the physical energy, to call back to them.

They would practically have to trip over him.

She could only hope there were more clues like the missing glove. That would help immensely; it would tell them they were still searching in the right direction. But so far, nothing had come up.

It was a short while later that Leo pointed to a pink flag hanging from a tree, and a marker on the ground.

Stopping, he turned to face her, making it easier for them to talk. "This is it. This is where they found the glove."

Jo was glad the other searchers had been smart and marked the location. It felt good to know not just that they passed the point on the map, but that they physically had reached the place where the evidence had been recovered.

She looked around to see if Dalton might be nearby. But the first pair here had likely done that, too. However, with the weather changing on them, the searchers hadn't made it far past this spot. She and Leo were moving into new territory now.

They turned all 360 degrees, looked up and down, and stepped off the trail as they called again for Dalton. But no response came except the howling of the wind and the rustling of the trees.

After a few moments of fruitless yelling, Leo motioned for them to keep going. Jo followed along in silence until he did it again—just started up a random conversation.

"Hey, Jo. Can I ask you something else?"

CHAPTER THIRTY-FIVE

Leo waited. It took a moment for Jo to respond to his question, but eventually she practically grumbled, "Sure, why the hell not?"

Okay, he thought, *she was clearly still angry, and deservedly so.*

But he was still confused, and he deserved to be confused, too. He was trying to think through every possible angle of it and coming up with nothing. Had Jo thought she would move to Redemption and start over and no one would find out about the assault?

Yet Conrad Phillips had dug it up relatively easily.

In that moment, Leo decided that he needed to tell her about Conrad. She deserved a heads-up that one of her coworkers had it out for her. And Jesus, *why?* What had she done to Conrad to make the man so angry?

They hadn't even been search partners, they'd only been together at the beginning in the group. He wasn't on her shift at the RFD, not that Leo knew about. Conrad had only the slimmest of excuses for investigating her in the first place.

Had she just been female and beautiful and uninterested in him? Conrad seemed like the kind of guy to think his interest was worthy of return. Leo didn't like where his thoughts were going. Maybe Jo *had* assaulted someone, but it sounded like she was getting shot down from all angles for no reason other than the circumstances of her genetics.

He didn't want to bring that up again, wasn't going to step into those murky waters right now. So he asked the other question, the one he'd intended. "Why go by Jo? Your name is Joely and it's beautiful. Why not go by that?"

He'd thought it was an easier question. Lighter. A simple conversation. But the laugh that replied was sharp and bitter and he realized that his innocuous question about her nickname wasn't an innocuous question after all.

He'd somehow stepped in it again.

There was a pause as the awful, angry laughter died down and he didn't think she was going to answer. But eventually she must have stepped up a little closer behind him. Because her voice was loud enough to startle him.

Leo had a flash of worry that she was going to do something to him or attempt it. She was certainly smart enough and strong enough to pull it off. But what she did was speak.

"Because no one wants to hire Joely to work in a fire department—"

"That's not true! They hired you. Redemption hired Leslie and Ann and ..." He didn't remember the other women's names.

He turned as he talked and looked directly at her. Jo just offered a far-too-easy shrug. "Of course, you're right. I'm sure *you* would know."

He felt her simply turn off again. *Fuck*. How could he just keep stepping in it with this woman? From what he'd seen, she was amazing. From what he heard, she was a nut job. And from what he said, he was being a right ass.

"I'm sorry. Tell me?"

Was her past record just an excuse to mistrust her? He really couldn't tell, everything was too tangled up to pull any one thread. And was letting her off the hook because he wanted her *badly*? He had no idea.

Leo wanted to kiss her again. He wanted to hand her off to someone else and get a new search partner. He wanted to have not met her and not feel what he felt.

"Women aren't as strong as men—" she started.

"But that's not true!" he interrupted.

Immediately, Jo held up one hand, palm out, and he watched her eyebrows rise. He shut up.

She started over. "Women aren't as strong as men. We aren't as tall—so we don't fit on the line holding the hose. Also, we distract the men. Also-also, we get pregnant, and then we need medical leave. We get hurt more easily and more often. So we require more workman's comp. We create sexual harassment cases by showing up to work each day. And we want to get promotions that we don't deserve. We prefer to sleep our way to the top ..."

Leo felt his brows pulling together as he waited for her to stop. When she finally did, he added "But none of that is true, I don't think."

"No," Jo responded forcefully, "*None* of it is actually true. Women file far fewer workman's comp claims than their male counterparts. Whether that's because we're more likely to do the safe thing and not be flaming idiots or simply because we know we can't file them, because we'll get looked down on for it, I don't know. There is some data that suggests it's more the first."

Leo nodded along, finally beginning to understand.

"We do take maternity leave, but it's because we *have* to. Men can be expecting children and not have to miss a shift, but no one's going to put a six-month pregnant woman on the line. Honestly, I wouldn't do it either. But don't we cause a hassle just by becoming pregnant?"

Leo felt his heart sink.

"And the sexual harassment cases?" she shrugged again, but

he saw the mockery in it. "I mean, there we are, demanding that fire stations build separate bathrooms for us, because we can't share with the men! And we entice and distract our workers by our mere existence."

"That's on the men," Leo said it as if she hadn't already figured that out herself.

What an idiot he was. But still. "They should fire the men who can't do their jobs."

This time when she laughed it wasn't a short bark but a cynical throwing back of her head. Her laugh was long and hard and seriously amused at his lack of ... What? Leo didn't understand, but his stomach knotted down tight because he figured he was about to learn.

When Jo finally pulled herself back together, she looked at him. "If we fired all the men who can't do their jobs with a woman distracting them, who would be left? You can't fire half the fire department."

Shit, he thought. She was making her way in a male dominated field as best she could. He wanted to argue the rest of it, but it didn't matter if he knew the women in the Redemption Fire Department weren't sleeping their way to the top. It only took one person to think that and spread rumors. It only took one person in the higher ranks—the ones making decisions about who got promoted and who didn't—to hold someone back.

The higher ranks were populated by the older firefighters. The older firefighters had come into the work decades ago, when it was an entirely male profession.

And what could he say? What could he possibly do now to make everything okay for her, because there was nothing he could do. He wasn't even a fellow firefighter. And, as she had commented before, if he stuck up for her, that would be different, and it would shine the light on *her* again.

He could only hope that his friends and her coworkers were

more on the ball than she expected them to be. Clearly, they were better than she'd experienced in the past, but were they good enough?

Was he?

He'd always worked hard to be the kind of leader that he would have wanted to work under. But Jo was shining the light on some hard truths. Had he put Bethany on the desk because she was female? He thought it was because she was naturally good at it. But was she naturally good at it because she was female? Did he just think she was good at it because she was female? And maybe there was somewhere else she'd rather be. He'd asked her if the desk was good, and she'd agreed. Had she agreed because she didn't think she could disagree? Bethany was also cheerful, not quite willing to push back the way that Jo was.

What about the women who'd worked for him in the past and left when they got pregnant and had children? He'd had two Rangers do that in the past. Had they not felt welcome back? *Jesus.*

He'd thought he was doing well, but a few harsh words and he realized maybe he hadn't even known what to look for. He tried the only thing he could think of to say. "I'm sorry that you had to deal with that."

But Jo was frowning at him, holding up a hand for him to stop. She motioned again for him to stop talking and then pushed an angry finger to her lips, signaling him further.

While he'd been having a disturbing little personal epiphany, she had been doing the job.

"I'm sorry," he said it more quietly.

Now she was angry at him, stepping forward and clamping her hand over his mouth as her other hand reached behind his head, holding him steady. She whispered a very low, harsh, "Shhhhhh!"

And then he heard it.

CHAPTER THIRTY-SIX

"Daaaaaltonnnn," Jo called. "Dalton!"

Next to her, Leo did the same. They tried to keep a brisk pace as they followed the sound, hoping to locate the missing boy.

Running was difficult with the packs on and they shouldn't be running anyway not with the woods growing dark. It was barely approaching midday. It shouldn't be this difficult, but they couldn't afford a rolled ankle or a twisted knee.

The winds were kicking up and every time Jo thought she heard something, she couldn't be confident that it was a child.

"Dalton!" Leo called out again, his feet crunching heavily along the path as he worked to stay upright. He kept his eyes up in case the child was visible or, maybe like Jo, in hopes of catching a flash of color.

Though Leo was usually agile, Jo could see he was slowing down. And she could feel that she was, too. She was ready to lean over, put her hands on her knees and just stop and breathe heavily for a moment.

"I don't think it was him," Leo huffed out the words—though whether he was exhausted or irritated, she couldn't tell.

Jo held one hand up, palm out. This didn't make any sense. "Why would he be running from us? The sounds always seem to be coming from equally far away."

"Do you think it's a bird?"

"I don't even begin to know what I think it is!" She was irritated, even if he wasn't. She kept hoping to find Dalton, alive and hopefully safe. The sound had kicked her wishfulness into high gear, only now she was growing more and more confident it wasn't a child.

The four hours of sleep she'd had seemed like enough when she woke up and was eating eggs. She'd felt fully rested despite the relatively short night, but now—between Leo's cold attitude and the desperate hunt for Dalton—that feeling wasn't panning out.

Jo was beginning to lose hope and, without hope, she was beginning to lose energy. Above her, the trees rattled as a harsh gust came through.

Looking up, she watched as the hints of already steel gray sky that peeped through the canopy above darkened ominously. "Oh, shit."

Quickly, she peeled her pack from her shoulders, watching as Leo heard her and followed her gaze. He caught on and suddenly did the same.

The two posts that anchored the bottom of her pack frame tapped into the ground and she leaned the whole thing against her leg. Once again, it became clear just how heavy it was. But right now, her hands scrambled, opening zippers and lifting flaps.

"Right side, back pocket," Leo called out, though they were only a few feet apart.

Her hands scrambled, the thick polypropylene gloves making her far less dexterous than she was used to being. She finally caught the tab of the zipper and tugged the pocket open, finding the promised rain gear there.

Hadn't they already done this once? she thought as she shrugged in again. She managed to get the front closed and checked that she was properly covered—for what it was worth. But then again, this was exactly why there wasn't a full crew out. They'd known this was coming.

She turned to look toward Leo, to see if he had any further instructions. But as she opened her mouth, a crack emerged in the sky loud enough to drown out anything she might have said. Loud enough to stop her from saying it.

It rattled her ribcage, despite all the padding she wore, and from Leo's expression it startled him, too. When it ended, she could feel her heart thumping and she put one hand to her chest. As Leo looked left and right, maybe wondering if another tree had been cracked and split like before, Jo followed his gaze.

Luckily, she didn't see anything. If the lightning had hit something, it wasn't close enough to them this time. For all the shock, it seemed to be just noise. She looked up at him and raised her voice over all the surrounding sounds. "Which way do we go?"

Stepping closer to her, Leo reached out to take her hand and told her, "We're not lost. Because we didn't have a specific direction to search for the noise, I kept aiming us in the same way. We're still on path to get to the caves. Let's see if we can get there and shelter out this storm."

Jo nodded. As the wind kicked up, Leo was raising his voice more and more just to be heard. She found she was watching his face, maybe even reading his lips as much as she was hearing the noise. When he turned away, he kept his hand in hers.

It was a far warmer and friendlier gesture than he'd offered all day. So she left them connected in this odd little way as she followed along, watching her feet, trying not to trip or stumble or be a burden. This was definitely beyond protocol, but Jo liked it.

The rain began coming down in earnest then, letting them

know they'd been none too hasty in whipping out the rain gear. The drops were large enough and heavy enough to pierce the top of the canopy, then splash on her. She was grateful for the gear. Dalton had no such safety measures. Dalton was four and Jo was becoming more and more afraid that they would find him dead.

She was likely now risking her life to offer his parents closure and nothing else.

The two of them hiked for what felt like another two miles. Usually, Jo was good at gauging distance, but these woods were not her natural habitat. She had been a city girl most of her life and as the path became muddy and mucky, it was harder to step cleanly. She was confident that her natural gauge was off track.

"We're close," Leo said, and in the distance she saw a gap in the trees.

Water sheeted down into the open space, not the kind of thing she was interested in stepping into and she wondered what lay up ahead. A burned-out gap of trees from some old fire? Perhaps a hidden wildflower field?

But *no*. As she stepped up, she noticed the ground getting rockier then dropping away in front of her. Unlike at the creek, this cliff had an edge. But the drop was maybe fifty feet, not fifteen. And there was no muddy bank with saplings growing sideways to hold onto.

This was a sharp drop to the bottom, where raging water was made angrier by the pouring rain, not that she could see it, but she could hear it. She shuttered wondering how much PTSD she might have developed from the mudslide that had come down when they finally found Jason.

Had that only been a day ago?

Not even.

Jo looked to Leo, wondering if anything people said about relationships formed under intense duress was true. It probably was. He could go his own way and she wouldn't be losing anything—not anything real anyway.

Still holding her hand, Leo took a few steps forward, out to the open edge. The rain pelted him as he slowly tipped his head and looked downward.

"Dammit!" he declared angrily. "This is exactly what I was afraid of."

CHAPTER THIRTY-SEVEN

In his head, Leo swore a blue streak. He had no doubt that if Jo could see his face she would be able to read all the words passing by—every foul thing he'd ever heard.

The caves were here, exactly as promised. But the reason he'd never stumbled upon them, was because nobody could actually *stumble* upon them. They might fall and hit a ledge and realize there was a cave below where they had stood previously. But right now, he had no doubt that he was standing over an entire network. The only problem was, he was going to have to repel down the side to get to them. They were not going to be the shelter that he and Jo had hoped.

Jo stepped up to join him at the ledge, something he didn't like. He'd quickly dropped her hand and pushed his own out across her stomach, as though he were a mother holding her back. Not that it would work.

He knew she saw the futile gesture and laughed at him. But still she maintained her protocol and a safe stance. With one foot forward and one back, the pack still limiting her mobility, she slowly tipped her head down to take a look.

"So we're not looking for Dalton in there, because there's basically no way Dalton could have gotten down there?"

"That's my current assessment. Well, not from here." Leo thought the four-year-old certainly was not known for his rappelling skills.

The rain pelted them as they stood out in the open. The caves were supposed to be their shelter, too, if they found themselves in a situation exactly like the one they were in.

Ivy was usually on her A game and—as she had suggested the caves—Leo had assumed she'd checked them out and that a kid could get there.

"Wait!" Jo said, tapping his arm to get his attention and hollering above the sound of the rain. It splatted against their gear and tapped on the rocks and the leaves nearby and drummed up a horrifying noise. The sound of rushing river washed up from beneath them. So Leo turned to watch her mouth—the mouth that he had tasted and wanted to taste again.

"Ivy said that Mr. Gentson said that he and his brother played here when they were kids! If these are the right caves, then there *must be* a way for kids to get down to them!"

She carefully turned her head, not wanting to get thrown off balance by wind or the extra weight. Then she pointed. "Look!"

Jo was right, of course she was.

Over to the side, there appeared to be a pathway downward. Of course the path was covered in dirt and all dirt was now mud.

Leo was contemplating all his options. Caves were solid, but the path was concerning and so was rappelling the side of a cliff in this weather. Also, the cliff cut much further down than the ten feet below him where he could see the first opening of the cave. Any errors could mean falling to their death.

He trusted that he and Jo could both easily make the distance, but the extra gear was an added issue. So was the wet surface of the rock. The limited visibility. The rain coming down ... and so on until it all added up to a bad idea.

But once he'd seen the path, Leo became more convinced that Dalton may have made the trek down to the caves. The path wasn't much wider than a sidewalk, and not even that in a few places. He wouldn't feel very comfortable walking casually on it, but a four-year-old who was running from a fire and bad behavior might fit just fine.

"Can we walk over and just shimmy our way down?" he asked. The cave would provide the best shelter. It was solid.

He had packed a tent but walls were better. Jo was already pointing and shaking her head, though. "One section of the walkway has been washed out! If Dalton went down, he isn't coming back up the same way."

Crap, Leo thought. He counted the hours again. Dalton had most likely run out of his snacks twenty-four hours ago at the latest. Unless he'd done some really great rationing for a four-year-old, he was very hungry and very cold.

"What do we do?" she asked, letting him make the call.

She had to be thinking the same thing he was.

If Dalton was down there, and they walked away, it would all be on them for leaving the child to die on his own. However, if they went down there and got themselves stuck, others would have to come rescue them.

At least, Leo thought, *If we go down, and we get stuck, we have all our food and supplies to survive.*

"Is the smart thing to wait out the storm?" she asked.

But Leo didn't know. He wished he could predict if the rain would be coming down for a long time or if it would let up. As bad as it was right now, it wasn't wise for them to keep going. He made his decision.

"Let's head back and pitch the tent. We'll see if we can wait this out until it lets up enough to get down into the caves and check to see if the kid is there."

She nodded along.

The more he thought about it, the more he realized it was the better decision. They'd seen no signs of a four-year-old boy. Aside from the marks left by the usual mountain creatures, there had been no signs of anything worthwhile. They'd left the designated hiking trails long ago. He'd only seen one discarded wrapper, but most of the ink on it had been rubbed away until it was only a shiny, clean slip a foil. It had been here since long before Dalton and his brother had snuck out of their home.

And, if the kid was in the caves, they'd have to climb back up with him. That would be even less wise in this weather. Leo would have looked upward just to confirm how crappy it was, but it would have rained into his hood and dripped beneath his gear.

Turning away from the edge, from where Dalton just might be, Leo tried to console himself that three of the four boys had been returned home.

He tried to ignore the similarities to his own story, but despite the ages being the same, so many things *weren't* similar. His younger brother had been out in good weather. Leo had loaded him up with snacks before they'd been split up because they were *hiking*. And a whole team of searchers had been out scouring the area for Garrett.

Now it was just him and Jo. As he looked left and right and down, and across the ravine at the dark gray sky, sending buckets of freezing water down onto them, he realized that even Jo could not search any longer. Her steps had grown slower. They were cold and tired, and though they weren't going back in, and they weren't giving up, it was time to tap out for a while.

They needed to rest and, if they were lucky, they could find enough tree canopy to create a relatively dry space. He hoped they could set the tent somewhere it wouldn't get washed away or shaken in the wind.

But even finding a patch of ground big enough was going to be tricky. He stopped and took a few steps back, catching Jo's hand in his again and tugging her with him.

He told her what he was looking for. "Hopefully a rise, a slope is okay. It won't puddle ..." and he wondered if he was completely explaining to her things she already knew. But when she suggested a completely inappropriate spot, he realized he wasn't.

She shrugged and pointed to herself. "*Urban* Search and Rescue trained."

She emphasized the first word and he laughed. They'd search for five minutes before Jo snapped up, tapping him on the back of his hand where he clasped hers.

"Listen!" she snapped out the word, suddenly excited again. "I heard something!"

He heard it, too. And this time it was getting closer, not further away. A soft, high pitch sound that could be a four-year-old carried to them, and they grinned at each other.

Together they turned toward the sound. It came and went, so this time Jo led the way, as clearly her ears were keener than his.

"It's over here." She pointed and stepped ahead. Then, "Over here!"

She tugged on him, pulling him behind her as she stepped through the branches and brush, taking them off the slim semblance of a trail made by creatures and not humans.

His hopes rose with each step. He kept hearing it, and it sounded like a child crying. His gaze darted side to side, trying to place the sound.

"There!" Jo seemed to have it pegged and she ran a few more steps until she stopped cold.

Leo ran smack into her, thunking into the bulk of her pack and throwing her off kilter. Jo managed to dig one foot forward, even as she grunted with the hit, and kept herself upright.

"Leo," she ground out the word in low, low tones. "Don't move."

But it was too late. He'd already peeked over her shoulder and heard the angry growl.

CHAPTER THIRTY-EIGHT

Shit, Jo thought. They'd found a child, alright. Only it wasn't Dalton, and it wasn't even human.

She'd read about mountain cats. She'd known there were maybe even a few bears up here, but she'd not really been ready to face a wild animal down. This did not happen in urban searches!

"Jo ..." Leo's voice wavered, and his hand came out slowly making its way in front of her as he cautiously pulled her back.

As if his arm would make any of this okay. She almost smirked at the idea.

She would rather get attacked than watch someone else get attacked. And, for some reason, she knew it'd be worse if that person was Leo. So Jo slowly reached out and grabbed on to his arm.

Her blood pulsed through her system with her adrenaline on high gear. Using the straight, stiff way he held her as a lever, she tugged on him, pulling the two of them backward away from a growling mountain lion.

Jo could tell that this one was female because of the tiny cubs she was guarding. Those had been the childlike voices calling out to them—the ones they'd been inadvertently chasing down. Bad idea to chase and follow a mountain lion's babies. Hell, they'd probably been mewling for their mother to stop the two people who kept yelling and chasing after them.

Unfortunately, for each step backward that Jo and Leo took, the mother mountain lion took one step forward. Her teeth were bared, a constant low rumbling came from her chest. Her ears slicked back and her fur stood upright. Not a calming look. She was ready to attack.

Jo was in full fight-or-flight mode. Her muscles tensed and she readied for fight but prayed for flight. She tried to see and hear the big cat, to assess how angry it was or if this was just a warning. But everything around her was noise. The wind in the leaves, the rain crashing down in buckets above them, even her own feet moving through the fallen leaves and branches hindered her hearing.

She tried to calculate the distance between herself and the cat, and then she berated herself a bit for not doing a good online search of "how far can a mountain lion jump?" Jo had been far more concerned about the local snakes. *But no, she and Leo got a mountain lion.*

"Slowly," Leo doled out the word as though Jo wasn't doing exactly that. But she didn't fault him, they were both running on fumes and fear. Was that her heart thumping in her ears or his?

They stepped backwards in tandem with Jo becoming concerned that they'd walk right off the cliff before the mountain lion stopped pacing them. But even as Jo figured it out, Leo's voice came softly to her through the pounding rain.

"Stop moving."

They were likely directly over the caves now, or at least where they thought the caves were. Jo once again tugged on Leo's outstretched arm that still hovered across the front of her, as though it would protect her from any of this. This time, her brain had churned to another idea and she pulled him gently to the side.

They'd have to start moving a different direction, if they were going to get out of this mountain lion's sight.

Jo took her first tentative sideways step. She still wasn't sure what was behind her and a step in the wrong direction could be a step off the cliff edge into nothing, if they'd moved farther than they thought.

A growl came with the first sideways step and Jo froze where she stood. She felt a cold line of sweat run down her back.

She hated it. It was a normal sensation if she was working out but out here in the rain and terror? No. She wasn't going to be this afraid. So she stepped again, slowly, distributing her weight with an even roll from her toe to her heel. It was the best she could do given the thick soles of her hiking boots.

She stepped with a soft, steady pattern, using the rhythm of her heart *thunking* against her ribs. As she moved, and tugged Leo along with her in slow motion, he talked quietly with every step.

"We're not a threat to your babies." He said it as though the mountain lion could understand reason or English.

Jo's mind raced, considering all the ways this could go so wrong. What about the packs they carried? She told herself that surely Leo would have packed medical supplies. He was far too prepared for anything else. But was she qualified to take care of someone who'd gotten attacked by a mountain lion? Her medical training was limited. What if he fell off the cliff? What if she did?

Every path was a new way to die or be maimed. Every deadly option was one she wasn't prepared for. Her thoughts churned a million miles a minute even as she took another slow step to the right, her breathing shallow and thin.

She wasn't trying *not* to breathe. She wasn't sure she was

even trying to move slowly. It was just a natural consequence of being stared down by a creature who could take out her throat in a single swipe or cover the distance she'd worked so hard to put between them with one leap.

Her lungs felt as though they were collapsing in on themselves as the harsh woosh of her breath escaped. The mountain lion was turning around. Jo fought the sound, wondering if the mother cat could hear it through all the heavy rain and the rattling of the wind in the trees.

But the mountain lion dropped her shoulders as she headed away. Maybe her babies required more of her attention than Jo and Leo did.

"Keep moving, Joely," Leo said in that low soothing voice he'd used on the cat. "Keep moving."

She did, knowing she was safer when she couldn't see the mountain lion anymore. They had moved far enough back to not be a threat anymore and it had turned and finally taken a few steps in the other direction.

She whispered, "We're too close to the cliff's edge."

She could feel it. The rain had changed. Maybe she felt wind rushing upward from the canyon behind them. It was terrifying, in case the growl of the mountain lion wasn't enough.

The rain pelted them heavier the closer they got to the edge. The trees grew less dense on the thick rock and the partial shelter of the canopy above disappeared. The daylight—as gray as it was—filtered through.

The forest was all sound and fury. But behind them, only five to ten more feet now, was empty space. She hadn't turned her head yet to check for sure, but she knew the edge was a sheer drop into ragged tree tops and raging waters.

Leaning forward, Jo whispered into Leo's ear. "Now what?"

CHAPTER THIRTY-NINE

Leo checked and double checked his knots. They didn't have the kind of rigs that the teams would bring for a well-manned search and rescue. This was just the two of them and ropes and—he pushed his foot against the tree—a sturdy trunk.

Looking up at Jo, he watched as she finished her own knot system. He motioned to her. "Joely? Swap with me?"

She nodded. They would check and double check each other's knots. Then they checked each other's harnesses, tugging on straps and carabiners.

The mountain lion hadn't shown back up, but the rain had gotten heavier. Scaling the cliff was going to be highly problematic, but it was clear they couldn't camp so close to where they'd seen a mountain lion, particularly one with tiny cubs. The slightest misstep and she'd rip them to shreds.

Pushing his attention to the work, he saw that Jo's knots were excellent, plausibly superior to his own. He nodded at her and watched as she finished her own inspection and she gave him a thumbs up.

Their packs came off and were ready to be lowered down.

Leo inspected everything again, even turning and leaning forward to peer over the edge of the cliff again. The river at the bottom of the canyon was difficult to see with all the gray rain pouring and obscuring everything. He could see just enough to know that the water churned angrily and that it wasn't a place he wanted to end up.

From what he could tell, it was a damn long way down. As he looked, he wondered if Dalton had come near here and mis-stepped. Leo's chest pressed in and the thump of his heart slowed with fear. Right now, Dalton didn't matter. It sucked to say that, but if he and Jo didn't get themselves safe, no one would be out here to find the boy.

This was not going to be an easy drop. He couldn't see the face of the cliff. He couldn't tell if there even were caves down there, they were just operating on the fact that there was clearly a partially used path and that the caves were reported to be here. Given the river below, the probability of a cave was very high. Given that this was the end of the path and they were going to have to turn back around, he needed the stories to be true. He needed to be standing on top of a usable cave. This was a bet he didn't like, but he didn't feel they had any other good options.

"You ready?" He asked Jo even though she clearly was.

They'd decided that Jo would go over first. He didn't like it. But when they worked their way through a plan where he went over first, then she was the one left up here possibly with a mountain lion watching her ass. It also meant she came down on the less secure rope system. He didn't like that either.

He hated his no-good-options. He double checked her harness and gear, all of it unwieldy in the heavy rain.

"It looks pretty good," she told him. "Lots of handholds and toeholds. It should be okay."

With that, she enacted a plan that he wasn't quite emotionally ready to run and stepped slowly backward, carefully sliding herself over the edge in a manner that he'd seen experienced climbers use.

Damn good for a city girl, Joely, he thought as he acted as a second anchor for her line. As he watched, she disappeared over the side.

CHAPTER FORTY

Jo reached out with her foot, searching for another toe hold.

There was nothing.

She tried moving sideways, but with the rope directly above her she could only move so far, too much of her weight was supported by the system they'd rigged. This wasn't a climb —she'd done plenty of climbing, though most of it was in indoor gyms. Some had happened out on real cliff faces. But in those cases, the rope was merely a backup for the climber's own strength.

This rock, the rain, all of it was far too slippery for a real climb. She was basically getting lowered and her weight was in the harness. Her hands and toes were just working to be a guide. She'd slipped enough times that anything else wouldn't have worked. Now, even trying to push herself sideways seemed too much.

The wet rock left her nothing for her foot and as she felt around for anything, adrenaline flooded her system. It seemed each time she managed to relax, she would slip again and be caught in the grip of full body fear once more.

Jo considered removing her gloves—not that she could now,

when she couldn't even find a foothold to steady herself. If she took her gloves off, she might get a better grip, but her fingers would slowly freeze, causing her grip to loosen. There were no good options here.

She tried to feel around with her toe carefully, though she suspected it would be more of a wild swing to anyone watching. She was grateful that Leo couldn't look over the ledge and see her, he had to stay farther back for safety. Her foot swung inward and still didn't hit anything ... which didn't make much sense.

Hanging on with her three other limbs, Jo fought her rising panic.

She wanted to say something and yell up, but it wouldn't make any difference. Leo couldn't come look and if he could, he couldn't see anything but the top of her head as she freaked out. She had to trust in the harness.

It was a tenuous trust, one born of statistics. She believed it would work because she'd never seen the webbing fail. Rope could slip out of belay lines, climbers could fall. Those were deadly options, but she was harnessed and Leo was on the other end of it, as was a sturdy tree.

So if she slipped, she would lose her hold and bash against the rock. But she almost could not fall to her death.

So Jo took a deep breath to steady herself and moved her foot in another slow awkward motion, before lowering herself another third of her body length, without anything under her right foot. This time her left foot found no purchase either.

Now, the lower half of her body was completely hanging free in open space. Her heart pounded. She told herself this could be good news.

People said *never look down*, but she needed to. Jo held on tight, her fingers catching into good crevices and outcroppings —now the only part of her holding on.

She slowly rotated her head, the rain gear crinkling around

her head and making all of it worse. The pattering of the drops hitting her drowning out the raging of the water below, the heavy thumping of her heart louder than everything else. But when she looked down, she saw that the rock had dipped away from her.

She was dangling over a ledge that was maybe eight to ten feet below her.

She needed to get to the ledge.

So she lowered herself until she was hanging from her fingertips. Her smile grew wider with each foot downward that she moved.

"It's here!" she yelled up. "There's a cave here!"

Jo scanned the inside quickly, looking for any evidence of a four-year-old boy, but found none. She then checked left and right, hoping to find evidence of a child's passage along the cliff path, but it was difficult to see. The rain had picked up even on her time downward.

Not good, she thought, still dangling. They still had to send down the packs and then Leo.

There was no way to tell from here if this was the only cave. Right now, she was glad they've moved over a bit from where they'd first looked down. If they hadn't descended directly over one of these openings, she didn't know how far down she would have gone without noticing that it was here. Even ten or fifteen feet away the rain was too dense to see through.

"Give me rope. I'm going to drop!" she called up and waited for his return reply.

Moving only on faith, she let go of one hand and then the other. All of her weight was now on the harness, with no control of her own and she began to twist slightly as Leo steadily lowered her toward the ledge.

The harness held her in an odd position. It was almost appropriate for climbing—a half-sitting stance—but it wasn't good for stretching and getting her toes to the ledge quickly. Jo reminded herself to be patient even as she made a full rotation, swinging out to face away from the cliff, looking out into the gray nothingness. The only thing she could see breaking the rain were a few branches of trees that had grown on ledges or maybe were just incredibly tall.

Her heart pounded out a rhythm she didn't recognize. She clutched at the rope holding her as if that would do anything and Jo looked down.

So close, she thought. She'd be okay even if she fell the last eight inches. She'd be okay landing on the ledge. She just had to tumble backwards into the cave and not forwards off the edge.

At last, rock touched her toe, pushing upward and letting her breath come out on a whoosh of relief.

"I'm in!" she told Leo, far above her where she couldn't see him. "I'm in!"

She wanted to just strip away the harness, but she couldn't. not yet. They had to lower down the packs. She would have to be out near the opening and that wouldn't be safe without her harness still on.

She felt the rope go just a little slack. Probably enough for Leo to tie it off, and enough for her to walk several feet away and into the safety of the cave. For a moment she breathed freely. No rain pounding down on her. Though she could still hear it outside, the cave walls muted the roar and the cold air was still. Jo could have shivered with the chill, but it felt peaceful.

Though she wanted to linger, there wasn't time. Jo scanned the cave, pulling out her light and hoping not to find any evidence of bear or snakes or worse. If she was lucky, she'd find a glove or a hat that belonged to Dalton.

"First pack coming down!" She heard Leo calling and Jo stepped back near the opening, watching as one pack dangled in front of her eyes. Slowly it came down where she could reach it, but Jo waited until it was almost on top of her before she put her hand out and controlled it.

She unclicked the two carabiners at the clock top and hauled it into the cave before hollering up, “Next one!”

So far so good. The plan was running just like clockwork. She watched as the second pack also came down without problem. It was Leo that was the concern. Jo would have to be his anchor from underneath him. Even that would normally be fine, but this was no indoor climbing wall.

Still, she reminded herself they’d planned it all out.

“I'm next!” he called down.

Jo knew she wouldn't feel better until he was here in the cave with her.

She quickly turned and looked into the last corner of the cave, trying to finish her interrupted scan for snakes or evidence. There still wasn’t anything.

But then Leo called down, “It's getting bad up here! Hold on, I'm coming down fast!”

CHAPTER FORTY-ONE

Leo stepped backwards toward the cliff slowly. He was grateful he'd already been in his harness, having climbed in when Joely did.

He was also glad that his yelling down hadn't made the cat any angrier than she already was.

At the time that they'd harnessed up, they'd simply both climbed in, checking each other over. It had seemed almost intimate, patting her down, sliding two gloved fingers under each piece of webbing and tugging to make sure it was secure. But now he was glad because it meant he was ready to move away from the angry cat stalking him right off the cliff.

As he stepped slowly backwards, his hand moved forward to grab the rope that would stabilize him. If the mountain lion jumped, he would have to leap backwards and off the side of the cliff to avoid her.

There was no telling how he would land or smash the rock or what that would do to Joely. He stepped backward, his heart pushing up into his throat. He didn't want to do that to Joely, she couldn't see him and was expecting a controlled descent.

He took another non-threatening, slow-moving step backward.

He'd expected to feel the earth disappear under his heel, but he hadn't expected it on this step. He was closer to the edge than he'd thought, his focus on the cat stalking him down.

His toe bore all his weight as he stepped backward into nothing and bent his knee.

The rope didn't give.

"Jo! I need line!" He was yelling the words as the mother mountain lion offered only a low growl as warning before she leapt.

Despite the wind and the rain that battered both of them, surely she could hear his heart racing. His pulse sounded like an army marching in his ears and the continuous low growl was a reminder that he would not be the victor if it came to a fight.

Just as she jolted forward with a swipe of a too-big paw laced with razor claws, the rope slid and Leo dropped out of range.

Had he not been petrified, he might have worried about pissing his pants. That was close. *Too close.*

Backing over the edge of a cliff was a perilous task on a normal day. Add wind and it got more dangerous. Add rain and it got significantly more perilous. Add an angry or hungry cat—fur soaked, fangs bared—and he'd been certain he wasn't going to make it.

Just as he breathed that he was off the edge of the cliff, she moved the last few feet, reaching out to swipe at him again.

He'd told Jo he was coming down fast, but that had been when he'd seen the cougar approaching again. She'd stalked him while he lowered the packs, and he'd thought maybe she was just curious. But something had changed as she came closer. He saw that she wasn't in the best shape, and she was looking to make him into a meal.

The cat stood at the edge of the rock, leaning forward and

swiping that huge paw out. He jerked backward with each motion.

"Are you okay?"

He heard Jo calling up, but he didn't quite process the question. His eyes were trained on the cat above him, his muscles far too tense for a controlled climb down into the cave.

As he ducked and the cat missed again, the growl turned to a scream.

"Now Jo!" he yelled and tipped slowly backward, settling all of his weight into the rope.

Jo was in charge of everything now, and whether he had a peaceful climb or plummeted downward, twisting an ankle as he landed, was all in her hands.

The rope gave a bit, as Jo slowly lowered him and he scrambled to get handholds and drop out of range of the big cat still trying to reach down and swipe at him.

Every search and rescue team member went through classes training them on the physics of ropes, pulleys, load weight, and more. And Leo forgot every single bit of it as he scrambled to get out of the way, his grip slipping and failing as water pelted him and ran down the rock face.

A sharp sting bit his finger and he was too stunned to yell.

He looked up to see the giant paw closing over his hand. Water tried to get into his eyes. He'd managed to move his right hand lower, and he'd been looking at it as he felt around for a hand hold, his left had stayed above him bearing most of his weight on the slippery rock.

The lone claw had caught his glove and from the feel of it, she sunk well under the skin. It tugged as he tried to pull away.

This time he did scream.

"Leo!" Jo called up.

The cat screamed down.

Maybe the fact that he'd been looking into the mountain lion's eyes as he yelled was finally enough and she removed her paw from his hand and stepped back. She disappeared beyond the edge of the cliff as he watched his own red blood drip down his arm. The rain pummeled him and tried to steal the blood away. Maybe that was an upside.

His foot slipped but the harness caught.

"Leo?"

"I'm okay!" He called down even as he watched his hand. Even as he knew that Joely knew better than to believe him.

Still, she didn't step out on the ledge to look up at him. That would have been dangerous. Despite the fact that he was yelling and screaming and tugging on his line in all kinds of crazy ways, Jo was keeping him safe.

"I'm okay." The words came out on a gush of relief as he managed to get a toe hold, then a good handhold with his right and finally pull his bleeding left hand down out of the cat's surprisingly large range.

He lowered himself a few more feet before he had a sobering thought.

He didn't know where the cat had gone.

The last thing he'd seen as he tipped over the edge, was the pulley they'd anchored to a sturdy tree. It held his weight and was perilously close to the ground ... and to the mountain lion.

He'd believed for a stupid moment that being out of her range meant he was finally safe. He'd breathed a sigh of comfort that the lion wouldn't follow him down the side. But he realized, as he moved the next step down, that she stood right next to a moving rope. If she was angry, it would be the place to attack.

He was out of her attack range, but he wasn't safe from her yet.

"Jo!" he yelled down, no longer even attempting to operate with standard belay format. "Bring me down, fast!"

Even three days ago, he would have told anyone that asked, hell no, he would not let Jo Huston hold his line ... certainly not in a storm with a big cat hovering over the side of a cliff. And right now, he couldn't think of anyone he'd rather have holding him.

Their set up was unfortunately a shitty system. Because she was belaying from beneath him, she needed to stay away from the edge and, because he needed an anchor at the top, the rope wound around several angles, rubbing against rock as it went. The line shouldn't wear and rip, but it wasn’t designed for this.

A growl sounded above him, and Leo whipped his head up to see the mountain lion’s head pop over the ledge again. She was no longer just defending her cubs. She must be hungry or threatened and he worried again about her turning her attention to the bright pink rope and the pulley that moved and twisted next to her.

He worried about going back up. They didn’t know how long they would be in this cave.

Leo kept moving downward, the rope going slack each time he tugged, but only enough for him to make his next move. He felt at the wet rock with his right hand, his left still bleeding, though it worked well enough to hold on. He guessed he was lucky the blood was soaking into the glove and running down his arm, and the heavy rain was washing much of it away.

He found another grip and wondered if his sat phone would connect. It should. He moved his left hand down, feeling the sting of the cut with the movement and then slid his foot lower. His boot slid along the wet rock a little too easily, until he found another foothold and finally let out the breath he’d been holding.

His brain was tugged a million directions. If he looked up again, he’d get rain in his face again. It would run inside his jacket, like it had the last time. He’d be freezing if he wasn’t exerting himself so much.

Leo worried that the cave might block the phone signal and he would need to come out toward the ledge to get contact. His left foot slid down. His right hand moved and then his left, the bite of movement reminding him again that he was injured and reaching the bottom was no longer the end.

He was imagining coming out and standing in the rain just to get a signal, trying to figure out how to let people know they were alive. But the fact of the matter was he wasn't really alive. Not yet.

He hadn't reached the bottom.

He didn't have anything to call in about.

"Watch your feet!" Jo called up as he slid his right foot down and the rock disappeared from under it, a petrifying sensation in any scenario. Only the best climbers went up inverted slopes. Only fools were out in weather like this. And Dalton wasn't even in this cave.

Leo risked the rain to look up and see the mountain lion still loomed overhead, watching him. He wondered for the first time if maybe she wasn't hungry, but maybe she was mad that they were taking her cave.

He looked left, down the long pathway. He'd thought it was a little narrow for an adult, but that Dalton would maneuver it easily. That meant so would a mountain lion.

He looked down to see the ledge beneath him connected to the path.

It was only one body length beneath him, something he would jump on a normal day on a normal piece of ground. But here, if he rolled backward, he would go off the cliff. If he hit too hard and twisted an ankle, he'd never get out of the cave on his own volition.

Using only his hands and relying on Jo on the other end for support, he slowly lowered himself down until the drop became but a few feet.

"I've got you," she said. "Let go."

CHAPTER FORTY-TWO

Jo's heart pounded. She could tell the moment Leo let go of the rocks and began to swing. His weight pulled on the rope and her hands and she fought to keep him steady.

Anchoring him was a problem from inside the cave. She'd done the best she could. They had known there wouldn't likely be much in here to use for counterweights, so the anchor was Jo and all the friction that the system produced from running up around the edge of the cave and the edge of the cliff and to the pulley system and back down. It wasn't the safest method, and—Jo suddenly realized—maybe why he'd insisted on coming down second.

Holding on tight, she did several things she wasn't supposed to, like wrapping the rope around her arm. If he fell, she could get tugged along with him. Watching Leo slowly descend by her own hand wasn't supposed to feel this way. It was supposed to be emotionless, steady work for her brain, not her heart. But it seemed everything had changed in the past twenty-four hours.

She let the rope out, slowly monitoring her own breathing and talking him through as he twisted to face away from her. She would have liked to step forward, grab his harness, and haul him in. But he was still swinging over her head and if she stepped forward, she would change all the angles.

If she let go, he would fall. Though the ledge would catch him, it wasn't wide enough to be safe. One wrong move and he'd tumble into the gorge. There would be no way for her to stop him. So Jo didn't step forward; she just monitored her breathing and slowly let out more line.

"Three feet!" she called up, and then Jo watched as his boots slowly lowered to touch the rock of the ledge.

Leo carefully stood on his own weight, the heavy pressure of the rope letting go of its bite on her arm.

She wanted to breathe easy, but she couldn't. With her relief at finally having him down, she suddenly realized she needed air. Her breath soughed in and out of her lungs. She was ready to leap forward and grab him, haul him toward her and kiss him.

She was also ready to grab for him if he tumbled backward. She would probably go right over the edge with him but, at this point, that might be the best choice. The rain formed a noisy gray curtain behind him and she watched as he stretched himself upright. The awkwardness of the harness hindered him but he took several steps forward.

Leo was suddenly in her space and in her arms. She hadn't even realized she was holding them out to him. He was soaking wet and their rain gear crinkled and kept her from feeling him pressed to her. Still, he crushed them together, their harnesses clinking the carabiners as he crushed her into a soul bearing hug.

Jo felt it in that moment—Leo felt the same way she did, despite how cold and standoffish she'd been.

She hugged him back now. Despite the fact that she painted him the worst possible picture as a dare or a challenge to hate her, he'd come through.

"Oh, Joely," he said, "that was terrifying."

She nodded though she hadn't been the one on the rope. It had been terrifying for her, too. It wasn't just the wind or the rain or the narrow ledge or the mountain lion. It was because it was Leo. Because she could handle a loss in a tough situation. They didn't always win. Rescue workers and firefighters died on the job, it was just a fact. It was harder when it was someone she knew and liked, but she knew they'd all chosen that path fully informed.

But Leo had somehow become different. Losing him would be a blow she wasn't sure now that she would survive.

As she lifted her face, not thinking about it but wanting to kiss him, needing to feel him, his arms loosened around her. Without him holding the doubt at bay, she stepped quickly away. Maybe she'd read it wrong. Maybe it was just the rush of the situation. He hadn't really trusted her from the start, had he? And she couldn't be with someone who didn't trust her.

The kiss in his kitchen—the one that had filleted her, that she still couldn't scrub from her memory—had been an anomaly.

Taking a deep breath, she stepped backward into the interior of the cave with him. And Jo tried to act as though she hadn't just realized she'd fallen so hard for this man. She talked to cover the emotions that were blazing through her, eating every ounce of self confidence she'd previously possessed.

"I looked around, but I didn't find any evidence of Dalton." Jo pulled herself together and became all business. She pointed backward toward one corner that was simply darker than the others. "The cave appears to lead further back that way. I don't know if we'll fit. And I don't know if it's safe right now. But he might be back there."

Leo was smart enough not to ask if she'd tried or if she had called out for the kid.

They'd come down far too fast for a full search. He began to look around. Luckily, the space was just tall enough for Leo to stand upright in most of the room.

He turned a full circle and announced, "Well, we have shelter."

He headed near the front and raised his hand overhead to touch the top slope where the opening was almost as high as he could reach. Blood dripped down his arm.

"Leo! You're bleeding!" Jo stepped forward, the wind splashing the rain into the opening and getting her gear wet again.

She looked him over more carefully now. His face was wet, and that meant there might be water inside his gear. He would chill too quickly if he didn't get changed and fast. Playing it smart, Jo turned away even as he protested.

"I'm fine."

He wasn't, and she was digging through her pack for the medical kit that she knew had to be there. The small, lightweight box was white with a red plus-sign on the front and she popped it open and pulled out a square of gauze. "Give me your hand."

He seemed reluctant to do so, and once she peeled his glove and wiped the blood away, she listened to him hiss with the pain, before she realized why. The cut was deep. "Leo, what happened?"

Sighing as though he didn't want to tell her, he said, "The mountain lion came back. Stalked me right off the edge of the cliff."

Jo was stunned. She'd known he was hollering that he was coming down fast. But she'd been unable to step out and look up to see what was actually happening. *Crap!* She examined him and saw the sharp slice that ran along the back of his first finger begin to ooze again. "Did she get you anywhere else?"

"Just here." He watched as she pushed the gauze back into

place and applied pressure. "I was below her range, or so I thought. She swiped down and caught me."

Holy shit.

She'd been in the cave, trying to help him down quickly, but with no idea that he was getting attacked.

Once she got the blood cleared, she took a good look at it. He should get stitches, but stitches had to be put in within six hours of the wound. Jo looked out at the rain. Even if they left right now, that likely wouldn't happen. "Let me clean it and get you bandaged up."

He only nodded and held the gauze as she directed while she got out the rest of the supplies. By the time she had the wound cleaned, the bleeding stopped and steri-strips holding it together, the light was gone. Jo covered the wound in a cut piece of elastic tape and figured it would hold.

"We have to get the place set up," he announced as he stood back up.

They'd been in intimate space with her bent over his hand, bandaging him. But he stepped away again, far too easily. Jo forced a nod and watched as Leo paced off a few steps.

"We need to make shelter at least halfway between here and the back wall." He pointed out the distance and Jo raised one eyebrow at him.

She finally reached up and pushed the hood of her rain gear off her head, realizing as she did it that she could take the whole coat off and the harness. He could, too. They were going to be here for a while.

She quickly began unclicking everything as Leo did too, explaining about his suggested positioning as he went. "We've already seen lightning and we've seen it close. Lightning can enter a cave up to half the distance back from the size of the opening."

"Seriously?" She heard the harness hit the dirt floor of the cave with a soft thunk. The metal clinked and echoed slightly off the stone walls. She breathed out a sigh.

"Yes, seriously."

Once again, she muttered, "Things you don't learn in Urban Search and Rescue."

They both peeled the rest of their rain gear and she saw that he was, in fact, wet underneath. Getting Leo dry became their priority.

"Is it really that different?" he asked as his fingers deftly moved and his gear dropped to his feet as he shed it and stepped out.

He, too, took an obvious sigh of relief.

But each thing they shed was another layer that had been keeping them warm.

Maybe their body heat could warm up the cave. She took off her jacket, only then realizing her sleeve was wet.

"It's different," she told him. "Urban Search and Rescue means you can drive a truck to a close place. We never had to hike out to a location like this. We were often looking in buildings and crawl spaces and boiler rooms. There are walls to break down and we had a lot more tools. But I've never carried anything as far as I've carried these packs these past few days."

Leo listened attentively even though he'd quit peeling clothing at his last layer. He'd turned and begun pulling carefully arranged pieces off his pack. He held up one bright orange roll and announced, "A tent. I think we might need it."

Then he pointed to the bottom where a blue nylon piece was rolled. "I have a sleeping bag and so do you. We can zip them together, if that works."

He didn't even give her time to respond to what was plausibly a hot invitation or maybe just safety protocol. He was pulling out water bottles, snack bars, and a thermos. The food looked like heaven.

But ... "Leo, you're wet. You have to change. Now."

He pointed to her shoes. "So are you."

Frowning—she wasn't wet—Jo looked down, only to see that the bottoms of her pant legs were soaked. She hadn't even noticed. She would have to completely change, too.

She wondered if she was up for this. She'd sat, nearly naked in a tub with him just under twenty-four hours ago. So she could strip down to her underwear in front of him without it being anything new. But it *was* new. She wanted more. She would look at him differently today when he peeled away the last of what he was wearing.

She wondered how she would handle the fact that everything was different for her now, when a noise cracked behind her, and both of them jumped.

CHAPTER FORTY-THREE

The crack of lightning that made Leo jump drove home the necessity of doing everything correctly.

"We have to set up first," he said even as Jo was pointing to his clothes, and once again saying, "But you're wet."

But if he got naked, he would get colder. He needed a warm—or at least not freezing—place to change first. "Yes, but it's safer to set up first."

He paced off the steps, calculating half the distance of the opening of the cave and figuring out where to put the things he'd brought. He'd hauled that pack for miles just in case something like this happened. He would make use of every piece of equipment he'd made them carry.

Taking the precaution of moving out of lightning range cut their usable space significantly. But he'd already had a tree struck near him yesterday, and that last crack was too close. They couldn't risk it. He toed a line in the dirt. "We stay back, past here, unless we have to do something important."

Like use the satellite phone, he thought, *or if they heard anyone.* There were a lot of reasons to cross the line, but they wouldn't do it unnecessarily. Lightning gave no warning.

"First, we need heat." He went to the bag and with just a few efficient motions pulled out and assembled a small camp heater which he quickly lit. "That should help. Next, sleeping bags."

They needed the tent, too. But while it would keep the heat in, it would be insanely confining. Difficult to do more than sleep in it, even changing clothes would be problematic given the small size.

Leo looked up, wondering if he could find a few spots to anchor some crampons so he could hang the tent as a barrier. It would give them much more space.

He'd probably spent about fifteen minutes gathering supplies and checking out their limited surroundings, during which time the cave went from dark to nearly pitch black. If he hadn't lit the heater already, he couldn't have seen anything.

He was just turning around to find a flashlight when Joely handed him his, her own flicking on as she looked around.

"There," she pointed to a good spot, though he hadn't said anything about what he was imagining. She clearly had the same idea, and even handed him a crampon to slide into the small crevasse.

He couldn't help but smile as he hung the tent. It covered most of the opening and the ripstop nylon was fire resistant. Also, the floor was dirt and, he thought—almost smiling again—he was stuck here with a firefighter. She wouldn't let him do anything too stupid.

He hung a line for wet clothing to dry. They rolled out the sleeping bags, set out the food, and then went on a second search for snakes, spiders, and anything that could bite. Leo was grateful they hadn't found more than just a few wolf spiders that had scurried away. This part of the country overlapped brown recluse and black widow territories, and Leo had been on the lookout since they'd first entered the woods.

"Clothing is next," he told Joely, taking charge in what was clearly his area of expertise. "Get the bag out and put it near the heater to warm up."

They both had full outfits, bagged, vacuum sealed and ready to go.

Then he added the next part, hoping he didn't sound like a skeeve. "Strip down to what's dry and climb into the sleeping bag."

Turning around before he could tell if she was watching or not, he started on his own wet pieces. Because if he got the slightest hint that she was interested he would want to turn around and watch.

He peeled his shirt and at last the thermal layer closest to his skin, before going for his pants and socks. Everything had at least one icy wet spot on it. *Not good.*

He headed to the edge of where the tent now hung blocking the outside, and he peeked around. The heater must be working, because the moisture from the rain clung to his face and tried to freeze. Leo stepped back. The rain had changed but hadn't stopped coming down.

"What is it?" Joely asked as he turned back. Though she was still facing the other way—now in her underwear, this set blue—she must have heard him moving or she'd taken a peek.

"It's not raining anymore," he said. "The bad news is that it's sleeting."

They were stuck. They couldn't even walk along the ledge or try to climb back up. Coming down wet had been dangerous enough, going up in icy conditions would be worse. He needed to hook up to a satellite or some distant cell tower to get a check of the weather patterns.

But right now, they needed food, rest, and he needed a prayer that Dalton was somewhere sheltered and doing okay.

Behind him, he heard the rustle of nylon, and though he knew what it was, Joely's voice came to him. "I'm in. Time to climb in before you get colder."

He walked over to where only her head and her hair—which she'd taken down—peeked over the top end of the sleeping bag. The blue nylon matched his, and he unzipped it only a little before sliding in.

The flannel interior was soft, but cold. That would change in a moment.

The cold wasn't the only problem, he thought. He could stay still and be the perfect, emotionally cold trail boss, or he could say what he wanted to. Leo picked the middle ground.

"You know, the sleeping bags can be zipped together."

"So we could share?" Joely asked almost slyly, but then she made a cautious sound. "Eh, better not. You're my boss."

"Ooof!" He made a noise almost as if she'd slugged him. "No. Out here we're partners."

Though, even as he said it, he wondered if he'd just made a horrible mistake, hitting on his trail partner.

"Do you share bathtubs and sleeping bags with all your coworkers?" she asked.

But Leo laughed. The zippered edges of the bags were aimed toward each other so that they could see each other's faces, if nothing else. "Sure."

Comfortable in her cocoon, despite the fact that there were no pillows, Joely grinned at him and he laughed again. "Yes, I do. I'll have you know, I've been in that tub with Kalan Smith."

She groaned at him. "And here I thought I was special."

She was, but he didn't say it out loud in case she was still thinking he was her boss. Then she offered up, "That was really manly of you."

He couldn't help the bark of sharp laughter that escaped him. "You know what's not manly? Losing our toes to frostbite when it was preventable."

This time she was the one who laughed, the sound echoing off the walls and warming him maybe better than the sleeping bag could.

He waited a moment, trying to think of something else to say, but Joely beat him to it.

"My sleeping bag is already getting warm. How do we put them together without losing the heat? Because isn't that the whole point?"

CHAPTER FORTY-FOUR

"Okay scoot just a little bit this way …"

Jo laughed as Leo gave her more instructions.

"Now unzip it all the way. You'll probably have to slide down inside to do it."

Though the bag wasn't just a big square, they did zip all the way down the side.

"I don't know … I feel like I'm losing heat." Jo talked to him even as she slipped down into the bag, pulling the zipper along with her.

The cold seeped in where she'd opened it. These appeared to be the good ones, probably rated to well below freezing temperatures, with their human-shaped form, puffy layers, and soft insides. Leo's handy camp heater was doing good work and so was the tent that blocked most of the opening. But with the gaps and the freezing rain outside, their gear could only do so much.

Clearly, Leo had deemed each of these items necessary, despite the added weight to the packs and the space they took up. But right now, as she heard the sleet hitting the rocks outside the caves, she was grateful they'd carried it all.

Wiggling until the two open edges of the sleeping bags were touching, she felt his hand reach across the space and find hers in an almost too intimate gesture that didn't end up quite intimate enough.

"Here, hold these together," he said, handing her the two top pieces. In the low light she felt the movement as he reached for the bottom.

She held the pieces he'd given her while he dove into the bottom of the bag again, now softly brushing her toes and gently caressing one leg in what could have been an accident but maybe wasn't.

He proceeded to very awkwardly roll around, first zipping the bottom layer together then diving back in to get the top zipper. The bags were puffy enough that the zipper stayed away from her skin, but Leo didn't.

The full body contact was more than she was prepared for, but it worked. Her breath sucked in and she felt the heat of him slide around her as they lay quietly in the joined cocoon.

She wasn't naked, still in her underwear like him. Unlike last time, there was no pristinely lit bathroom, no Victorian claw foot tub. No heat other than their own.

Then again, she also had almost no inhibition this time.

That concerned her. The last time she'd been nearly naked with him, she'd found him attractive. This time she was imagining having sex with him—hot, steamy, crazy sex. Sleeping with her boss was always a bad idea.

But, there was a concern about not ever escaping this cave. Though Jo was confident they could survive just fine here for a few days—and that eventually someone would come and rescue them if necessary—there was always the possibility that they didn't make it out.

It was a risk that was true of every rescue.

Jo would be damned if she fell off that cliff and she hadn't taken the chance in front of her.

Leo lay still, having accomplished the goal of getting the bags zipped together. He wasn't pressuring her further. The nylon of the tent snapped slightly as it fluttered from pressure outside the cave changing. There was a constant drum of the sleet hitting the rocks and the occasional change in pattern as the wind shifted. All of it was music against the silence that had fallen between them. It wasn't uncomfortable, but it was heavy with possibility.

He rolled a little, moving just inches closer, his mouth near enough that she could kiss him if she wanted.

"There. This is definitely the smarter move." He grinned at her, a heart stopping smile that offered too many possibilities.

She tossed off the moment with attempted humor. "Have you also shared a sleeping bag with Kalan Smith?"

"No." The one syllable was somehow seductive.

His hand came up and slowly and softly pushed her hair back out of her face. He gave her every opportunity to pull back, eventually even whispering, "You can say no if you want."

When Jo whispered back, "I don't want to say no," she barely finished the sentence before his lips touched hers.

CHAPTER FORTY-FIVE

Leo's tongue swept into her mouth. His arms came around her and pulled the two of them together in an embrace that seared her everywhere he touched.

And he touched everywhere.

His legs wound between hers and she found herself wrapped around him, entangled before she even realized she'd made a move. The hazy fog in her brain had only one clear focus: Leo Evans.

Jo kissed him back, her hips moving against his and she tasted the heat in his mouth as he groaned softly at her movement. So she did it again.

"I want you, Joely."

The words were soft and not demanding at all. But though the tone wasn't harsh, the words pulled her under as surely as a riptide. There would be no rescuing her from this. The only reasonable thing to do would be to protect her heart, and she wasn't sure that was possible.

For someone who readily hung from ledges and climbed the scaffolding of unfinished skyscrapers, falling for Leo Evans was maybe the scariest thing she'd done.

But Jo tended to fight fear with action, and she ran headlong into it, the way she often did. Her hands slid down his bare back, and she sighed at the play of muscle beneath warm skin. When she reached the curve of his very fine ass, she squeezed. It wasn't her fault if the move pulled them closer and his breath sighed out.

She traced his jaw with her lips, soft and gentle as she moved to the shell of his ear. For a moment, she'd believed she was the aggressor—a good thing so he would know it was fully mutual. But as her tongue rounded the curve of his lobe, she found herself on her back, the full weight of him pressing her downward.

It was evident how much he wanted her.

He slid his fingers down her arms, the soft, soft touch stealing her breath and making her surrender. But then, he held her wrists down, pinning her into the fluff of the bag. Her surrender was no longer her own.

His lips nipped at hers and he spoke in gentle terms. "If you keep touching me like that, this is going to go a lot faster than I intended."

"Mmmmmm," she grinned and rocked her hips upward, her heart racing at the idea of what she was doing. "What's wrong with fast?"

She hadn't intended to fall into bed with anyone in Redemption. At least not until her new position was solidified. But everything had gone to hell and she was wet and Leo was almost naked and definitely hard.

He groaned. "There's nothing wrong with fast. I just wanted to show you what we can be."

That was interesting ... but she refused to grab onto it and turn it over in her thoughts or make it into anything other than words. The shell around her might be disappearing in Leo's presence, but it would be smart to maintain whatever self control she could.

She tugged her hand free and trailed her fingers up his side, enjoying the look of bliss on his face in the low light. But his expression quickly changed and he made a move of his own. His fingers traced her hip, up past her ribs until her breast was firmly in his hand. His thumb brushing across her nipple let her know that she wasn't in control here. And she wasn't going to be.

His mouth came down on hers, his weight heavier now that he no longer propped himself up. Somehow, he simultaneously moved his leg between hers, managing to press in exactly ... the ... right ... spot ... as he kissed her.

His deft fingers traced her breast again, the feelings somehow more potent the second time around. When Jo gasped and opened her eyes, she saw the top of the sleeping bag was slightly unzipped, the cool air moving across her now uncovered breast.

How had he ... ?

He'd distracted her and peeled the top down. But she couldn't complain.

"I know it's a little cold, but I wanted to see you better." His words and the expression on his face made her believe.

For just right now, she could tumble headlong into his arms, into his touch, and let him take everything away. Because she was doing it anyway. It was time to stop fighting. Jo smiled up at him, his return smile assuring her that they were in sync. This time when she rolled her hips she let go of a breathy gasp as she watched his eyes roll back.

It wasn't just her.

When his eyes opened, she saw a new fire in them. Leo had clearly thrown "slow" to the winds and managed to move both desperately and gently as he peeled them both clean. She didn't know or care where her underwear wound up, only that they were truly naked next to each other and his hand was sliding softly between her legs, his body wedged between her knees. But it was exactly where she wanted him.

As his fingers trailed over her folds, she felt the hit of his contact with exactly the right spot. "Yes, there!"

He might have moaned or said something wicked, she didn't know, because he was touching her and she was writhing against him. It took all her focus to reach down and wrap her own hand around the length of him.

It made his fingers still and his head lift, his mouth drop open with pleasure.

She stroked, once, twice—

"Shit!" His eyes blinked and he yanked himself back and out of her touch. Hard to do in the confined space of the sleeping bag, but he did it. He stared at her. "No condoms. I don't fucking hike with condoms!"

Oh, thank God. She'd been afraid this was serious.

"I'm on birth control."

She reached for him again, but he executed a swift dodge and evade maneuver that made her frown.

"We've been out over twenty-four hours. How would you … ?" He didn't even seem to be able to finish the sentence and it was at least good to know that he was as addled as she was.

But she had to get herself together or he wasn't going to finish this … *her*. "Hey, guess what?"

"What?" he sighed, heavily, not seeming to appreciate her lighthearted move.

"I'm in firefighting and search and rescue and I work twenty-four hour shifts on the regular and I'm not a dumbass."

"Of course, you're not—"

"It's an injection. We'll have to be out here for another month before I'm fertile. We're gonna have a lot more problems like hunting our own food and becoming feral before birth control becomes an issue."

He was laughing by the time she finished, but she was glad

for the change in his mood and hopeful that they could get back to where they'd left off. But she didn't have more than half a second to wait before he was kissing her again, before he was close enough for her to stroke the length of him again and pull another groan from him.

Leo moved slowly, maybe too slowly. Jo was on the verge of begging by the time he was positioned to slide into her. Even as he brushed against her and sent her nearly flying, he stopped. "Yes?"

"Yes!" But she finished the word on a groan as he pushed into her in one smooth, hot stroke.

Her back arched, her legs lifted and she wrapped herself fully around him as he moved. Jo rode the tidal wave that came quick and hard. The sound of both their groans and cries echoed off the cave walls until she hit the precipice and fell over.

A moment later, Leo's voice cutting through her still pulsing fog told her he'd toppled over the edge, too. Then he gasped and collapsed forward, somehow not falling onto her, but coming to rest with the two of them breathing heavily together.

She could only relax here for a moment, Jo told herself.

Once he came around, things could get awkward. But she breathed in the cold air, needing it to quell the heat still churning inside her and she waited.

CHAPTER FORTY-SIX

As Leo slowly came back to his senses, he took stock.

Jo's warm, naked body was curled into his, her ass spooned in against him, his arm snug across her stomach. Every inch of her was warm. Every inch of him was tingling.

He'd barely gotten his breath back after the first time when he'd simply started touching her again. It seemed the right thing to do, as if her skin simply called out to his hand. The way she moved against him confirmed it. They did belong together.

The second time, he'd gone slow. Maybe he hadn't let her catch her breath so she couldn't protest. Knowing Joely, she would have protested if she'd wanted to. Instead, she'd offered up soft sighs, seductive groans, and finally herself again.

They'd certainly made the most of keeping warm, he thought. They'd even had to unzip the bag a bit, they'd gotten so hot. The sting of freezing air was yet another sharp sensation on his skin. Joely was a bundle of contradictions.

She shifted slowly against him. *Give him another few minutes and that would turn him all the way on again.*

She hadn't quite slowed her breathing enough to make him believe she was asleep and he wondered what that meant. Was she avoiding talking to him? There was no place to go to get away, being silent was her only option. Then again, he might have simply worn her out.

Leo hoped it was the second one and he thought about where to go from here ... He knew his way around Redemption and Lincoln, and he considered what places to take her on a real date after they got out of this.

Because he desperately wanted this to continue after this search was over.

Ridiculously, he found he didn't quite know what that would look like. So he opened his mouth, and went with simple. "There's a really great brewery grill in Lincoln. I'd love to take you ... if I could talk you into being my date."

Her head turned quickly, looking over her shoulder at him. No, she hadn't been asleep at all. He would have grinned, but he had no idea what her response was from her expression.

"When?" she asked.

At least it wasn't "What?" but it didn't let him know if that meant yes or no or ...

"As soon as we get out of here? As soon as we get warm enough and get enough sleep ... and you're not on shift." *Damn, there were a lot of caveats.*

She laughed. "Yeah, I'm missing my shift, or at least I'm pretty sure I will."

"Trust me. They've taken you off the roster."

Leo felt her stiffen at that statement, maybe a little too much. Did she regret coming out and missing her shift? Or was she mad that he'd gotten them stuck out here? He was opening his mouth, when he felt her relax back against him.

"Well, I'm only here for two more weeks anyway." She said it casually, but it was like a bomb in the stillness of the cave.

"What?" The very idea was ridiculous. "Two more weeks where? Not in this cave." Though he might like being stuck here with her, her answer was far too concerning.

"Nebraska."

What? She was leaving? Moving away? *That didn't make any sense*. He didn't even know how to respond.

But Joely offered up more confusion. "My mother decided, since I live here now, that she could attend a charity event nearby. So I have an appearance in Omaha with the Reiner family."

"I know them. They're funding a missing persons initiative with one of the local detectives."

"I think it's my mother's attempt to build a bond between us." She paused then patted his hand as he tried to absorb everything she was saying. Leo was just trying to connect the puzzle pieces, but it sounded as if she was leaving in two weeks ... Jo confused him further. "Do you want to be my date? Do you have a tux?"

"Of course I have a tux," he replied, still confused.

"Not a rental. A good designer."

"I have a really good tux. And yes, I'll be your date to a charity event, but ..." He trailed off and Joely filled in.

"After that, I'll be moving. I have to find another station."

"Why?" He was just so confused, and his chest hurt at the thought of her moving away. He shouldn't be that invested yet. Sex wasn't love ...

But, damn, with her it was close.

"I can't stay here." Her words were clear. The emphasis between each of them told him the idea should be obvious. "They know about the assault. *You* just told me that they'll have taken me off the roster."

"No!" he almost yelled it, glad to have been wrong. "They'll take you off the roster just for the next shift or whatever recovery you need. Because you've been out on a search for forty-eight straight hours ... maybe longer by the time we get in."

In his arms, Joely froze for a moment. Her words were

halting. Soft, but serious. "No. They'll take me off entirely. That's what happens when they find out you have an assault like that."

"They won't just fire you." They wouldn't? Would they? He hadn't read the report. So he didn't know the details, or at least the details that had made it into the report.

"You can't go." Leo declared it as though he was in any way shape or form in charge of this. At best, he could tell Taggert he was being an idiot for firing a firefighter with a record. Not that that would go very far. Taggert would listen to him, but probably not take his advice about a woman Leo was clearly interested in. Leo said it again, as if he had some authority. "They aren't going to let you go."

Her head turned, and even glancing back over her shoulder, she managed to raise one eyebrow at him. The expression told him he was being an idiot. But he wasn't.

"They like you."

Her bark was sharp and cynical. The one he'd heard before. The one he thought maybe yesterday had erased. Clearly it hadn't.

He tried another tack. Not a good one, but the one he had. "You remember the first time we worked together, with the two lost hikers? I went down and pulled them back up and the winch slipped."

"Oh, I remember," Jo told him. "You blamed me."

Fuck.

She wasn't one to brush things under the table, and she wasn't wrong. It would have been nicer if he could have admitted that maybe he had made a mistake sometime *before* seducing her ... or being seduced by her. "Yes, I did. And I was wrong. But the thing you need to know is that afterward, when I made a comment about how you'd let me slip, Sebastian Kane read me the riot act. He made it clear in no uncertain terms that it was the winch and not you that caused the problem. And he told me that you were the only one who caught the issue beforehand and had actually tried to stop it from happening."

Once again, she turned her head, looking over her bare shoulder at him, her expression clearly saying she didn't believe him. "Kane read you the riot act?"

"He gave me a stern look and told me the facts." Leo clarified. Because she was right. Kane wasn't the kind to yell or dress anyone down. "That *is* the riot act from Kane and you know it."

He felt only the slightest muscle relaxation beneath his touch. So he pushed forward. He had a goal now. "I don't know if you can tell them the truth about what happened or not, but RFD isn't the kind of crew that would hold that against you. If you've got a good record with them—and you *do*—"

She cut him off. "But it's *exactly* the kind of crew that would hold it against me. Redemption is the crew that *specifically* went digging into my past and when they found something, they *passed it around* and took it to the chief."

"No," Leo told her. "That was all Conrad Phillips. It wasn't your guys; it wasn't A-shift. If you do good work here, you'll belong."

He realized as the words came out of his mouth that he wanted nothing more than for her to belong in the Redemption Fire Department, to belong in Redemption Nebraska. To belong in his arms.

And that was maybe a mistake. She was wiggling away. Everything with Joely seemed like one and done. He'd had one kiss ... and then he learned something that made him pull away and re-evaluate. They'd had one night together now, albeit on hard dirt and flannel sleeping bags, with no pillows, no clean sheets, and no heat except their own. And Joely was already pulling away.

But instead, she rolled over and faced him. She was looking at him for a moment as if assessing him. He had no idea what questions she was asking about him in her mind, but he tried to look worthy, whatever the answers might be.

"I don't know," she finally said. "I have no clue if they'll keep me. It's a pretty tough charge on my record."

"It is. But nobody's seen any evidence of that here." He paused for a moment, and added, "and they won't."

"How do you know that?" she said.

"I've just spent the last two days with you. I've put my life in your hands more than once. And I have a hard time believing that what's on that record is both correct and unprovoked."

"Nobody else was even written up," she said, "Well, the 'incident' was written up, but no one else was charged or sent to another station."

He nodded. Once again, she looked at him. Her eyes didn't narrow or blink, but the deep blue assessed him.

She was fully on the other side of the sleeping bag, and he was still warm from the heat they had produced together, but no part of her was touching him anymore, except maybe her words.

"I'll tell you."

CHAPTER FORTY-SEVEN

"I was in the shower," Jo started. This was the easiest part, the statement of facts. "There was a separate women's bathroom. There were five women at the station, full time. I was the only one on my shift ...

"The guys gave me crap all the time. I wasn't a rookie, but I was new."

She was glad that Leo didn't say, "They give everyone crap." That was true. But hers hadn't been new-kid stuff or even Jo-related ribbing. "They thought it was funny to suggest that I scrub the toilets or clean the kitchen."

"That's everyone's job," Leo said, knowing full well that all-male stations did those jobs and never complained.

She nodded and swallowed, hoping he didn't speak again. It was easier if she just blurted it out. Her pause must have concerned him, and she could almost see the moment when he looped back around to the fact that she'd opened with *I was in the shower.*

Jo could see he was getting ready to ask, and her heart was thumping. It was almost like being back there, some kind of PTSD probably. She started over. "I was in the shower, so I didn't hear anything. The first warning I got was a hand on my ass, and another that grabbed my breast."

She watched his face, her chest collapsing inward, her heart forming into a tight little knot, thumping slowly as if it could escape.

"I turned around, too quickly, and I slipped. I hit my elbow and my knee."

And that had been the easy part. But she'd been naked and surprised and then she was down. Her muscles clenched at the memory and she was terrified and furious all over again. So she took a deep breath before she continued. "There were three of them."

This time, when she glanced at Leo, she saw his lips press tightly together. He'd figured it out. He would stay quiet now and just listen.

"When one of them reached out to touch me again, I just got mad. I cracked. And that's the problem. You can't crack. But I cracked ..." Her hand opened and closed in front of her. She sucked in another breath, but this one was as angry as the one she'd taken that day. She could almost feel the steam in her lungs and the shame at being caught unaware and assaulted. "I stood up fast and I planted my feet. The shower stall was a tiny space, and he was blocking my exit. I didn't even think, I just acted. I put my hand on the side of his face and I shoved his head into the tile. It cut him."

The records were right, she thought. She *had* assaulted a fellow firefighter, she *had* slammed his head into the wall. The noise of it had brought the other firefighters—and then her chief—into the tiny bathroom. The shower had been a stall with an open end, which normally wasn't a problem—not in an all-female room. But the room had grown crowded. The chief had first asked what was going on in here, and then quickly spotted that Jo was fully naked and he told everyone to leave.

"The chief cleared everyone out and told me to get dressed,

which had made so much sense at the time." She'd been shaking by then, and only wanted to get herself covered. So she'd rinsed her hair and calmed down. "But by the time I got out, the three of them had already told their story. And they backed each other up."

"What?" The word burst out of Leo's mouth, unable to stay inside him anymore. "How could they even back that up?"

"Have you forgotten? There were three of them. Three assholes who all entered the women's bathroom when they knew I was alone and in the shower. You think those guys are going to suddenly become upright citizens?" She didn't wait for him to answer. Leo needed to get his head on straight. Some men were assholes and other men needed to start watching out for it. "They told the chief that I invited them in."

"And he believed them?"

"To this day, I don't know if he really believed it. But there's no proof that I didn't. My fellow firefighter has a cut over his eye. His blood matches the blood on the tile and the tile is cracked where I slammed his head into it. I have a bruise on my elbow, and my knee, from where *I* slipped in the shower. There are no marks on me from what they did, and I can't prove any of it."

Her hands were waving around as if flinging off the excess nerves as she tried to explain. Her shoulders felt tight, and her back rigid, even in the confines of the sleeping bag. Her movements kept making the sleeping bag gap at the top and letting the heat out, but she couldn't stop until Leo reached out and grabbed her hands.

Slowly, he slid his fingers through hers and she gripped on tight. Too tight.

Forcing herself to take a breath, she tried to keep her voice from shaking. "I couldn't stay."

"Of course not."

"The Chief said he suspected what happened, but he couldn't

fire them when *I* had so clearly assaulted *Rob*. He offered me a rec letter, and he offered to bury the charge. It would exist, but he wouldn't forward it or anything like that. So of course Conrad had to go dig it up!"

She was angry all over again, squeezing Leo's hands too tight. Jo could feel herself shutting down. She hated it. She hated the retelling, every single time. It burned like fire down her neck. Her anger that even though she'd fought back and saved herself, she hadn't had the "appropriate response." She'd been told she should have screamed and let everyone come in. Then, standing there naked in a full room, she should have calmly stated that she'd been assaulted.

Instead, she couldn't prove any of it. Hell, even if she'd been a model citizen, she couldn't prove anything anyway. She just would have sacrificed all dignity and all defense for having the first word. All her options had been beyond shitty.

She was shaking. She pulled her hands out of his, needing to not be touching anyone. She was naked and angry and shaking, stuck in a cave with a man she just had sex with, and now she was confident that she should leave.

What she wanted to do was throw on her clothes, stuff her feet in her boots, and just walk off. She'd go for a run, except she was completely stuck. Even if she put on her clothes and got all her layers on correctly, there was still nowhere to go.

She hadn't even realized that she was clenching her jaw and squeezing her eyes shut. Her fists were curled so tightly that her nails were biting into her palms. She hadn't felt any of it until she felt Leo gently opening each hand and touching the side of her face.

"Hey. Look at me."

She didn't want to. She didn't want to face up to the story she'd told him, to the fact that she knew where she stood and what she had done. She didn't want to know how he judged her for it.

"Hey." His voice was soft and this time, when he touched the side of her face, she felt the warmth of him sliding closer, sliding against her, skin on skin, warm and kind. Always waiting.

Jo opened her eyes and saw his mouth open. She had no idea what he was going to tell her. Because Jo Huston threw herself at Leo Evans.

CHAPTER FORTY-EIGHT

Leo awoke to an odd sound. It took him a moment to place the screech and chirps as birds.

He would have sat upright but remembered that he and Jo were zipped together into the sleeping bags. Sitting up would have moved everything and woken her awkwardly.

So he laid still and enjoyed the sound that wasn't just birds, it was also the absence of rain. Leo's eyes flicked to the opening, where the tent allowed daylight around the edges for the first time. Not only could he see sky, but the entire orange fabric held the glow from the light behind it.

He checked his watch. 6am.

They'd slept long enough. Not that they'd managed a single full night since the search started. But, once again, they had enough rest to get back on their feet.

He would have liked to stay here, but they couldn't. So Leo rolled over, hoping to gently nudge Jo and regretting that he couldn't wake her up the same way he had last time, when the rain and sleet had still pelted outside and they'd been stuck with just their confessions and the small space. Instead, he found her eyes open and clear.

"It's time to go," she told him, beating him to the punch.

Leo nodded, anxious to get on with the day. Maybe the weather had finally turned. But still he couldn't quite make himself move, it was easier to watch Jo as her hand sneaked out and grabbed the pack of clothes that had been warming by the small camp light. She pulled the whole bag down into the sleeping bag with her, and he felt her squirming around. He wasn't surprised when she emerged, fully dressed, save for her boots and jacket.

"Get cracking," she grinned at him and tossed him his own pack of clothing. But then her expression turned serious when she added, "We've got a kid to find."

Dalton had been out for over forty-eight hours now and, while this wasn't the worst weather Nebraska could see, it also wasn't the kind you wanted to be lost in. Not stuck in the mountains alone and certainly not at age four.

By his calculations, Leo figured the child could still be alive. So the two of them had work to do. He dressed as quickly as he could. They ate energy bars and used a little water to brush their teeth.

He stepped beyond the tent, almost to the ledge and waited for the satellite phone to connect. Behind him he heard shuffling and the recognizable sounds of Joely completely dismantling their camp.

A few minutes later he ended the call and turned back.

"Are there teams out?" she asked.

He smiled and nodded. He and Joely would be getting retired, at least for a while. Their only assigned job now was to make it back to the base camp the team had set up.

He was opening his mouth to say so when Joely said, "We have to check out the other caves. We're already here."

She was right. They were good to go and it would take the others too long to get here and get down the side of the cliff. Though he'd told the team they were heading in, she was right.

So Leo asked one word. "How?"

But she didn't have a ready answer for that. "We'll have to figure it out. Someone will, might as well be us."

She moved efficiently, boots already on her feet, hands full. She reclaimed carabiners and pulled the tent down, holding it out for them to fold it back up together. Leo stuffed it back into its rightful place in his hiking pack before they both stepped out toward the ledge.

The brightly colored rope they'd come down on still dangled from the top. Hers was anchored to a tree, his looped over the pulley and came back down into the cave where it was coiled and waiting. He gave it a tug and found it held fast, letting him know that at least the mountain lion hadn't completely dismantled his system.

Wrapping his arm in a loop through the rope, he tugged harder, letting it take a little of his weight. When it passed the test he watched as Joely did the same thing. It wasn't a solid anchor, not like a harness, just a slight safety measure as they both stepped out toward the edge.

The rock out here was wet and glistening in the daylight. But it wasn't icy.

Small blessings, he thought as he took another step forward, double checking each step before putting his weight on the rock. He didn't trust any of it. Then together, he and Joely leaned out a little bit and looked side to side.

"There's one over there." Jo pointed "And another one beyond. The trail ledge leads right to the two other openings."

It was almost as though Mother Nature had intended people to use these caves ... or maybe mountain lions, he thought. He pointed the other way. "I don't see anything over here."

To the right, the ledge trail sloped back up toward the top. That was the way out, if they could walk it. He wasn't sure they had enough rope to get far enough and there was a chunk of the ledge missing, which meant the whole thing had to be treated as unstable.

"Going straight back up means maybe encountering the mountain lion," he commented, though he hoped that they'd been gone long enough that the mama cat would have moved on to some other source.

He really wanted to walk out on that trail. So he examined it as best he could from where he stood. The piece of rock that had sheered away was relatively large—another bad sign. Maybe it had been due to a crack, where water had seeped into the space and then expanded with the freeze.

He fought the horrifying idea that perhaps Dalton had been on the ledge when it went. If that was the case, they simply wouldn't find him for a long, long time. No one would be voluntarily going down into the ravine below. Still, Leo looked down, seeing no clues to a fall but hearing the sound of the churning water reaching up to him. The glimpses of the river that he could catch, still showed brown and muddy water raging through.

Trees jutted up, a few of their tops almost reaching high enough to touch the bottom ledge of the cave. There was enough foliage to break his fall, but also break his bones.

He was mentally working out a way to get to the next cave safely, when Joely began tapping his arm.

She looked up at him, catching his eyes as she moved her finger to her lips. Her eyes went wide as, once again, it seemed she'd heard something that he hadn't.

Her expression grew excited and Leo felt it pulsing into him, even though he didn't quite know what it was.

Her grin grew broader and her cheeks flushed. She'd heard something, even if he hadn't. Joely opened her mouth and called out, *"Dalton!"*

CHAPTER FORTY-NINE

"Shit. I'm stuck!" Jo called back to Leo, frustrated. Her harness restricted her at the same time it kept her safe.

She moved slowly along the ledge, facing the rock, holding on tightly, trying to step softly and test each foot placement as she went. She desperately wanted to move faster but any accident she had would make it take longer to get to the boy.

"I'm coming Dalton!" Jo called to her right, hoping the sound would travel around the corner and into the cave. It had traveled to him before, and his voice had traveled back, so she kept calling out. However, this time, the boy didn't answer. He hadn't for a while. His initial return call had been equal parts clear and scared, but then he'd quit responding.

She took another tentative step before slowly putting more weight on the spot. It was a painstaking process, but not only did at least one of them have to survive getting over to Dalton, someone also had to survive the way back with the kid.

They'd argued, fiercely and quickly, about who would make the trek and who would anchor. Jo had finally won. "Leo, I'm smaller. You need to be the anchor, you're heavier. And whoever gets across the ledge has to come back with a kid strapped to them. Dalton and I will fit better, it's not a wide ledge."

She could tell he'd tried hard to form a counter argument. He had valid points: Being on the ledge was dangerous. Being on the anchor was important. Nobody wanted to be the one to watch your partner slip or fall. It was always considered better to be the one doing the falling.

She took another step to her right, planting her hand and moving until she tugged the rope.

"More line!" It was the harness holding her back, and the last thing she should ever do was unclip out here on the ledge and free climb all the way over. She fully intended to scoop up a four-year-old child on the other side.

"Hold on," Leo told her. Though his tone was outwardly calm, she could tell there was an underlying sense of urgency. He, too, knew they were working against a very tight clock. And that they hadn't gauged the ledge distance very well; she was much farther away than she'd intended to be.

Jo didn't know what he'd done, she only heard his voice say, "Okay, go" at the same time that she felt the harness finally give and let her move further.

She was taking her steps when he told her what he'd done. "I've got rope tied to rope, Jo. It's stupid and awful and you only have until the knot hits the pulley."

She wondered if the knot might go through the pulley, but that was unlikely. "How far do I have?"

She imagined the knot sliding its way up the trail as she moved out, she certainly wasn't going to look at it. And she was close, so close to the entrance to the next cave. She told herself it would be enough. "What have you anchored it to?"

Both ropes had been hanging down into the cave from the top. Hers was fully anchored to a tree; his had both ends in the cave, with the middle looped through a pulley at the top. A shitty system, but the only one they could form at the time. If he tied her rope to his, that bought her a little more distance now and he could hold on to the remaining loop … she then decided not to figure out the physics of it.

Stepping sideways, she got farther from their own cave entrance and closer to where they had heard the child. He'd never said that he was Dalton, though he'd answered to the name. Jo figured any kid would if in need of rescue, still, she would be disappointed if it was a different kid.

Two more feet.

She stopped again, slowly stepping out and testing the ground for sponginess or give. It was rock beneath her feet, and the freezing weather could shear it away in a split second, leaving her hanging if she wasn't careful. She pushed with the ball of her right foot. When it held, she added pressure, then more of her weight.

Then her entire system jumped as the rock gave way beneath her. Jo couldn't help but watch in terror as a piece the size of her head tumbled and fell silently beneath her. It was maybe worse that it didn't make noise, that the distance was far enough that she couldn't even hear it hit.

She must have yelled out, because Leo called back, "What!?" and the rope suddenly snapped tight as he held on to her.

"I'm okay!" It was the first thing to call back, to let him know he could stop worrying. "A bit of the ledge slipped away."

"How much is a bit?" he asked, the words harsh.

Jo knew that if he deemed it too much, he would pull her back. "Not big. Five, six inches, I'm just going to step over it."

And, while her answer was true, any missing part of the ledge was concerning. Given the missing chunk on the trail back up to the top, this wasn't the only piece that had fallen out or come loose, and the whole thing became more precarious. But she couldn't wait.

"Let my line out, Leo," she told him, still moving sideways. None of this was real rock climbing and Leo had just violated belay systems to hell and back. But there already were more rescue teams coming out into the woods, combing the area for Dalton. Once she and Leo had him, they'd hook up the satellite phone and call it in.

She had to keep going.

Jo felt her way around the edge as the rock slowly dipped in forming the cave. It took far too long to get enough of her body past the opening to where she could see in, and then another moment for her eyes to adjust. She called out, but no one called back as she blinked and tried to see.

When her eyes finally adjusted to the dim cave, lit by the bright day behind her, she called back, "Leo! Leo!"

CHAPTER FIFTY

Jo held onto the ropes, once again unable to watch as Leo moved along the cliff above her. This time he climbed upward, and her job was to take up the slack and not let him fall if he slipped. She tried not to hold her breath, but it was a constant battle between nerves and need.

They had reconfigured the harness and rope system yet again for another bold and risky maneuver. They'd argued again about who would go first. This time Leo insisted that it was him. She would have to carry Dalton up to the top with her. This time it was because he wanted to clear the area and make sure the mountain lion was gone before anyone else came up. He would also need to be the anchor for the two of them to ascend, that would be safest from the top, not the pulley system they'd jury rigged.

So she pulled up the slack as Leo climbed the side of the cliff. All of the maneuvering was much easier now. The rock wasn't dry, but there wasn't water actively running down the side. The sun had made her warm in all of her gear and she was oddly on the verge of overheating. As the temperature swung wildly, she was grateful though. Maybe it would help Dalton.

They'd unpacked one of the sleeping bags, wrapped him in a foil blanket and stuffed him inside. He'd been so cold that he wasn't able to stay awake. It was an early stage of hypothermia, though neither of them had to say it.

Jo pulled the line again, this time feeling it suddenly slacking in her hands. So she wasn't surprised when Leo called down. "I'm up. I'm up."

She knew he would need to clear the area. While he did, she stayed efficient and used the time to rouse Dalton and try again to get him to eat. He was already strapped into the smaller child's harness they'd brought and clipped firmly into the rope form they'd made so she could carry him up.

Jo needed him awake if he could be. She shook his shoulder as she unzipped the bag, hating that she was letting some of his precious heat go. He still wasn't warm to the touch, but they couldn't bring the sleeping bag with them. In fact, Leo had stripped the most essential items from the packs they'd carried and put them into a smaller bag that he had carried up with him. This meant Jo only needed to bring Dalton.

He was far too big to strap to the front of her, and she was going to have to wear him. Instead, they had to rig him to fit onto her back, and they had to rig it so that it would hold if he fell asleep or even if he decided to fight them. They both knew he wasn't alert enough to hang on.

Jo couldn't climb with a child in front of her. So, while it was the safer option, it was off the table. She didn't like it, but she trusted the ropes and the carabiners. She always had. So now she hoisted Dalton onto her back and strapped him on. Double checking everything before stepping closer to the edge.

She was weighted backwards in the worst possible way, but this was what she trained for. This was the reason she lifted weights at the gym and why she ran miles every day. This was the thing that her family would never understand. Her heart thumped heavily, her breathing rougher than it should be, because she could lose big on this climb. Or even if they made it back, Dalton might not. He was in bad shape.

But ... if he did make it ... that would be a victory she could hold for the rest of her life.

So Jo anchored herself firmly to the rope and called up. She waited for Leo's commands and then headed toward the ledge and stepped carefully to the side where she could climb.

She had to be extra careful. She and Leo were running on fumes and their own excitement at having found Dalton ... and their own fear that they might still lose him.

Starting upward, she felt the limp weight on her back, threatening to tip her and making the climb that much harder. But Jo fought for every foot. The harness and heavy line helped steady her. She worked to not get ahead of herself, but keep a slow, steady pace.

She had to get them both to the top without injury or accident. She had no idea how long it took, but she eventually felt the top edge almost as a surprise. She had been watching only the rock in front of her, paying attention only to the weight on her back—the occasional movement was the only thing letting her know that the boy was still alive.

Leo must have anchored the rope, because suddenly a hand was on her harness and she was being lifted. Along with Dalton, she was hauled up and over the edge.

"Agh!" She banged her knee into the edge and even stubbed a toe as she cleared the top.

"Are you okay?" Leo's sharp question gave the injury more gravity than it deserved. It had simply been a surprise.

"Just got bumped." And none of it mattered. She was on her hands and knees with Dalton sprawled limply across her back as she crawled a few feet farther onto the ledge before Leo helped her upright.

"Further," he said, taking her hand and still pulling her back away from the sharp drop into the treetops and river below.

He was right. She hadn't thought of it before, but the other ledge had given away. What if the top edge was already faulty, too? It was all the same rock.

Only once they were both well back from the ravine did Leo begin stripping his harness. It came off easily, falling at his feet. He reached up to help her unclip Dalton and swing the boy around, gently setting him down. "Leave him in the harness."

Jo nodded as Leo explained. "We have to carry him out and do it fast."

Dalton was fading. She was no expert but even she could see that. So Jo slid quickly out of her own harness. There was no time to enjoy the sensation of being able to stand fully upright again. She took only one full body stretch, one glance behind her at the still cold but finally bright, sunny day, before Leo was nodding.

He already had Dalton slung across his own back. The little boy's head still lolled to the side and Jo hoped it was from sleep and nothing more.

Leo held out the sat phone, pushing it into her hands. "Call them."

But he'd already taken off down the path. Jo dialed, staying in close pursuit.

CHAPTER FIFTY-ONE

"Leo, it's my turn." Jo insisted for what was probably the fifth time.

"I've got him," he protested.

But Jo stopped still and planted her feet. "No, you fucking don't. Protocol is that we trade him off regularly so that we constantly carry him on a fresh back."

Leo knew this. And, no, they hadn't followed protocol all along—they'd cut a damn lot of corners along the way, and they'd cut some of them very sharply. But in this instance the protocol was exactly the right way and she knew it.

She might not be as physically strong as Leo for carrying the heavy weight of a passed out child, but trading off the weight and trading it in shorter intervals was definitely the way to go. "Leo, trade him now."

He'd moved several yards ahead of her, not quite realizing she had stopped until that moment. They were both working up a good sweat despite the chill in the air. It felt warm compared to what they'd been searching in before, so Jo didn't mind. She only minded Leo not being willing to do the trade.

He looked at her and she knew—she just *knew*—he wanted to say, "I'm fine," or "I've got it," but she stared him down, hard.

Her turns carrying Dalton wouldn't be as long as his. *Fine.* Though she was relatively tall for a woman, her legs weren't as long as his. It was still her turn and he still needed a rest. Leo seemed to sense her stubbornness in the glint of her eyes, and at last he conceded. Stepping back toward her, he reached for the carabiner in front that held the boy tightly to his back.

Jo met him halfway in between, exactly as it should be. She understood his stubbornness. She had it, too, but for now she was grateful to help Leo out of the extra weight. She lifted at the makeshift pack, watching as Dalton's head lolled from where it had rested against Leo's shoulder.

That was concerning.

Helping to pull the weight off of Leo, she tried to check the child. The pack they'd designed was both ingenious and pretty shitty. She didn't think they'd been considering the distance they would have to carry the boy. Also, they'd intended for carrying Dalton to be a backup—a way to get him to safety if he became exhausted or if he passed out. At one point she'd even imagined Dalton walking along with them, her holding his hand and telling him they would be going home.

But the child had been far too weak from the moment they'd found him. He'd barely even been awake for small stretches of time. So—though she hated the sight of the small child passed out as Leo carefully set him down—it was only what she'd expected.

Watching Leo's shoulders roll with the freedom of not carrying the pack, she realized the ropes were very uncomfortable though they'd done their best with what they had. It was going to be her turn. She'd been smart and tucked a few small towels into the pack Leo had carried up from the cave. Now she watched as they fell to the ground from where they'd been offering whatever padding they could for Leo's shoulders. She grabbed them to use for herself.

Though she wanted to take a few moments and set everything up carefully, they needed to act quickly. Getting Dalton to an ambulance, and the ambulance getting him to a medical center where he could be treated, was of the utmost priority. His small body splayed on to the ground, the foil blanket falling away in spots. They couldn't afford for him to lose any heat and both she and Leo reached out to tuck it back into place.

His hand came out and laid, palm up, and still the boy didn't seem to notice that he was crinkling in a foil blanket on the ground in the forest.

"His lips are a decent color ..." Leo commented.

But Jo shook her head. "On darker skinned people if you wait for their lips to turn blue, you're waiting until their oxygen is way too low."

She carefully lifted the child's lip, but he didn't move. Not a good sign.

Shaking her head at Leo, she watched as he reached out and felt for a pulse at the side of the child's neck, his eyes growing wider with each passing second. "I don't feel anything, Jo."

He pushed the foil aside and Jo recognized the movements as he found the sternum and counted up one finger space because this was a child. He was about to start CPR, but she pushed him aside.

"Let me." She peeled her own glove and reached out. The little boy's neck was far too cold.

She didn't like it and she, too, didn't feel a pulse. It didn't mean it wasn't there though. Holding her left hand up to stop Leo, to make him wait while her exposed right hand grew chilled in the open air, she tried to drown out every other sensation except what her fingertips could feel.

"Oh my God." The words came out on a gulp of air. "I felt it!

It's slow and weak, but he does have a pulse. We need to put him on the front of me."

She was already unzipping her jacket and peeling it off. She explained how she wanted to put Dalton in front of her, baby sling style, and wrap the boy's legs around her waist to keep him warm.

Jo was confident that she was okay, body heat wise. The way they'd rigged the tent, their space had been fine—not like a fireplace in a cabin warm and cozy, but warm enough. With the small camp heater and the sleeping bags, they'd stayed at a normal body temperature.

She pushed aside the thought of how they'd kept their body heat up and how they'd not discussed that at all this morning, but there sure as hell wasn't time for a dissection of their relationship now. There were far more important things on the table.

Jo's hands worked rapidly, as she tugged her glove back on and wrapped Dalton up quickly. She watched as Leo searched the small pack for extra materials. And slowly they crossed the boy's arms in front of his body, tucking them in under the foil blanket. They placed the padding on Jo's shoulders, and put the pack on her, this time in front. Leo helped her slip back into her jacket, pulling it around her and the boy. Then they wrapped Dalton's legs around her and tucked them up, pulling the elastic ripcord at the bottom of the jacket to tighten it and hold him in place.

She couldn't zip the jacket all the way up with him inside, but he was surrounded by a foil blanket. Slowly, Jo moved her arms, testing the pack and how the extra weight would make her move. She took a few tentative steps and once she found her rhythm, she wrapped her arms around Dalton as if he were her own child.

"You ready?"

She nodded. "Let's go."

The hiking was definitely harder, carrying the child. Jo did her best, but by putting him in front of her, she'd made it difficult to see where she was stepping. She wondered if this would be what it was like one day when she was pregnant, and she couldn't see her own feet. She hugged the boy tighter, grateful to feel what little breath she could on her neck. He was still alive ...

"Jesus, he's cold, Leo."

But Leo only nodded back. They'd done everything they could, there was nothing more they could make happen out here with their limited resources. The only thing now was to get him back to base camp and medical help faster.

Unfortunately, the new base camp was farther from where they were now. So the two of them kept moving forward, knowing they had ground to cover before they would even meet up with the team coming to intercept them.

A little further along, Leo started carefully pointing out things to avoid stepping on, like roots and rocks that might twist an ankle. It seemed he'd recognized that she couldn't see where she was going. There was something about his natural care-taking that Jo felt deep in her soul. Was she a care-taker—a firefighter—because no one had really ever watched out for her this way? This simple, non-intrusive, non-insulting version of "I've got your back" that Leo seemed to just naturally exude was the most comforting thing she might have ever experienced.

She spoke up, almost as if she needed to fill the space, lest Leo realize she was becoming so attached to him. "Dalton's either warming up, or I'm getting used to how cold he is."

Leo turned back and looked for a moment. They truly didn't have time to stop.

"How much farther?" she asked.

"I think three to five more miles. Depends on how quickly the other team moves."

Jo crossed her fingers. The team had been launched from the

base when they called in that they'd found Dalton. But even with everything in place, no one was moving quickly. Jo and Leo were carrying the boy. The team coming their way was carrying medical supplies. They would meet in the middle and do everything they could to save Dalton.

Jo kept moving, one foot in front of the other, and wondering when it would be time to trade him back. The child was heavy, but she was determined to finish out her turn. And honestly, she hadn't even probably done half of it.

"*Joely*!" The word was harsh, not the soft lilting way he usually said her name.

Leo had come to a complete stop. It was harder for Jo to change her momentum on a dime with the extra weight. But she managed to not plow into him, as she came up right behind him where Leo held his hands wide on either side. One hand was splayed open, the black glove a clear stop signal. The other held the sat phone, clutched tightly. He'd been holding it, waiting for any communication, but now his fingers appeared to try to crush it.

What did he see?

Leo was just a little taller than her, and she couldn't quite peer over his shoulder to see what had made him stop so suddenly and bark at her. But, though she couldn't see anything, she clearly heard the low menacing growl.

CHAPTER FIFTY-TWO

"Joely, Back up!" Leo tried to say it in as soft a voice as possible, but also one firm enough to actually make her do what he insisted.

He, on the other hand, didn't move. He'd planted himself between the mountain lion—who seemed to have found them once again—and Jo who was carrying Dalton.

The last time they'd encountered the mountain lion, he'd counted Joely as a teammate, a fellow fighter alongside him. But now, she was carrying a wounded kid, one whose pulse was already light and thready. Leo, able to move swiftly and also stay behind and fight, was going to have to hold off the big cat on his own.

This time, as the creature raised still-wet fur and bared her fangs at him, he realized what the problem was. In fact, he wasn't sure how he'd missed it before. The interaction had been so unusual the first time. Mountain lions didn't chase people down. At the time, he'd attributed it to the cubs, but now he understood ... and that made the whole thing worse.

"Jo. She's rabid."

"What? Does that even happen up here?"

He almost laughed. For the last twenty-four hours it had been easy to forget that Joely came from big city rescue departments. She'd hiked enough and traveled enough that she fit in fine here, but then she asked something like that and made him smile despite the fact that he was probably about three yards from death. "Yes, I assure you animals in Nebraska can absolutely get rabies. And this one has."

"What do we do?"

Shit, he thought, because he didn't have an answer. For a moment, he just felt his tongue curl into the back of his mouth because he didn't have anything to say to her, but then he did. He held the sat phone out behind himself and told to her take it, grateful when she did. He was going to issue a short series of instructions, and at some point she would stop following his commands. He knew it.

"Step backwards," he told her and then waited until he heard the soft crunch of her footsteps. He watched carefully for the reaction on the lion's face. It was clear that the big cat saw Joely moving slightly away. The mountain lion's growl deepened, her head lowered, and her shoulders shifted—not quite ready to pounce, but closer than she had been before.

Leo slowly moved his hand down, trying to draw the animal's attention as he spoke. "I need you to reach into my pack and get the hunting knife. Put it in my hand."

He held his other hand out, open palmed, behind his back, hating that he was carefully organizing his words, because at some point Jo would refuse. He needed to get her to do as much of it as possible before she balked.

He heard her rummaging through and felt that she was trying to make slow movements—probably both because she had a child strapped onto her and because she was trying not to startle the cat. Knowing Joely, she was looking over his shoulder and assessing the big cat's nasty expression for herself.

But soon enough, he felt the unsheathed handle placed

firmly into his palm, and he closed his fist, getting a grip on the blade.

Ready for when the cat leapt, he spoke again. "Now slowly walk backwards, away from me."

"Leo?" she asked, her voice tentative, and he knew this was where it would start.

He said it again. "Joely, walk backwards. Get Dalton out of here ... please."

It was the please that made her go. He heard her footsteps as she moved back. Though he couldn't see her, he seemed to feel the loss of Joely Huston stepping away from him. *For the last time?*

But he made himself say more, to push her. "Go backwards on the trail until you can't see me anymore. Then I want you to cut ninety degrees to your left and just go off path. Keep walking until you hit another trail and then head to your right, back toward the team."

Her footsteps stopped as he'd known they would. "I'm not leaving you here, Leo."

"Yes, you are."

"No, I'm not," she told him once again, her tone stern.

"If you don't, Dalton will likely die. This isn't going to go any better because you're here. And I think I can maneuver and get out of this if I don't have to deal with anyone else." The last part wasn't entirely true. Though he did think he would have a better chance of getting out of it if he didn't have to account for a person who wasn't fast and also a child who wasn't moving, he wasn't confident he could escape the cat intact.

But the fewer distractions, the better he would do. "Walk away."

He kept his eye on the cat as she paced in front of him and he slowly shrugged his way out of the pack. There was more in there than just the knife, anything would help.

"Leo," Joely protested again though, this time, her fight

wasn't quite as clear. He could only hope that the threat to the one thing they'd come out to find would galvanize her enough to make her move.

"Leo." She said it again, but this time the tone let him know that he'd gotten through.

With the knife at the ready, his free hand rummaged in the pack, searching for a few things that he hoped might help him against a rabid mountain lion. Plausibly the worst part was that so much of what he needed was still back in the cave. Tools he should have, but had stripped for weight and speed, would have saved him now.

It didn't matter. He couldn't get them, and he would have to make due with what he had. He kept his eyes forward.

The cat would not be making rational decisions or even predictable ones. A mother mountain lion defending her cubs would have left him and Joely alone until the cubs were clearly threatened. Leo had believed they only encountered her in the first place because they'd chased her cubs down thinking they heard voices. Any normal day he would have told himself it was a ridiculously stupid error to think an animal was a child. But, between the rain and the wind and the leaves rustling, it had been truly difficult to distinguish.

But now he saw it for what it was … And here was the cat, her rabies-addled brain seeing him as only prey. With the mountain lion ready to jump at any moment, he couldn't even turn around and say goodbye to Joely.

Leo thought of so many other things to say as he heard her moving farther away. The occasional crunch of a twig made the mountain lion's eyes twitch. And each time Leo swayed, he hopefully blocked the cat's view and brought her attention back to him.

He almost called out, "I love you."

Instead, he didn't look, but said, "I'll see you back at the camp. Go!"

CHAPTER FIFTY-THREE

Jo ran, her breath soughing in and out of her lungs, her arms wrapped around the child now bouncing against her.

With each precarious step, she moved blindly forward, unable to see where she was planting her feet. So she simply had to be grateful for good hiking boots that she'd laced tightly, and she could only hope that it held her ankles in place.

In front of her, Dalton let out a soft moan.

Thank God. It meant he was alive still. She'd moved sideways between trails as Leo had instructed. Picking her way through dense underbrush already burdened with a passed out child had been slow going, but she'd pushed forward, keeping one hand on Dalton to steady him and the other reaching out to brace on tree trunks. All she could do was pray that none of Nebraska's poisonous snakes were in her path. She wouldn't see them until it was too late.

The moment she'd run into the new trail, she'd breathed a heavy sigh of relief and took an immediate right. Jo picked up her speed. Now, her fingers fumbled with the satellite phone. She had to connect, had to tell someone what was happening.

"I'm on another trail! Not where you're expecting to intercept us," she told them.

"You're Joely? I'm Bethany."

The introductions were a waste of time. Jo issued more instructions. "Your team needs to split. We ran into a mountain lion. Think she's rabid ... Leo stayed behind with her."

The last words were the hardest ones to get out. *She'd left Leo behind.*

She hadn't told him how she felt, or what she thought. She didn't even know if she'd sacrificed Leo to save Dalton, because she wasn't sure that Dalton would make it.

"What?" The voice came back across the line. Whether it crackled or whether she just couldn't hear clearly because she was crashing through the woods and making her own noise, Jo couldn't tell.

She fought for the air to say it all again. "We split up! Some of you need to get to Leo."

She was desperately afraid he would need medical attention ... maybe more than could be provided on a trail. And at the same time she *hoped* he would need medical attention—that the medics didn't find a situation where there was nothing they could do.

A mountain lion was not an easy fight on a good day, not when the cat was acting under normal parameters. A fight against a *rabid* mountain lion. Hell, even if he survived it ...

Jo decided to stop thinking about it. She couldn't afford the mental stress about something she couldn't now do anything about. If Leo had been the one holding Dalton, she would have told him to take the kid and go, too. There had been no time to choose the better courier and switch out roles. So she had to believe that Leo's decision was best. She hated it, but it was the same one she would have insisted on were the positions reversed. Her brain churned trying to tell herself she was doing the right thing.

So maybe it was her own fault that her ankle rolled and she went crashing down onto her hands and knees. One hand snapped up quickly to cradle Dalton's head before it jerked and rolled too hard.

As Jo pushed upright, she felt the sharp pains in her knees, both of them. The pants hadn't ripped—they were far too sturdy for that—but, at the very least, she'd bruised her knees and she was pretty certain she'd ripped the skin.

Back on her feet, she made herself run as best she could. It was faster but not easier. Faster was what Dalton needed. Faster was why she'd left Leo alone, so she pushed forward.

She tripped and fell a second time, this time smacking against a tree. Once again, she'd not quite stopped herself before she did any real damage. She only managed to twist a little so that she took the brunt of the hit on her own shoulder, and not on the little boy.

He groaned again, and she hated that it was a welcome sound. He wasn't doing well, but maybe if she'd gotten him warmer, he was doing better. And Lord knew with the way she was running, she was heating up.

"Where are you now?" the voice carried through the air for a moment before Jo realized she'd left the line open. But maybe that was a good thing.

"I don't know."

"Where is Leo?"

"He's on the original path that he laid out for the team. If they keep going that way they'll run right into him."

But it had been Leo who set everything up. He'd designated the meeting point. He knew the names of the trails, and the distances. Jo didn't know any of it and she sure as hell didn't know the name of this other trail that she'd cut over to, but she tried to explain the instructions Leo had given her. Her only hope was that the person on the other end knew more than she did.

"Hold on," Bethany told her. Whoever Bethany was, she was a goddess, Jo thought now.

Bethany named the trail Jo was on and a moment later came back and said, "I've relayed your information to the medical team. They're close. Keep your eyes open."

Jo tried—she really did—but she was sprinting blindly along a trail that wasn't made for running in the Nebraska wilderness, where she was unfamiliar with everything, and apparently could run into a rabid mountain lion at any point.

Ten hard minutes later, she saw a flash of yellow through the trees. She called out breathlessly. "Hello! Hello?"

"Hastings Search and Rescue!" they called back. "Joely Huston?"

Her own name had never sounded so good.

"I've got Dalton!" She cried out, "I've got Dalton."

Then, over the phone Bethany told her, "It sounds like they have you. I'm disconnecting now. We're going to find Leo."

As she moved closer, Joely found that the yellow flash she'd seen was more than just a single person. Multiple bright vests, catching what little sunlight came through the canopy, made their way through the trees toward her. They ran and she ran forward.

She was out of breath, but two minutes later she collapsed, exhausted and nearly defeated at the feet of three search and rescue workers.

CHAPTER FIFTY-FOUR

Leo kept the hunting knife in front of him, blade out, the handle firm in his grasp. He slowly waved it back and forth, using it to hold the mountain lion's attention. Jo had disappeared behind him a while ago, but the cat had kept him in its sight.

While he wasn't keen on being held hostage by a rabid mountain lion, he was glad that it hadn't followed Joely and Dalton.

With another sudden move that shot Leo's adrenaline through the roof, the cat growled at him, low and fierce. Leo offered his own growl in return.

In his left hand, he held the flare gun, the bandage Jo had put on his finger blocked his ability to control the weapon the way he would have liked. He'd thought he'd get a doctor to look at it and get some antibiotics when he got back to central camp. The cat growled to let him know he'd be damned lucky if his hand was the worst injury she inflicted on him.

The gun was in his non-dominant hand, as the knife seemed more important. Unfortunately, he didn't truly know what the flare gun would do. Would it startle the cat? Make her angry enough to leap? Or could he actually hit her and wound her with it?

Leo hated wounding an animal, but he also understood there wasn't much he could do in this case. And he wanted to live. He wanted to get back to Joely. He was already regretting all the things he could have told her as she walked away.

Part of his brain tried to run on another track, as though normal thoughts would make any of this normal. So he lamented that there were now rabies infections in his park. But right now, he needed to fight to keep his brain focused exactly where he was. He needed to stay on the task of survival.

The big cat paced slowly in front of him, and he tracked her movements obsessively, ready with both the knife and the flare gun. He had stuck an extra flare into his back pocket, but it would be difficult to reload in a hurry. Right now, he only had the one shot.

As far as he knew, no one was coming for him. No one would until Joely found someone and sent them to him.

He needed to figure out how to get away from the cat. But she wasn't letting him get by. Her cubs would be a great distraction, but he didn't see them or even hear them now. He worried about their safety ... though they would need to be dealt with, too.

Maybe he hadn't gotten enough sleep. Maybe he hadn't eaten enough, but his brain kept wandering. Leo forced it back to the present and contemplated what would happen if he simply backed away.

But how far back could he go? The cat had every advantage if he was moving backwards. He could try to get past her by getting on another trail, like he'd had Joely do. But he didn't want to follow Jo. The whole point had been to get her and Dalton away from the danger.

If he went backwards then sidestepped the other direction, that wouldn't necessarily be any better. One problem was that there weren't as many trails in that direction. It headed back toward the area where the caves had been, back to the places marked off limits to hikers and campers. It was also farther away from the medical teams.

Another problem was that once he went off trail, the cat had an advantage.

Well, he thought to himself, *the cat had an advantage anyway.*

She was strong, with deadly jaws, and as of right now, she knew no fear. But he didn't have any other weapons and with his hand bandaged, he was using everything he could handle.

It wasn't much.

Leo rolled forward onto the balls of his feet, knees bent, ready to spring, defend, attack, whatever was needed.

She turned at the end of her very short path and headed the other way. She moved like a caged lion.

His brain wandered again. There was going to be so much cleanup from this, and yet none of it would matter to him if he didn't survive this encounter.

The cat turned back the other direction and Leo felt a glimmer of respect. She was caging him in, moving slightly closer with each cross path she took.

Fuck. Did that mean she was getting ready to pounce? If she did, it would happen with lightning speed. Leo had already flinched a number of times when she'd jerked a muscle or hunkered down at him, eyes glazed, then maybe changed her mind. Maybe she wasn't as far gone as he thought, and she was messing with him.

Should he move backwards, or should he counter her and show strength by stepping forward? Could he just take one solid step, switch the flare gun into his right hand, take aim and kill her?

He didn't want to kill her but right now, all he wanted was to get back to Joely. He wanted to see Dalton and tell the kid he was going to be okay. He wanted to go home and sleep in his own bed. Stoke a fire in the fireplace and curl up on his sofa and tell Joely how he really felt.

The cat stalked again, and this time Leo took a step backward.

They were at a standoff, neither of them quite in a position to strike. Only now she was close enough, that with what little effort she needed to get into position, she could reach him in one leap. He'd only get the warning of watching her crouch to spring.

He counted the distance between them. She wouldn't just reach him, she'd be on top of him.

Knife or gun? Knife or gun?

Gun first, then knife, he thought, rapidly switching the weapons from hand to hand. His motion triggered the cat and he had only the momentary warning of her bowing slightly before she leapt.

He tried to do everything he'd heard about from friends who hunted. He tried to stop his breath so it didn't interfere. He thought about snipers shooting between heartbeats. Could he do that? There wasn't time.

Everything moved in slow motion as he pulled the trigger and watched as the too-bright light of the flare aimed toward the cat. Only later did he register the sizzling sound of it sailing through the air.

He was too stunned to do more than watch it bounce off her. His aim was true, but had it burned? Was she hurt?

The cat almost didn't even react, there was just a cry that had a slightly altered tone as she pushed off her back feet. Wide front paws splayed and aimed directly at him. There was no way to dodge the blow. He simply couldn't be fast enough.

The gun fell from his fingers, and he shoved the knife into his dominant hand even as he registered everything. The cat was airborne. The flare gun clattered to the dirt, too far away should he need it again. Bad decision. The knife was in his hand and it was the only thing he truly had.

So he held it forward, his other arm coming up across his face. This was going to hurt like a son of a bitch.

Leo tried not to look. He couldn't leave his face exposed, but he needed to see to fight. He jabbed outward, feeling the knife rip into soft flesh. The cat twisted as her claws shredded open air, and then his flesh.

Her body slammed into him, and he landed on the ground, the blow stunning him for a second. A second too long.

He'd fought. He'd stabbed her harshly. And it hadn't been enough.

Leo felt another white hot flash of pain as her claws bit into him.

CHAPTER FIFTY-FIVE

Jo walked into the station at 7:45. She was fifteen minutes early and hoping to slip in unnoticed.

That was impossible though, as she came in through the back bay door and was jolted at the applause that greeted her. All of A-shift stood in a line, as did C. They were coming off of their twenty-four hours. Instead of the usual trade out, all of them stood clapping. *At her.*

She was stunned.

She'd missed one shift being out with Leo on the rescue. Then she'd been granted another shift off to recuperate. She'd thought she was walking in today to get fired.

"What?" she asked them, staring oddly and scrambling to figure out why they were doing this.

"You found the kid!" Kalan Smith told her, his hands finally coming to a standstill, as he reached out and clapped her on the shoulder. "Good work, Huston."

"It was just a regular SAR." But even as she said it, she saw the looks on their faces and admitted that it wasn't.

Ronan Kelly stepped forward. "From what we've heard, that was some very intense rescue work. Rock climbing in an ice storm? And we heard you ran the kid five miles on your own to meet up with the medical team."

Had it really been that far? She could only shrug. This was not what she expected. In fact, she had been braced to be called directly into the chief's office. It could still happen.

She waved them haphazardly away, her hand sloshing back and forth through the air, uncomfortable with the praise let alone the applause. "This is absolutely unnecessary. Thank you."

But they grinned and, one by one, patted her on the back. C-shift workers headed to their cars in the lot. A aimed their way inside.

It had been a rough five days.

She'd gone home and stood in her very expensive, multi head shower, and not quite gotten warm enough. It was absolutely not the same as a claw foot bathtub big enough for two.

She had been treated for lacerations on her hands and knees. Only later—when medical insisted that they check her over—did she remember that she'd had several falls. They'd bandaged her and questioned when she'd gotten the cuts. Since they were new, and wouldn't need antibiotics, she was allowed to head home.

Dalton had been run on ahead by two of the medical team who'd met her on the trail. The third had stayed behind with her, slowly walking them the last miles in. Before she and her handler had arrived at base camp, Dalton had been rushed to the hospital and the second team had come in with Leo on a backboard and stuck him into a second ambulance that had been summoned by Bethany for exactly that purpose.

By the time she'd stumbled in, her arm slung around her rescuer for support, her energy flagging by the moment, Dalton and Leo had both been long gone.

She'd been fed and had water forced on her until they felt

she was adequately hydrated. At home, she'd bathed then slept for almost a full day.

When she'd woken up, she'd immediately headed to the hospital where she'd been told Leo was in recovery. He'd needed surgery on his leg and his arm, and the messages that had pinged her when she'd awoken told her he was expected to need time to heal but would get up to full strength soon enough.

She'd breathed a ready sigh of overwhelming relief and rushed straight to Lincoln to a hospital she'd never been to before. But as soon as she'd navigated the maze of hallways and arrived at the waiting room for his floor, Jo had run into an older woman with a cap of white curls. Mrs. Evans had informed her that Leo did not want to see her.

That had not been what Jo expected to hear.

Maybe he had decided he didn't trust her after all? Or maybe he had decided he'd gone too far and this was the easy way out …

She'd stumbled through the words, "Will you tell him I stopped by?" then muttered a quick, "I'm Joely Huston," as if that mattered.

She'd almost shocked herself at the use of her full name. Leo was still in the hospital, and they expected him to be sprung in a few days. The guys were planning to head to his house as he went home, and check anything he needed accommodations for. Jo was invited.

She couldn't say yes. She couldn't say no.

Maybe he would message or call soon.

So she occupied her time by checking her locker. She inspected every piece of her turnout gear that had gone unused for well over a week. And she tried to make her day normal. Within just a few minutes, the bell rang, and it was a welcome relief as the Chief stepped out of his office, naming off the trucks they would take and who would be in what position.

Jo, grateful to be on the list, hopped on the rig and gladly went on the call. It turned out to be nothing more than smoke coming from under a car hood. The battery had come loose, slid next to something too hot for batteries and caught fire. The flames were three inches high, and a small fire extinguisher had done the trick, but it had been everything to Jo.

She'd been sent on a *normal run,* she was still on the roster. And she was trying to hide the fact that she was both disturbingly happy and disturbingly vulnerable waiting for Leo to say something as they looped back to the station.

No one had made any comments about the assault charges. In fact, they didn't seem to be an issue, as Jo got no strange vibes as she worked with the rest of the team. They came back in, checked over the truck, and laid hands on every piece of equipment. Like clockwork, they put their turnout gear back, ready for the next run.

But as she filed back through the doorway to the main room, the chief stepped out of his office and pointed at her. "Huston. Can I see you?"

Son of a bitch. She nodded sharply though her insides churned. She'd just gotten to believing that everything was going to be okay. And of course it wasn't. *It never was.*

It took her almost a full minute to get her features schooled down to somewhat normal. During that minute, she argued back and forth with herself. Did she need to look normal? Would it be okay to be angry that she was getting pushed out of yet another job?

That last run, she'd felt so much a part of the team. It seemed almost cruel to let her come back in, fit in, and feel good about what she did, before taking it away again. But she did manage to get her expression together.

She walked into the chief's office, confident—or at least full of simmering anger that she was keeping a lid on it—with her hands clasped behind her back. Taggert motioned for her to take a seat across the desk.

"At ease," he seemed to tease her, as though she were a soldier. She couldn't relax, but she did unclasp her hands and attempted to look natural.

"As you know," he began a little too solemnly, "It has come to our attention that there was an assault charge filed at your last station."

She nodded. What else could she do? Even as her throat clenched down, she tried to offer an accepting smile. She could feel the hammer swinging.

Taggert leaned forward, fingers interlaced, ready to deal some serious news.

Son of a bitch, she thought again, and Jo opened her mouth to resign her position before he could fire her. But Taggert was faster than she was, almost as if he were *trying* to beat her to the punch.

"Conrad Phillips dug it up, and it made me curious as to why he'd gone to so much effort to discredit you. I mean, he'd barely worked with you. So I asked around."

What?

He leaned back, clearly disgusted. "And let me tell you, every female worker at this station had an earful for me about Phillips, particularly Leslie and Ann who've been on shift with him for several years."

Joely fought to keep her mouth from dropping open. That was not what she'd expected to hear.

"I have instructed everyone to come to me with allegations like this in the future. That's my failure that they thought they just had to deal with him. I had no idea, and it's on me. That will change going forward. In the meantime, Phillips has been placed on administrative leave. He will not be back working at this station, ever. If he continues to work fire rescue, it will not be here nor in the state of Nebraska."

This time her mouth did drop open. "Are you serious?"

She shouldn't have said that. She shouldn't have acted so

stunned. This was her job, and she was supposed to be a professional.

"Not only that, I've reached back out to your chief in Dallas. I've discussed with him his promise to bury the assault charge. He said he didn't think the charge was legit—" Taggert waved some paperwork that she guessed was the printout of the charges against her. "Well, he clearly did a shitty job of burying it, since Conrad found it so easily. It will be getting *removed* from your record, though I have no idea if that will do any real good for that station and the other firefighters in it. I would love to tell you there's some grand happy ending here," Taggert waved his empty hand this time. "I told him he needs to clean up the shit in his firehouse, but I have no idea if he will."

He wouldn't, Jo thought. Her old chief had not been willing to go up against the guys under his command. He was more willing to sweep things under the rug than deal with them. But what Taggert didn't know was that even this cleanup that he offered was already some grand happy ending.

"So I can stay?" she asked tentatively. And she didn't realize until the words were out that she'd flayed herself open. When word got around, probably all of them would know just how much it meant to her to stay in the job, and she could only hope it didn't get used against her in the future.

But the Chief stood up and held out his hand, as though welcoming her for the first time. "Please stay. We're proud to have you, Jo."

She stood, too, luckily a natural reaction to his gesture. Because she was blinking back the tears forming at the corner of her eyes. She could not cry here, but she held out her own hand, and shook his and said, "Joely, please."

"Glad to have you at the RFD, Joely Huston."

CHAPTER FIFTY-SIX

Leo straightened his bow tie, his heart pounding as he checked in the rearview mirror. Then he had the stupidest thought: this tux was Calvin Klein. Was that good enough for her?

Joely had questioned him about whether or not it was a 'good tux,' and the fact of the matter was, he had no idea.

What would he find? Would she be here with another date on her arm? She hadn't reached out to him. It had been two weeks and he'd not heard anything from her. Even when the FD had come over to check out his house and put in any ramps he'd needed, she hadn't been there. Leo hadn't needed ramps, and the evening had ended with the guys staying for pizza and beer instead of carpentry, but without Joely there it hadn't been as great as it could have been.

He'd been through surgery and then in the hospital for five days recovering and dealing with painful physical therapy. He'd been continuing it like a good soldier at home, mostly because he was bored out of his gourd while he was on medical leave and he was alternating between depressed and angry that he hadn't heard from her.

Leo had picked up his own phone maybe five times each day, but she hadn't reached out to him, so he hadn't reached out to her. It was a bit childish, but he was too mad to have a real conversation anyway—especially when he thought that conversation would just be her telling him that it had been fun, but she didn't want anything more.

Only a day ago had he been able to take the gauze bandage off the back of his leg. He'd gotten permission to go without the one on his arm two days before. The mountain lion had managed two or three terrifying swipes before Leo got in a good second knife stab that had eventually stopped her.

He'd been found on the trail, bleeding out, the dead cat nearby. Leo had been breathing heavily—which at least had told him he was still alive. But had the team not arrived when they did, he didn't know how it would have gone. His leg gushed enough blood that he would have bled out sooner rather than later.

Luckily, they had arrived relatively prepared. They'd left camp expecting to meet up with a child in need of heat and food. Instead, they had a grown man with open wounds. The one on his leg had flayed down to the muscle and on his arm, the cat had cut almost to the bone. He'd had tendons reattached so that his hand would work again. He'd have scars forever. But better that than his face or his neck, he reminded himself as he took the freeway into Omaha.

He was breathing a little hard at the prospect of what he was doing tonight. He couldn't seem to call her, so throwing himself into Joely's path and at her mercy seemed to be the next move. And while she could flay him open worse than the cat had, the very public venue should limit how badly she could kill him.

He'd granted himself two very lucky points in the cat attack: First, the cuts had been clean and the things she'd cut had been easy to reattach. The second was that—as a park ranger—he'd already been vaccinated against rabies. The doctors liked to tell him how lucky he was while he laid in that bed, bandaged up, wondering if the first surgeries had done enough.

But Joely hadn't reached out. She hadn't come by. She hadn't even sent word. So he hadn't counted himself all that lucky. But Leo told himself that he was, so tonight he had a hitch in his step from the recovering leg and the recovering slash to his heart.

The drive to Omaha wasn't short. Aside from a few jaunts to the grocery and the dry cleaner to get his tux ready he'd not really been out and about. Bethany had worked the phones until her back felt well enough to get into the field again. The others had been covering for him. In the next few days, he'd return to the job full time. The question was: would he have Joely at his side or would the work be cover for a shattered heart?

He knew that Jo and Bethany had saved his life. Jo had called in his location and Bethany had pinpointed him, sending a medical team to him as quickly as possible. They'd also saved Dalton. He'd heard the story that, when the team had intercepted Joely, she'd run so hard that she was on the verge of collapse herself.

He hadn't run tonight at all, but as he pulled up to the Reiner mansion and got in the line of waiting cars, he breathed as though he had.

What was he doing?

But another car pulled in behind him and it was too late to back out now.

Dalton was okay. So Leo would cling to that win, no matter what Joely told him. In fact, the boy had bounced back much quicker than Leo. And if tonight didn't go well, then Leo wasn't certain he was going to bounce at all.

Handing the keys to the valet, he tried to look normal, to look as though he belonged in this overly opulent world. He climbed the marble staircase without a date and stepped into the ballroom. His eyes scanned the crowd searching for brown hair in tight braids, blue eyes, and a wide mouth. But no one here looked like that.

He was quickly intercepted by Lando Tavares. "Leo! Glad to hear that you're okay!"

"Me, too!" He tried to look past his friend but he couldn't. He hadn't seen Lando since the first grant had come in and he and Chloe Goodman had left for their first case. Leo nodded at the redhead on Lando's arm. "You must be Chloe."

He'd seen her picture in the paper, and he wanted to catch up with his friend, but he was too distracted. Only a moment later, Lando and Chloe were pulled away, and Leo began scanning the room again.

There were long sparkly gowns, shimmering skirts and shiny coiffed hair. Was one of these women Joely? It couldn't be.

Only then did it occur to him that maybe she hadn't come. She'd asked him to be her date. He'd said yes, but there had been no further discussion. He'd simply showed up. What if he'd showed up and she wasn't even here?

But as he turned to leave, he heard her voice.

His head turned quickly but as he looked, he found it wasn't her. It was a woman who looked a lot like Joely and sounded almost exactly like her. But his Joely wasn't here.

Disappointment flared through him. This had been a mistake. He reached up, tugging at the lapels of the tux. Because he had nothing else to do, he grabbed a passing flute of champagne just to keep his fingers occupied.

This whole evening was one stupid decision after another, he thought. The crowd and the conversation that flowed through clear lines of etiquette made it clear that the guy in the house his friend's mother had decorated didn't belong here.

He'd seen the other cars when he pulled in. He didn't have the kind of money to donate to the Reiner Family missing children's charity. His good old Calvin Klein tux was clearly low end for this crowd.

He bit down on his tongue, regretting that he'd wasted the evening, but as he turned to leave his eyes swept the ballroom one last time.

Somehow, he saw what he hadn't seen before: the shimmery fabric and the shiny curls cascading down the open back of her gown weren't what he'd expected. But the big blue eyes and the wide smile were.

Without quite realizing what he was doing, Leo strode across the room.

CHAPTER FIFTY-SEVEN

"Leo." Jo said his name in a tight voice. She hadn't meant to, it was just the surprise of seeing him here.

She'd told herself she was getting over it. Over *him*.

Seeing him here—in that tux—told her she was a liar.

Everything had been going so well at the station. Work was the best she could expect, the RFD the best place she'd ever found. And yet, it hadn't been quite so satisfying. She hadn't realized when she'd gone out on that search, that she'd come back nursing a broken heart. Joely Huston was not one for broken hearts. She realized she wasn't handling it well.

"Joely," he offered back just as tightly.

She fought a frown. Galas were not the place for sour expressions. Her mother made sure she knew that she was here to make an impression and donate money and encourage others to do the same—not to fight with the man who wasn't her boyfriend.

"Why are you here?" She tried to ask it softly. Jo took a sip of her champagne and attempted to make it look to anyone who glanced across the room as though this was some perfectly normal conversation.

"I thought I was your date." The words had a little bit of a bite to them. He was clearly upset.

"Why would you be my date?" She stepped away, her chest clenching. This wasn't going to be pretty. He hadn't wanted to see her so why the hell had he gotten dressed up in a tux to come tell her?

Everything had been made clear to her a week ago. She didn't need this. She already felt shitty enough as it was. Even the champagne tasted sour now and she quit sipping at it, just used the glass as something to keep her hands occupied.

"You couldn't even come see how I was doing, after ..." His accusation started strong but trailed off, as he clearly wasn't quite willing to say it out loud. *After what.*

But Jo knew. She felt it often enough in flashes and flares of memory and longing. She offered a tight smile to a passing waiter and set her half-finished champagne on his tray with a thunk. "I *did* come visit you at the hospital."

Then she grabbed his hand and turned, stalking away dragging him along. It was hard to make an angry exit in four-inch heels and a gown that literally swished as she walked. She must look like a fool, she certainly felt like one.

He followed along until she turned the corner, finding what she hoped was a relatively private hallway. Turning back, she dropped his hand like it burned and glared at him. She would have put her hands on her hips and stared him down, but she would have looked silly standing like that with her curls and glittery makeup. The ruby red of her lips was for smiles and small talk, not anger and heartbreak.

Instead, she rolled her fingers into fists that disappeared into the shimmering tulle of her skirt, the bulk of it trailing behind her each time she moved. But Leo didn't seem to take her anger, or if he did, he transformed it into anger of his own.

"What do you mean you came and visited me? I didn't see you!"

"I didn't see you either!" *Well, that was a dumb thing to say.* Jo hated being flustered and hated being angry when she was really just hurt. "Your mother made it very clear that you had no desire to see me. So I left. What the hell else was I supposed to do?"

She figured her mother was probably looking for her. And the only thing worse than dealing with Leo while she stood here in this stupid ball gown was having her mother come hunt her down to play the society girl. She couldn't do it right now and she only hoped that her mother didn't find them here.

She stalked further down the hall, away from the ballroom, hating that the too-fluffy dress stole her anger and made her look ridiculous. She tried to paste a society appropriate smile on her face but, just as she thought she was getting herself together, Leo grabbed her hand. If he hadn't held her so tightly she would have toppled over. She was more than capable on heels, but she didn't like them and this whole conversation was throwing her for a loop.

"What?" He sounded genuinely confused.

Jo huffed out a breath, tipping her head back and praying for strength—absolutely the wrong thing to do in a ball gown. "I went to see you. I was informed that you didn't wish to see me. So I left. Are we good?"

"No. No, we're not good. I never said that. Why would you think I didn't want to see you?"

"After ... the cave, I mean ..." She struggled to find words. "Who knows what that was? It's the spur of the moment thing you probably want to walk away from." She was looking at the carpet in the hallway, at the plants placed every ten feet and wrapped in fabric for the party. "Your mother made it perfectly clear to me that you didn't want to see me. And some of the guys had gone to see you ... *They* were allowed in!"

She waved one hand, making sure he understood she wasn't being an idiot. She had evidence.

He looked lost, and frowned, and she almost left him there to deal with it himself. But his hands came up, palm out as if to say he had no idea. But the guys had gone to visit while she was still sleeping. *They* were the ones who'd kept her updated on how he was doing. Leo had visited with *them*. Just not *her*.

She hated that she noticed the twitch in his left arm as though the simple movement had bothered him. Jo reached out for his hand, holding the warm skin against her own and starting to push up the cuff. "Are you okay?"

Leo jerked his hand back. "I'm fine. I'm going to be fine. My mother told you not to come in? Why would she tell you that?"

"Hell if I know!" Jo was mad. This wasn't her issue. "She specifically said you didn't want to see me."

If he wouldn't let her look at the arm, then what was there to do? Should she just stand here and glare at him? So he didn't know why his mother said that, but did that mean something more? She didn't have the bandwidth to wait while he sighed to himself and looked out the window.

"Shit."

"I told her to tell you that I'd stopped by. So you should have known that I came."

"She didn't tell me."

Jo put her hands out to the side. Well, there was nothing she could do if his family was actively getting in their way. And he hadn't said he *did* want to see her either, only that he hadn't known. This was too much and in entirely the wrong place. She could have made it through tonight if he just hadn't shown up.

"Don't hold it against her," he said softly.

"Why would I? I don't even know the woman."

"But I want you to," he whispered the words into the space between them. "I had too many visitors and the doctors told her I needed to rest. I think she just turned everyone away. She wouldn't have remembered who came and who didn't. I thought you didn't even check in on me."

She froze. What should she say? "Well, I did." She paused, but he didn't say anything else, so she tossed out the one thing that was making her angry still. "You didn't check in on me either. You've been home for a week now and ... I've heard nothing from you."

He took a sigh and a moment and she started to swish past him, but he grabbed her hand again. They had to stop doing this. She was about to lose it and she had to get out of here.

"You're right. I didn't. But since I spent five days in the hospital, and you didn't check to see how I was doing—"

"But I did!" She insisted. It was all a big mess and she told herself that any man who wanted her would have reached out. So she made a preemptive move and watched as her own hand reached out to clasp his forearm. He twitched as she touched him and she knew it was still healing. She'd heard the cat had gotten him there. "Tell me you're going to be okay."

If he told her, she would leave and let him go his own way.

"Tell me I can be your date for the evening." He countered, reaching up to push her hair behind her ear.

That was a horrifying move, she thought, as clearly Leo did not understand the effort that went into gala hair, and that he was not supposed to touch it. But it was maybe the sweetest thing anyone had ever done for her.

"I was mad, and I shouldn't have been. You did come."

Shit, she was mad and she shouldn't have been. But how did she undo the anger she'd carried for almost two weeks?

"Okay." She dropped her acceptance into the middle of the awkward silence. It hung between them, but something soft and undefined and awkward began to fill the space.

"We should be seen." It was easier than standing here and trying to define what they were. She still didn't know if he would be anything beyond her date for the evening. Leo seemed like the kind of guy who would show up simply because he said he would. So she started to turn, waving at him to come back out onto the floor.

But Leo stood, unbudging, and once again grabbed her hand and tugged her back. "Be my date—"

"I said yes." Her impatience bled through.

He grinned. "—For everything. There's a brewery to go to. Movies to watch. Promotions to celebrate." But then he looked chagrined as he glanced down at his tux. As if maybe he wondered if she would want more of *this*. Or maybe he thought the things he was offering wouldn't be enough.

"A brewery date sounds wonderful."

"You could stay over with me tonight."

"I could?" she asked as warmth bloomed in the middle of her chest. Was he really asking?

"I mean, you have some medical training. You can inspect my wounds." He offered it up ridiculously and she found herself laughing.

"Surely Hernandez should stay over if you want a medic."

But Leo was looking into her eyes and she didn't dare hope she was reading him right. She was probably just seeing what she wanted to see.

"I don't want a medic. I want you."

"Joely!" the voice hissed from around the corner.

Shit. Her mother could certainly ruin a nearly perfect moment. "I'm coming, mother."

But then she took a chance and dragged Leo along with her. She stopped in front of her mother and tried to play the part. "Leo, this is Marcia Huston, my mother. Mom, this is …" she paused, *what was he?* "Leo Evans."

"Her date for the evening," Leo said, holding on to her with one hand and holding the other out to her mother. Somehow, he knew to respond perfectly when Marcia managed to slide her hand out, palm down as though she were the Queen of

England. "In fact, I'm Joely's date for everything from here on out."

She couldn't help her surprise. Her head turned and her eyebrows lifted and Leo just tilted his head at her as if challenging her to tell him he was wrong.

Marcia, of course, raised one sharp eyebrow, as if to say *what is this?* But what she said was, "I have to get back out there. And you do too."

She pointed at Joely, making sure her instructions were clear regardless of whatever this thing might be with Leo Evans. Jo would have laughed but as her mother disappeared around the corner, Leo pulled her into his arms and kissed her, once again violating gala protocol.

This makeup took far too long to mess it up with a kiss. But she didn't care. And she leaned in, kissing him back until Leo finally pulled away, taking her face in his hands and saying carefully, "I love you, Joely Huston."

CHAPTER FIFTY-EIGHT

Sitting in the back of the rig, facing the tail, had never bothered Luke Hernandez before today. But now, as the team raced out toward yet another house fire, his stomach clenched, his lungs ratcheted down, and his throat tightened.

The engine was coming to a halt. He didn't have much view back here, but he had a feeling they were close. In fact, maybe they were already here.

He should say something!

He told himself this over and over. From the moment the chief had called out the address he'd known this would be bad. But he'd lied to himself and said the address was wrong. Told himself he misremembered it, that it wasn't what he thought.

But now, even through the heavy gear, he heard the latches clicking as the crew threw open the doors and began to pour out of the large red truck ready to hit the ground running. If he didn't follow suit, it would look odd.

So Luke climbed down one big step, and jumped the last bit in a move that, despite the heavy boots, jarred his ankles. He took the landing hard, because the rig had pulled up directly across the front of the house. The first thing he'd seen was the confirmation that he'd been right the first time. And he should have told the chief.

He did a quick scene check along with the others. But he did it poorly, he knew. The first thing Luke *should* have seen was the smoke pouring out of the windows, the orange glow in the far left corner, and in the periphery of his vision, his fellow firefighters already unwinding the hose, laying it across the yard. He knew some of them would be at the other end, pulling the hose and hooking it up to the nearby hydrant.

He didn't register anything like he should. He just stared. The first thing he did see was that it was exactly as bad as he'd feared.

"Hernandez!" his chief snapped. And that was it—that was his chance to tell the chief what he knew, what he now *believed,* rather than merely suspected. But instead, he automatically ran and put himself into place on the line.

His arms and his brain worked in sync with everyone else and he could only hope his movements didn't reveal the turmoil inside him. Together the team got the water flowing hard and heavy. They aimed it near the base of the house and soaked the front yard, wetting it to keep the fire from spreading to nearby buildings and trees while another team headed to the small house and began venting it.

His team waited with the hose until they got word then, as a unit, moved forward. Normally, his pulse pounded from the adrenaline of the fight, this time it was from fear.

He felt a sinking sensation as, behind him, he heard frantic noises of a neighbor, screaming. The Chief's voice boomed through the comms.

"The neighbor thinks she's still in there. Said her car is in the garage, that she always closes the garage door, but the neighbor saw her come home this evening."

Luke didn't know who they were talking about, but the entire line paused for a moment, letting him know that they did.

Even with the face shield and the hood covering so much of him, Ronan must have caught his expression.

His friend leaned closer, "This is Ivy Dean's house."

That wasn't how Luke thought of the place. Clearly, Ivy didn't think of the house the way he did. It seemed she'd been fixing it up. But the chatter around him now gathered more weight. This wasn't a random resident, not someone he didn't know.

He'd wondered if the homeowner had been targeted specifically, and now he felt his blood turn to ice as he feared that maybe this was about Ivy.

Ronan Kelly was already calling into his comm, "Send me in, chief!"

Luke's brain must have truly been scrambled, because it took him a moment to realize that Ronan was volunteering to go into the house and conduct the search and hopefully a rescue. Before he knew what he was doing his own voice followed suit.

It was too late. The captain was already saying, "Kelly, Huston. Inside!"

But Luke knew something they didn't. In fact, he might know a lot of somethings they didn't.

He waved over Sebastian Kane, who was standing back, having just stepped away from his spot on the second hose. Luke motioned him to trade positions, and Kane began the intricate moves of taking over his spot on the line.

"Chief!" he announced, even though it wasn't his place to give such a command. "Send me in!"

He watched as Ronan Kelly and Joely Huston approached the front door and checked it out. But Luke was running across the open yard, toward where the chief stood, still hollering as he did. "I know where she is!"

There wasn't time to explain.

The chief looked him up and down and must have seen something in his face. Hernandez had to admit that he'd always liked working for Taggert. The man had a special knack for putting people in their best positions, and for understanding and reading them. He knew when there was more to a scene than caught the eye. He followed his firefighters' hunches and managed to make most all of them pay off.

Luke only prayed that Taggert did the same now.

He held his breath until he saw a slight frown and a glimmer of understanding. The chief motioned with just his thumb. "Kelly, back on the line. Hernandez, you're going in."

Far more grateful than he should have ever been, Luke bolted toward the house. He had a feeling this would be his last act with the Redemption Fire Department. He would be fired at least, if he didn't go down for the arson.

Thank you for reading! I love romances with real love and believable characters, and I hope you found all that in these pages. I want to fall in love right along with the characters, and I do, while I'm writing it.

About Savannah

I started writing when I was eight--I hand wrote an 80-page novella that I believed to be (adult) romantic suspense. I'm proud to say, I've gotten a lot better since then. I've grown up to be a nerd at heart! I love neuroscience and people watching, and if you look, you'll find some of that in each Savannah Kade book. Most days you'll find me in my office, looking out my window at a handful of the neighbor's cows, or watching my dogs or my cat roam the backyard.

Follow me, find me, ask me questions! I would love to hear from you.

www.SavannahKade.com

Savannah@SavannahKade.com

www.ingramcontent.com/pod-product-compliance
Lightning Source LLC
LaVergne TN
LVHW091033080826
845145LV00002B/475

* 9 7 8 1 9 4 8 0 5 9 7 5 6 *